I0651436

Edward Vaughan Kenealy

Edward Wortley Montagu

An Autobiography. Vol. 3

Edward Vaughan Kenealy

Edward Wortley Montagu
An Autobiography. Vol. 3

ISBN/EAN: 9783337116637

Printed in Europe, USA, Canada, Australia, Japan

Cover: Foto ©Raphael Reischuk / pixelio.de

More available books at **www.hansebooks.com**

EDWARD WORTLEY MONTAGU.

.

AN AUTOBIOGRAPHY.

IN THREE VOLUMES.

יאבד יום אולד כו

"Let the day perish in which I was born."

VOL. III.

London:

T. CAUTLEY NEWBY, PUBLISHER,

30, WELBECK STREET, CAVENDISH SQUARE.

1869.

EDWARD WORTLEY MONTAGU.

CHAPTER XXVII.

" I am weary with my groaning; all the night make I my bed to swim. I water my couch with my tears. Mine eye is consumed because of grief; it waxeth old because of all mine enemies."

I WAS now under my father's roof, and intolerably wretched. Lady Mary treated me with coldness and contempt, and mockery. My father was immersed in politics and money getting. With him indeed the first was only a means to the second, for he was above all vulgar notions of patriotism or public duty. He never came near me. I secluded myself with my books. He did not ap-

pear to remember that at the top of the house
such a person was in existence. I could not bear
to go out or even to look into the bright open air.
Francesca was lost to me for ever. This was the
fixed conviction on my soul. I should have run
away again and sought Manasam and the encampment, but I had undone myself by my flight with
Francesca and my encounter with the Gypsy
Queen. I should have wandered back to Sale
and Cave, and my literary friends—but why
labour now at the oar when I had no incentive
to work?—when I had no Francesca to cheer me
—no companion whose wants I might supply? I
sank into a species of lethargy; all my powers
were wrapped in lassitude. I could not bear to
see or speak to any one. I ate my meals alone
and in silence. I did not suffer the servants to
address me. I signified my wants by signs. I
was quiet only when I was wholly solitary. I
could not endure to look upon a human face. It
seemed the outward visible sign of villainy and
falsehood. I then thoroughly, for the first time,
grew a hater of my species.

At the end of a year I woke out of my dreams
and began again to mingle with ordinary life. I
laboured hard to store my mind with knowledge,
and I think I succeeded to some extent. My
position was strange. I was the only son and

expected heir of a great Commoner, yet I was allowed only something like ten pounds a year for all my wants. I was not absolutely expelled out of my father's house, but this was all—I was just tolerated there. If I pleased I could have gone; if I pleased I could stay. This was the cheering sort of alternative that was every day presented to me. For sympathy I did not look, for I was conscious of the hate of one and the indifference of the other, and I ardently reciprocated both sentiments. They thought, I suppose, that as I was dependent on Mr. Montagu for wealth, I should fall down prostrate and worship when ever his name was mentioned; but I scorned himself and his money equally. I would not enslave myself or degrade my soul by a lying pretence of a love which I did not feel for all his wealth, or for all the wealth of England. While I pursued my present course I respected myself, but if I became his serf, I should have so loathed my own meanness that I should have cut my throat to avoid the horror of reflection. But the fashionable world could not understand why I did not adore the man who owned a million; and so it was kindly set down by the mass of boobies to my own perversity and wickedness, and folly—a notion which my mother kindly encouraged. Wherever she went she represented me as a rogue, blockhead, weathercock, and liar. Fortunately she was now so well understood that her calumnies did me no harm; and there were some who even judged for themselves. The women, by their advances, told me I was handsome; the men, by their sneers and envy, and affected coldness, convinced me that I was learned; but I needed not either the women or the men to give me this pleasing information, for my looking-glass informed me of the first, and my conscience whispered me of the second. For a year I lived as I have described; after this I went into the "gay world," where everything was false, hollow, and melancholy. There was a perpetual hunt after pleasure, and as perpetual a disappointment. It was sought in routes, balls, ridottos, and masquerades; in the opera, at auctions, and in great supper parties; in races, china shops, lotteries, and gambling. This latter virtue the women carried to an outrageous extent, and my mother was perpetually involved in money squabbles, in consequence of her reverses at cards; in stock jobbing, also, in which the leaders of fine society mingled with the basest covetousness, and the most shame-faced boldness; in gallantry and intrigue, with a total scorn of the seventh Commandment. But though quested after in these various spheres of joy, happiness eluded her votaries; and the haggard face, the wrinkled brow, the sickly smile that never sank beneath the surface, attested the disappointment and the vanity of human wishes when centred only in externals.

I take pride in myself that I always despised these follies; nor did I less bitterly scorn their wretched votaries; what to me at this period were the painted smiles of the vain things in brocade and gold, who—I had almost written *which*—paraded the drawing-room, or sparkled in the dance? I tested them only by one woman, who was perfect, and I need not add they would not bear comparison. The innocent beauty of my Francesca every day rose up before me like a vision of Paradise upon some enraptured mystic; those eyes, full of virgin light, that hair that sparkled so lustrously over her snow-white neck, as I have since seen the golden beam of sunset rest upon an Alpine peak; that mouth, so full of beauty; that voice, which was like harp strings agitated by the summer breeze, so soft, so sweet, so musical, so exquisitely thrilling; that sound sense and exquisite understanding which, though a child, she manifested in all things; her elevated ambition; her sympathy with all noble and pure aspirations. These were what I had lost in her, and feared that I had lost for ever. But how discover her? How ascertain if she was not even at this present moment in the hands of the gypsies, subjected to the chance of death, wrong, outrage?—I knew not what, and scarcely dared to think.

There was not one of those women who moved around us that would not have surrendered herself body and soul to the young heir of the wealthy Wortley Montagu. I was now eighteen, tall, lively, enterprising; my descent was good, my connections powerful. What more did I need to become their god? Nothing. But I did not profit by my opportunity. A profound grief kept me and preserved me sacred. No morning dawned that I did not devise some scheme to discover tidings of my beloved; no sun sank without witnessing my baffled hope, and renewed disappointment. Yet I rose again next day, confident as before, but still doomed to the vesper mockery of my hopes. I employed emissaries, as much as my scanty means and credit would enable me to do, and dispatched them in all directions for tidings such as I desired. I sought out the mad-house, or private prison where I had been confined, but the place was untenanted and desolate. The persons who had occupied it disappeared immediately after my liberation, and left no trace that could lead to their discovery.

I went myself and saw the landlord. He appeared to be a sort of Quaker, and like Hogden, and others of my electioneering hypocritical friends, made great pretensions to piety; he even affected to sympathise with me—for I hinted my sufferings—but he could give me no information of his former tenants. I knew by his look that he lied, but it was useless to tell him that I thought so.

Among those who saw me frequently at this period, was my cousin Fielding—the chance companion in my first wild escapade to Oxford. He was now a literary character of some repute. His father, General Fielding, had thrown him loose upon London almost without a penny, and he began to live by his wits, or rather to starve by them, for nothing could be more precarious than his mode of subsistence. He was scarcely twenty, when in 1727, four years or so before the period of which I am now writing, he picked up a sort of scrambling acquaintance with the players, to whom wit, conviviality and gay humour are always a recommendation, and became intimate with Wilkes and Cibber, who introduced him to Mrs. Oldfield, then preserving by her bounteous generosity, the wretched Savage from starvation. He described his exact position in one sentence. " I had no alternative," he said, " but to become a hackney coachman, or a hackney writer, and I chose the latter." Ah! me, methinks he would have been more fortunate, had he taken to the rein, or even to the road, than to literature in this accursed era. The poor youth, driven to his wit's ends to pay his tailor, or buy a dinner, or supply his father, scribbled off a comedy called *Love in several Masques*, which was produced at Drury Lane, and dedicated to my mother in virtue of her relationship to the distressed author. Like all writers, he fooled her to the top of her bent, as far as flattery was concerned; and had she possessed only a tithe of those magnificent qualities for which he gave her credit, I should not have written these Confessions, nor would my father have left his hardly-hoarded money to a Scotch scoundrel like Bute. But poor Fielding was not the first who mistook a cloud for a goddess; for he got nothing from Lady Mary but a smile. His relationship, and connection with the papers however, produced him an introduction into our house, which was of some use to a young fellow struggling hard in the wild sea of London. Lady Mary, I suppose, discovered from him our accidental meeting when boys so many years ago, and she now threw us together. I rather suspect her object was to let Fielding drag me into his own headlong course of dissipation,

as a means of making me forget my Francesca;
for my lady well knew by this time that I was
married, and though she could have no doubt
that Francesca was of noble birth, still she always
spoke of her as "a washerwoman," which would
have been laughable for its absurdity, only that
it was galling for its insolence. From several
circumstances I began to fancy that Lady Mary
herself was privy to the plot which had rudely
separated us both; for she exhibited so much
malignity and feminine spite whenever that loved
name was mentioned by me, that I could scarcely
attribute either to exist against one who was an
entire stranger. I subsequently learned that my
suspicions were correct, and that while Lady Mary
well knew nearly everything relating to
Francesca, she took care to give them such a
colouring to my father, that he also believed like
the rest of the world, that she was of ignoble
birth, and little better than an impostor who
inveigled a rich man's son into a marriage with
the most sordid view.

But Fielding was too noble a fellow, and too
sharpwitted also, to be made a complying tool of,
even by one so ingenious as Lady Mary. Himself a man of quick and ardent sensibilities, and
notwithstanding all his grossness, of the purest
sentimentalism when true love was in the debate;

he was so moved by my artless descriptions of
her whom I had lost, and of the felicity we had
enjoyed in our brief summer time of rapture, that
I have seen the tears roll down his manly face,
and he would sit for several minutes in a
thoughtful reverie, in which sympathy for me
had a large share, and hatred of my enemies, a
still larger. So far from conducting me into those
scenes of boisterous madness, in which he was
nightly indulging, and which finally destroyed one
of the finest constitutions ever given to a man,
he dissuaded me from any such resource, and
deplored his own failings with a bitterness that
was sincere at the moment, but which melted
away in the first glass of generous claret that he
swallowed. He even aided me in my enquiries,
under a solemn pledge that I would not discover
him to my lady; and from his versatile acquaintance with human nature, and his profound sense,
wherever his own passions did not interfere, he
gave me advice as to her discovery, which would
probably have been successful, had Francesca
been in England. But an incident that occurred
soon after, by putting me in the right track for
discovering her, proved that all my efforts had
been misdirected, and that I failed, because to
succeed was an impossibility.

Fielding was in the habit of talking to me

about his literary projects, and I communicated
to him in time what I had learned from Akiba
my Gooroo. We had many disputations on the
metempsychosis, or transmigration of souls, and
it was after one of the conferences that he mentioned to me his notion of writing a little novel
on that subject, in which, using this Brahminical
doctrine, he might give expression to that curious
medley of observation and experience which he
possessed, and conduct one of his characters
through a variety of scenes as mixed and as sur-
prising as those of Gil Blas, or Asmodeus. I
approved of the notion, which had everything in
it likely to attract a youthful imagination, and in
a few weeks he brought me that sketch of the
Emperor Julian, which he afterwards introduced
into his strange work entitled, " *A Journey from
this World to the next.*" I read it and was pleased.
The motley nature of the scenes through which
the deceased Emperor transmigrates, operating
on an imagination half Arab, half gypsy, deeply
impressed my mind, and I thought to myself if I
were free this is just the sort of life I should like
to lead. I should traverse many lands and appear
in many characters. To day a pilgrim, to-morrow
a gentleman, now a soldier, now a merchant, this
time a sailor, the next a physician, a Jew one
week, a Mohamedan the following, a priest, a

fiddler, a quaker or a buffoon,—there was rapture
in the idea, and I fed my fancy upon it till I had
lived through a whole romance.

In the midst of our discussions, I one morning
proposed to him an excursion to Portslade, and
an investigation personally into the condition of
my gypsy friends. We had a few guineas, and
we went by the coach. Some odd adventures
befel us, which Fielding afterwards used in his
romance of "Joseph Andrews," but they are not
worth referring to in this place. We got to
Brighthelmstone, and I took up my quarters
there at an inn, while Fielding proceeded to the
encampment. He was away the whole afternoon,
and when he returned late in the evening, he was
a good deal excited. He then gave me the following account of his adventures.

"I took the route you pointed out, and after
lingering about the lanes sometime, I pulled out
a pocket book, and began to sketch that old ruin,
on which the camp of your friends abutted. I
had not been very long employed, when a very
pretty gypsy came up to me, and asked me to
cross her palm with gold. I looked at her sparkling eyes and roguish face, and faith I half envied
you your sojourn among these engaging
Ishmaelites. Ah, Wortley, you must have seen
some strange amusing sights, and you must give

me an account of them in detail some day, for
some great and wonderful work of fiction in which
we shall go shares. You may suppress all your
own intrigues, or dish them up under another
name, but you must at least give me a full, true
and particular narration of the—

     " ' Battles, dangers, sieges you have passed.'

    " I told the wench that gold was to me one of
the rarest commodities in the world, but that I
would give her a kiss or a piece of silver, if she
could tell me where I could find one Manasam,
one of her people, as I had a message for him
from an old acquaintance. Now by one of the
rarest chances in the world, this girl had known
your wife, and had a sort of wild attachment to
both of you, and before I had quite finished my
sentence, she divined what I came for, and burst
out with—

    " ' Ah! I know you. You came from Zala-
Mayna. Is it not so ?'

    " I was so taken by surprise, that before I had
time to invent a lie, I was forced to confess that
it was so, and when I had so disburdened my
soul, she said—

    " ' Well, I am glad you have come. We have
all been sorry for the poor boy, and have wished
a thousand evils on that accursed Dom Balthazar
for interfering with them ; but Zala-Mayna did

wrong to strike the Gypsy Queen, and it will never
be forgiven by the tribe. Had he been seized
that night, he would have been stoned to death—
such is the penalty by our law; and even still if
he should be in their power, I know not but that
they would inflict it. But if you give me the
piece of silver you spoke of, I will seek out
Manasam—though I should be sorry any of the
tribe knew what I was doing. However, Dom
Balthazar is gone, so I don't fear much.'

"I gave her the silver, but when I offered her
what I thought would have been the more agreeable half of the present, namely the kiss, she gave
me a smart slap in the face, which I assure you I
feel still.

"She then told me that I must not linger in
the place, but get back to the town as speedily
as I could. 'It would never do,' she said, 'for
Manasam and myself to be seen together.' There
were a dozen prying eyes always about the camp,
and Manasam had always shewn so much sorrow
for Zala-Mayna's misadventure, that he was
narrowly watched by the tribe, and would get
into trouble if he were seen conversing with me.
She asked me where I stayed, and I told her. I
expect the gypsy here to-night."

And ordering up a fresh bottle, he opened wide
his legs before the fire, and threw himself back

in his chair, with the apparent determination of
a man who has made up his mind to enjoy himself for the remainder of the evening with the
best that he could get. The wine appeared, and
after a hearty glass, Fielding resumed—

" Wortley, my dear boy, I don't know what
your lady mother will say to me if she ever finds
out I have been your companion in this adventure.
If she should, no more Twickenham for me ; no
more sugared compliments. I shall become as
odious to her as Pope, or Swift, and she will
pursue me with unrelenting lampoonery—

> Women you know do seldom fail
> To make the stoutest men turn tail,
> And bravely scorn to turn their backs
> Upon the desperatest attacks.

" But I suppose I must risk all, for there is a
spice of adventure about this love-feat of yours
that pleases me, and I verily believe it is just the
sort of thing I should myself have liked above
all others. For there is so much paint, folly,
and flippant falsehood about our court and
drawing-room dames, that I would any day
prefer a haymaker, or a milk-maid to the finest
duchess in the land—so long I mean as I had
the price of a dinner and a bottle in my pocket.
But that is a rare occurrence," and my cousin
sighed from his very heart. He solaced himself

with another glass, and as he did so, Manasam was announced.

The gypsy was but little altered since I had last seen him. I rose up and shook him warmly by the hand. I looked into his eyes, and could see that his friendship was sincere. He felt an honest interest in my welfare, that was written there as plainly as it was possible for Nature to write. For Nature pens his character on the front of every man in letters plainly legible to all who use their eyes, and they who do not, deserve to be deceived. I have never yet seen that face which was not to me as an open book wherein every trait of the soul, every passion of the heart, every habit of the spirit was clearly traced by the unerring hand of Nature, or rather of God; and as He cannot deceive or be deceived, it is we only who err in our estimate of humankind for want of bestowing proper attention upon those with whom we come in contact. Were I a monarch or a prime minister, I would undertake that no man should ever enter my immediate service until he had passed through my close scrutiny; and this obtained, I should not be deceived. No man or woman has ever misled me, for where my observation fails, instinct comes to my aid, and I know them all thoroughly and well, though under the most artful mask. And this probably

is one of the reasons why I take a more gloomy
view of life, and indulge in more sarcastic obser-
vations than pleases the many. For as *they* judge
by the mere outside, they are every moment
deceived by their own superficiality, taking mankind for what they appear to be ; and as it is the
interest of the majority to *seem* good, the shallow
suppose them to be what they seem, and all those
who have penetrated deeper, they call misanthro-
pists, evil minded, and detractors. But I who have
the art of piercing beneath the false outside, and
beholding, as in a map, all the true nature of a
man, delineated unto even its finest strokes, speak
of them as I find them, and as God will see them
on that dreadful day of judgment, when the secrets
of all hearts shall be disclosed. Hence, if in this
narrative I please, I shall please but few ; the
great mob of readers will run after him who
paints man in genial colours, and thus contributes
to those delusions which delight us all, even when
they mislead us most.

I invited Manasam to be seated, and poured
out a glass for him : but with the abstemious
habits of his people, he declined the draught. He
took a biscuit and began.

" Much, O Zala-Mayna, have I longed for this
hour ; much have I lamented that I knew not
where you could be found, or that I heard not

from you. I returned some days after you had
fled. Dom Balthazar had broke his leg when his
horse fell on him; he lay on the road till day-
break, when he was discovered by some of our
people who had tracked your course. He said
that he had ascertained your real name and position—that you were of great and noble blood,
and had deceived our trusting people with a false
device. It was rumoured also that he was to
receive a sum of money for bringing you back to
your father and mother; and a large reward if
he could separate you and Francesca for ever. I
rather fancy he knows her uncle; I rather think
he is in his employ to find Francesca out, and
that if he can by any means place her in his
hands, great will be the treasure he is to receive.
Guard her therefore, O Zala-Mayna, as the life
blood of your heart from Dom Balthazar, for he
will part you if he can."

I groaned, but remained silent. Manasam was
evidently ignorant of the loss that I had sustained.
I did not interrupt him.

"The Gypsy Queen also vowed a vow of
vengeance against you. It was resolved in full
assembly that if you were discovered and brought
back you should die. Akiba and I were not
of this council; if we had been, we probably
should have felt ourselves constrained to sanction

it, for it is a law of our people, and cannot be
broken. The person of the Queen is sacred. Dom
Balthazar disappeared from among us for many
moons; at length he returned and announced
that you were a prisoner. He was asked why he
had not brought you to the tents, that you might
die? He laughed, and produced gold—gold
immense—the price of your bondage. This, he
said, the tribe gains by his life—but nothing
should we secure by his death. The gold was
divided. Yet were there many who would have
preferred vengeance, and the law. Dom Balthazar
said no more. In a few days he departed for
Spain, where he now is. He dropped mysterious
hints, but we understood them not. Since then
we have lived as before; but no one has enquired for Francesca; she is safe with you. Is it
not so, O Zala-Mayna?"

Alas! I could not answer. Fielding told him
of my loss. Manasam was affected. We consulted what was to be done; but nothing seemed
to offer us a chance of discovering where Francesca
was. She had evidently been lured away by Dom
Balthazar—but whither?

A light flashed on me.

"You said he went to Spain, Manasam.
What business bore him thither?" Manasam did
not know.

" Depend upon it," said Fielding, " Francesca is in a Spanish Convent, and Dom Balthazar was her convoy. I know the gentlemen of these places, and what they will do for gold. Many of the abbots are Zingari themselves."

I restored Manasam his pistols, and offered him five guineas. He accepted the first, but peremptorily refused the second. After a long interview we separated for the night. He promised to see me again next day. On the morrow he came with Akiba. I was pleased to see this old man. Fielding was greatly struck by him. He said, he made him think of the ghost of Samuel appearing to Saul. We dined and passed the whole day together. I invited him to divine for us. Akiba at first refused; but he could not long withstand entreaties urged so passionately as mine were. He called for water, and dropped a small quantity into my hand; he then threw me into a magnetic trance, such as I had once before witnessed when he used the mystical Wâren. And this was what I then saw.

A small cell of hewn stone was opened before me, the light penetrated dimly through iron bars. There was a wretched pallet and a jug of water. It seemed an apartment in some vast building. An air of gloom pervaded the whole scene; it was in the shadow of mighty mountains.

Everything seemed still, desolate and monotonous.
A small book lay on the floor; a rosary was on
the bed. It might have been at first sight, a
dungeon, but there was no warder's tread, nor
clank of chain. It impressed me with the notion
of one of those immense convents that are found
in such great numbers all through the Peninsula;
prisons indeed, and full of dungeons, and horrors
and dread secrets; but guarded by a force
stronger than that of sentinel or fetter—the
force of ignorance and superstition. As I looked,
the idea of solitude, silence, desolation and
wretchedness became more and more impressed
on my mind. I could feel them like a heavy
weight upon my heart; they loaded me; they
weighed me down like atmospheric pressure. I
could discover in that pressure the sad and fearful
mass of sufferings, sorrow and despair that were
congregated within that dreadful place. My heart
was filled almost to bursting.

Suddenly a door in the cell opened. O!
Heavens, how shall I support this sight? It was
my Francesca—my loved, my adored, my lost
wife. Gloom and wretchedness were printed
deeply in every feature; her eyes were red with
weeping; they were fixed with a cold despair.
That young face bore the tracks of tears—the
furrows of age were already methought traced

upon it. She entered with a slow step—the step
of one who moves despondingly to the scaffold,
and who seeks to protract every minute between
himself and fate. There was a whole volume of
misery in that measured walk—she who had been
so light, so buoyant; like the thistle down that
swims on the summer breeze—like the winged
beautiful moth that floats in sunshine, and dances
on the passing winds; like the sparkling wave
that rises to the sunbeam, and is wafted with a
motion like that of music to the strand. I would
have spoken, but I could not. I would have
stretched out my arms to enfold her, for she
seemed within my reach; but the magnetic force
held me tight within its grasp, and I was power-
less in every limb. Eye and brain alone were
free; for the rest I was a marble statue. Her
heart heaved; a heavy sigh burst forth, but it was
not followed by tears; alas! that sweet fountain
must have been drained dry. She took the
rosary; looked at it for a moment, and put it
away. She raised the book, and strove to read,
but I could see that though her eyes were turned
upon its page, her thoughts wandered away, and
were afar off. She raised her head to the bars;
and sighed again deeply. Then leaning on her
hand she covered her face, and bursting into an
agony of woe, flung herself on the hard floor.

Akiba saw my agony, and released me from my trance. Oh! who can tell what misery I felt? I was again mad as I had been before. It required the strength of all three to hold me. The paroxysm lasted for some minutes; at length I fell exhausted. Next day Fielding told me what had passed, and accompanied me to London. When I got to Twickenham, without a moment's pause I rushed into my mother's room. She was reading a letter, which she hastily crushed up when she saw me.

"Woman," I cried, "give me back my wife of whom you have robbed me. Give her back to me, or tremble."

She seemed frightened at my energy. It was enough to make her so. She grew white as death. But the clever woman conquered her fears immediately, and half smiled.

"Mad boy," she said; "what do you say? How know I anything of that person? I suppose she is making up fine linen somewhere. If she wanted you she would have found you by this."

"Woman," I answered, "not worthy of the name of mother; cold, heartless, and wicked as you are; have you so utterly lost all human feeling as to see me die before your face by inches and not stretch forth a hand to save? You have ever been my bitterest enemy. You have poisoned

my father's heart against me. You have sought
to drive me forth for ever from his roof. Well,
exult, rejoice, be glad at length, for you have
succeeded. Give me but a hundred pounds, and
I will leave your sight for ever. Give it me this
moment, for I am half mad."

" A hundred pounds ! and what for ? To give
to your pretty laundress ?"

I could have stabbed her that instant. But
I answered coldly, " I want to go to Spain."

She started involuntarily, but almost instantly
recovered herself. I watched her with an intent
calm gaze. I thought I saw her guilt in that
unconscious state.

" To Spain, fool, and why ?"

" Madam," I answered, " you know. Give me
the money."

" I have none," she replied, " and if I had I
am not going to let you squander it in frenzy.
We have had enough of this already. Leave the
room ; I am engaged."

" What," I said, " you are engaged ? With
what ? And how ? With love letters from your
Hervey "—she gave another start—" with assignations and intrigues ; with satirical verses on all
your female friends and male pursuers, and all
the devilish machinery that makes the fabric of
your whole life ? Well, go on. But there shall

come a day when *I* also shall have my hour of retribution. I go; I leave your presence. Solace yourself with your daughter. Deceive, plot, scheme, to enrich *her* with all that is justly mine, and let that heartless cully, who thinks himself her father, endow her with imperial wealth. Even this shall not break my spirit, nor make me bend to either. But Nemesis will avenge me, and in the gloomy evening of your life, when frivolity shall fail, and folly cease to charm, you shall curse this hour, and pine amid a land of strangers and of foes for the soothing presence of your son."

CHAPTER XXVIII.

"Behold now I perceive that this is a holy man of God, which passeth by us continually."

I WENT straight to Fielding. That admirable philosopher was then living at Buckingham Street, in the Strand. By a rare chance I found him at home. He was usually denied to all enquirers. He was stretched on a sofa, a bottle of wine by his side, and a plate of cold meat. A lady's black silk mask and a pair of gold fringed gloves gave evidence of some affair of the heart. His table was covered with papers, and he was evidently hard at work at a comedy or a love letter when I entered. I informed him of what had just happened. He laughed a good deal at the scene with Lady Mary. Filling out a glass of

wine, which he pushed towards me, he said,
" This is my cure for all troubles; let me recom-
mend it also to you ;" and he almost forced me
to drink it off. He helped himself to another
and another, and then asked me what I meant to
do with myself.

" I mean to leave England and seek Francesca."

" A very good resolution," he answered. " How
many thousands have you got out of the old
gent? I hope you have bled him finely. Faith,
I should not mind going with you."

" Thousands !" I replied, " why I have come
to borrow a few pounds from you. Thousands,
indeed, from Mr. Montagu—you must be jest-
ing."

Fielding looked at me with great gravity; he
seemed to doubt whether I was in my senses.

" Upon my soul, Wortley," says he, when his
amazement had worn off, " if mine were a jest,
your notion is far more comical. To think of
borrowing a few pounds from me, who live by
borrowing pounds, shillings, and pence from
everyone else, is right good, and I congratulate
you on the bright idea. It was worthy of the
Chancellor of the Exchequer. Why, how do you
expect I live ?"

" By your wits, doubtless, and they coin gold.
Besides, your father allows you an annuity."

" I wish to heaven, my boy, it were so, and none
should share it sooner with me than yourself ;
but though my father makes me an allowance,
he always forgets to pay it. I have not had a
shilling which I could call my own for the last
six months. I am now driven to my last shift,
I should take a rope, or go on the highway, but
for this comfort—claret. Colley will no longer
lend me anything, and though Mrs. Clive wants
me to become her debtor, it is a thing I never
will do. She has a father, a husband, a sister,
and herself to support. Why should such a
worthless fellow as Harry Fielding be added to
the number ? Yet it is with difficulty I can
refuse her generosity ; and it gives me pain to
see her feel my refusal as a slight. But, poor as
I am, I will never act in a way unworthy of a
man of honour. But let me see—let me see—
can't we swindle some damned tailor out of fifty
pounds ?"

" I do not possess so rare an appendage as a
tailor. My father has never suffered me to order
my own clothes ? he has always kept me like a
boy, and I do not know a single tradesman."

" It is a most infernal shame," says Fielding,

" for if you had, we could easily have got plenty of money out of the rogues, and would have a trip together to the dominions of His Most Catholic Majesty, where we might get something from the priests for turning Papists. What then is to be done?"

" Why, I suppose I must go away without money."

" A capital notion—excellent—excellent. You mean, I suppose to get out of England as Sinbad did out of his diamond cave, by tying yourself to a rôk. Isn't that it?"

I shook my head.

" Well then, I know no other method for a man without money to get into Spain. What's your project?"

" I intend simply to go on board ship, and work my passage out as a common sailor."

Fielding looked at me incredulously. He laughed, and took another glass of wine. The notion seemed to take him by surprise. He had evidently never before thought of such a thing.

" Well," he said, " if you who can raise un-limited thousands by *post obits*, or by going in debt to the Jews, are such a regular nincompoop as to prefer working your passage out before the mast, by the labour of your hands, why I will put you into my Common-place, among the most remark-

able eccentricities in England; and would certainly introduce you on the stage in one of my
farces, only that, if I did, I fear it would be
damned by the critics for being false to all
modern notions of nature and reality."

"However that may may be, I will cheat no
one, except myself, and will never raise a penny
on *post obits* or by the Jews. I should be a common
swindler if I did; for I know my father will
never leave me a sixpence."

"And is there a young man of fashion in
England or out of it, who would not swindle a
Jew or a tailor if he could? Are not *they* ever
engaged in swindling *us?* What then is the
lex talionis for?"

"For rogues, no doubt; but not for you or
me, Harry."

"Well, Wortley, I believe there is some good
in you still. But who the devil is that?" and
Fielding half rose, as if about to retreat, and
turned rather pale, as he heard rather a loud
knock at the door. His fears, however, were as
instantly dispelled, for a vulgar, bull-puppy-
faced, short man, with a hard, cunning, sensual
eye, and coarse mouth entered. It proved to be
our old acquaintance, Colley Cibber.

"I protest to Heaven!" says the dramatist,
"you frightened me. I thought you were a

bailiff; and faith if I did not know you, I should have taken you for one when you entered."

" Mr. Fielding," says Cibber, " I am obliged to you for the compliment ; but I want to know whether that foolish farce is finished which we have been so long expecting? I think it is now some ten months since it was paid for."

" Oh, you old rogue," replied Fielding, " sit down ; have a glass, and let me tell you what Kitty Clive said about you t'other day." And he immediately, with infinite liveliness, invented a scene, in which Mrs. Clive had professed the greatest admiration for Cibber, whom she described as a perfect husband, father, wit, fine gentleman, actor, and I don't know what else besides. The old fool swallowed it all down, like honey, and forgot to pester Fielding about the farce—or what was really as bad, to remind him that it had been paid for. He drank a glass or two, and then, for the first time, began to recognise me.

" My good Mr. Smith," he said, " I did not remember you. Pray excuse me, and let me know how you are getting on."

Fielding stared at him with great amazement. Cibber, however, did not notice it, and I gave the dramatist a look. He smiled archly.

" Colley," he said, " what in Lucifer's name

do you mean by calling my cousin Montagu by
that rascally misnomer? Smith—Smith—allow
me, sir, to present you to him, and then make
one of your best stage bows. Mr. Colley Cibber,
patentee of the Theatre Royal, Drury Lane, I
present you to Mr. Wortley Montagu, Junior,
only son and heir of the Right Honourable
Edward Wortley Montagu, Lord of the Treasury,
&c., &c., and Lady Mary Wortley, daughter of
His Grace the Duke of Kingston. Cousin
Montagu, know Mr. Colley Cibber, who is one of
the most refined rakes, rogues, and wits in Great
Britain."

I was covered with confusion. Old Cibber
almost humbled himself in the dust before me.
Never was seen a more wonderful change from
patronising politeness, into crawling subserviency. Cibber had always behaved to me as a
respectable elder, with a position well established,
to a poor devil of a junior with no position at
all, or probably with even no prospect of one.
But here was a magic change indeed. The only
son and heir of the richest man in London was
before him, and he at once grovelled in the dust
at my feet. Fielding saw, and enjoyed the rapid
metamorphosis—but I was wholly confounded.
The old rogue saw it and hastened to relieve me.

" Ah," he said, " I see an intrigue—sly,—

sly—damnably sly. In the city too!—as Mr.
Smith—capital! capital! quite a dramatic incident, full of novelty and fire, damme—but who
would have thought it? Mr. Wortley Montagu,
I am proud and honoured in renewing—or rather
I should say, in making so distinguished an
acquaintance. May I present you with a pinch
of snuff?"

We talked on various matters. Cibber was
great on his friend Lord Chesterfield, and other
noble lords whose toady he was. Rumour said
he supplied them with actresses; but all managers
of theatres do this for their patrons,—so that
there was nothing wonderful in that. I have
known one of the most charming, modest,
talented young creatures in the world, who
sought employment at a royal theatre; her
recommendations from country managers, under
whom she had eminently distinguished herself,
were first rate. The director looked at them
scornfully, but at herself impertinently.
"Well," he said, "all this is very fine, but if I
engage you, you must get somebody to take a
private box—we have some remaining at a
hundred guineas." The young creature was
silent. It was her first visit to London, and she
did not understand him.

"Private box—hundred guineas," she murmured. "Why, dear sir, I don't know what you mean? I have come to ask employment, and you tell me I must take a private box."

The manager looked at her with curiosity. Such vestal ignorance was rather new. At first he did not believe it possible that anyone should be so benighted in these polished times, but a searching glance into her clear eye shewed that she really was so.

"Madam," he answered, "We have applications every day from scores of young women, all as clever, pretty and well recommended as yourself. We are in no want of talent—the town is pleased with what it gets. But you want to make a name in London—to win a reputation. Well you must pay for it. It is worth your while to make some sacrifice to get on the boards. Get some nobleman or gentleman to take a private box, and if he does so, we will then take you on. If you can't do this, you can't act here."

Even still she did not understand him; she replied, "But, Sir, I don't know anyone in the world who would do such a thing for *me;* I have none to depend upon but myself."

"Very well," said the manager, "good morning; but you need'nt come here again."

And this system to my absolute knowledge

now prevails almost universally at all the great
theatres—and I suppose it will extend to the
minor ones in time. So refined a people have
we become! But the honourable writers and
critics connected with these haunts of infamy,
take good care not to let the gentle public into
the secret ; and I believe I am the first who ever
did so. I have no doubt I shall receive my
reward—abuse.

In all these matters, Colley was of course a
proficient. Oh, how the old rogue crowed,
laughed, rejoiced, revelled in his scoundrelism.
If you could believe himself, he was the most
desperate villain alive. No age or rank, or sex,
or condition was sacred from his profanation.
Every man was a scoundrel ; every woman a
wanton. Thus he ran on. And he furnished
examples as he went along, that his views were
not merely theoretical—but founded on solid
facts. Did he weep, lament, or sigh over this?
Not he. He gloried in it ; he triumphed in the
universal baseness. He enumerated his own
debaucheries, gaming, subserviency, and filth,
until it made me sick. Here was an old
man, upwards of seventy, who seemed a walking
demon, and was proud to be considered so.

Fielding at length came to the point at which

he had evidently been running for half-an-hour.
With fine irony he began as follows:—

"After all Colley, from what I have known of
you, you are a good man, a feeling man, a kind
man, with all your eccentricities. Just hear me,
and when I have done, say whether you have not
an opportunity of performing one of the noblest
acts that ever man did?"

Cibber's eyes sparkled. He was evidently
glad of this encomium on his merits, thus made
in my presence.

"Mr. Fielding," he said, "I shall be glad to
know what you mean."

"It is not for myself I speak," resumed
my cousin. I know if I were in the lowest
pit of Tartarus, or even worse, in the Fleet
Prison, you would not get me out if ten
pounds paid down would do it. Nor do I com-
plain of that. Nay, don't look so surprised, but
help yourself to another glass—I shouldn't ask
the money, and you wouldn't give it, so no harm
would be done; but I now speak to you for
another."

And Fielding narrated a most piteous tale that
would have drawn tears from the hardest congregation, and melted even a company of professed
Christians. I only recollect the outlines. A young
girl in the country, the daughter of a painter,

beautiful and innocent, engaged to be married to a gentleman whom she devotedly loved; the day fixed for the wedding; the father thrown into prison by an unrelenting creditor, who took advantage of the approaching union; poor old man seized with paralysis: another week's confinement will destroy him; the debt is only fifty pounds; the daughter takes the whole liability on herself; the father is released; the lover is disgusted at finding they are so poor, and basely repudiates the match; the young girl is now arrested by the scoundrel who imprisoned her father; she is lodged in prison for the debt; the old man dies when he hears the sad news; will no one release her? Will no one fly to the rescue of this perishing virgin? Yes, there is one generous man who will do it — to whose heart charity never appealed twice; whose bosom is the shrine of pity. That man is Colley Cibber."

My cousin stopped. The tears were in his own eyes, so moving was the pathos of his narrative. But he spoke to a rock.

"Mr. Fielding," says Cibber, "I should be glad to assist this lady, indeed my heart feels for her"—the old rogue wiped his eyes, into which he called some theatrical tears—" but money, sir, money is very tight just now, and I really cannot do it—I really cannot. In a week or so—"

"Zounds, man, in a week she will be dead. She cannot survive her father's loss."

"Well, then, if it is only a week surely that will make little difference. It is a great pity she was so imprudent. I feel for her—I feel as if she were a daughter of my own—the dear child; but money is tight."

Fielding looked at him and changed the conversation. He rattled on love, gallantry, the stage, the green room. Lord Chesterfield became the subject of his discourse, and he kept us in a perpetual laugh. Suddenly he kept his eye upon Cibber, and said—

"Apropos, Colley, what do you think brings young Montagu here to-day. His old screw of a father won't lend him fifty pounds, so he came to me to borrow it. Was not *that* an excellent notion?"

"Impossible," answered Colley, "I know hundreds who would lend him thousands."

"To be sure they would," says my cousin, "but he is a prudent youth, and don't intend to run into their nets. Besides, this is a little private affair of gallantry, and he wishes to be sly—quite sly. You understand, Colley; don't you, you elderly sinner?"

I protested with my eyes against all this; but Fielding wouldn't see it; so he went on in his mad way. Cibber licked his lips.

"Such a pretty little rogue; only fifteen, fresh from rural scenes, budding into perfect loveliness. But her mother has some scruples; she won't let him have her unless he pays fifty pounds down to the wretch, and faith he hasn't it. So he came to me. Absurd, Colley, wasn't it? I tried to persuade him to be moral—but youth, youth—you know. And he is quite in despair about her."

"Ah! yes, youth, youth, and only fifteen did you say. Upon my soul they would be nicely matched. But that old haridan of a mother; was there ever anything so unreasonable, so wicked? I did not think there were such wretches in the world. Not sell her daughter to so pretty a young gentleman for less than fifty pounds? Won't even take his word for it? Oh! horrid; the age grows quite blasphemous. Mr. Montagu," he added, turning to me, " I shall be for ever your debtor if you will honour me by the acceptance of this trifle. It would be cruel to disappoint so fine a young gentleman. There is the money; repay it at your leisure. No, no, not a word. I won't take a refusal." And he pulled out his pocket-book and wrote me an order on his goldsmith for fifty pounds, which he thrust into my hand, and before I could prevent him left the room.

My first movement was to knock him down and kick Fielding himself; but the latter winked at me, and I determined to wait awhile and see whither all this tended. When the door was closed on Colley, Fielding flung himself back on his sofa and laughed for an entire quarter of an hour. He was quite beside himself. I could not make him hear or answer a word. At the end of that time I put the order into the fire. My cousin saw it, but too late to save it. This at once changed his laughter into the most profound gravity.

"Zounds! Wortley," he said, " what have you done? You have thrown away fifty pounds."

I explained to him that I did not approve of the jest; he saw that I was really angry, and he offered me a hundred apologies.

"Upon my honour, cousin," he said, " I could not resist the temptation of showing up the old vagabond in his true colours. I think I did so; and you must forgive me if I made you the stalking horse. The thing is done—I wish you had kept the money. I beg your pardon." And he held out his hand. I could not refuse it, and we were friends again.

"Now," said he, " in the name of Lazarillo de Tormes, Gil Blas, and Sir Robert Walpole— as good a beggar as any of them—how shall we raise money for the Opera House to-night? I have made up my mind to go, and you shall accompany me, as Falstaff says. But what money hast thou in thy purse?"

I produced it; it was only two guineas.

"Bah," said he, "that will never do. Stay here a moment," and he ran into another room, from which he immediately returned with a perriwig, a blue velvet suit edged with gold, not quite new, a silver hilted sword, a pair and a half of silk stockings, two shirts finely laced, a cocked hat, a ring belonging to his grandmother, a family Bible, a pair of red heeled shoes, and a lady's satin petticoat.

These he arranged with some neatness, and tied into a bundle. I asked him what he was doing.

"Oh!" he said, "only going to a kind friend, who obliges me with money sometimes, but as I don't like to be outdone in generosity, I usually deposit some little superfluous articles like these with him, and he generally gives me his note of hand."

"Do you mean a pawnbroker?" I asked.

"Yes," said he, "that is what the vulgar call him. How on earth were you clever enough to make the guess?"

The parcel was now tied up.

"Remain here, Wortley," said he, "for a few minutes." And galloping gaily downstairs, he called a coach, into which he popped with his bundle, singing and whistling like a big school boy.

In about a quarter of an hour he returned capering with joy.

"Hurrah! hurrah!" he said, "Evöe! Io Bacchus! never was anything so fortunate. I am the luckiest fellow on earth. I am richer than Crœsus, or your father. I am the happiest fellow in the world," and he ran up, and putting his arms about me, he kissed me in the excess of his madness. Opening his hand, he produced ten guineas, the gleam of which set him capering again.

"There," he said, "did I not tell you I was Dives himself. Now come and let us prepare for the Opera House. No time is to be lost. We shall go in dominoes. All the fine people in the world will be there."

CHAPTER XXIX.

"Now as they were making their hearts merry, behold the men of the city, certain sons of Belial, beset the house round about."

I was scarcely in any humour to go a-mas-querading, but Fielding's genial manner was difficult to resist, and he half thrust me into a mask and domino, amusing his fancy all the while with images of the adventures we should have. We called a coach and got to the Opera House about ten. The rooms were already full, and we resolved to take a survey of them at first before we engaged in any more particular pur-suit. There were Soldiers, Monks, Demons, Jews, Priests, Cardinals, Harlequins, Clowns, Shep-herdesses, Kings, Turks, Pantaloons, Bandits,

Negroes, Fox-hunters, Princesses, Nuns, Fairies, Frenchmen, Corsairs, and Maids of Honour—a motley assemblage, symbolical in its variety of the real world about us. Twenty masks one after another ran up to us, and saying, " Do you know me?" were rather disgusted with our ignorance of one and all; for we spoke in feigned voices, not intending to reveal ourselves until we had performed the entire circuit of the place. This was at length achieved, and we sat down at a table for some refreshment.

" Your present condition," said Fielding, who was half sentimentally tipsy, "reminds me somewhat of Cornifix, Count of Ulfeld, Great Master of Denmark. For this noble person was like you, the son of a great nobleman—indeed his father was Lord Chancellor of Denmark; and like you his spirit was so lively that at the age of ten, the old gentleman being wholly unable to control him, or reduce him within any reasonable bounds, was obliged to send him to Paris under the care of a governor, with strict orders to curb the growth of a most licentious temper. But although he laboured in this honourable employment for five years, he was unable to check the young Count, and at the end of that period he wrote to his father, resigning the task in despair. The old man, enraged at such perversity in his son, dis-

carded him for ever, and Count Ulfeld, thrown
on his own resources before he was sixteen, was
little better than a wandering outcast, though
whether he went in masquerade among the
gypsies hath not been recorded by the historian.
In his last extremity he travelled into Germany,
and made his case known to Count Oldenburgh,
who was a distant relation. The Count was
pleased with his wit and figure, and entertained
him for three years, at the end of which period
half the husbands were jealous of the young
Dane, and all the women, particularly the wedded
ones, were pulling caps for his favours. But
when the war broke out between King Christian
and some of the Germanic princes, Count Ulfeld,
being tired of Venus and longing after Mars,
solicited letters from his kinsman to General
Fowlk, one of the greatest captains of the age,
under whom he campaigned for five years, until
he became as thorough a soldier as he had before
been a courtier. On the restoration of peace he
went into Italy, and became acquainted with
Signor Cremonini, a noble Venetian, who made
him an accomplished diplomatist, and by his influence he was sent into Denmark in the train of
an ambassador, from the Republic. At Copen-
hagen he was present at all the conferences which
the Chancellor, his father, had with the Ambassa-

dor, and the former began to feel a wonderful
liking for the young stranger, whose ready wit
and general knowledge were of great advantage
to the Ambassador's councils.   He took occasion
to solicit a private interview him, and after offer-
ing him all the services in his power, and en-
treating earnestly that he would enter into the
service of Denmark, he begged to know of what
family he was?   The young man at first refused
to satisfy him on that point, but being pressed
much he at length said, 'My lord, I am that
unfortunate son of your own, whom you discarded
for his youthful follies on his governor's report.
May I hope that I have sufficiently atoned for
them?'   The Chancellor was delighted with the
discovery, and made the King acquainted with the
whole story, so that in a little time Count Ulfeld
became the idol of both count and kingdom.
May I venture to hope a similar termination
to all your escapades?"

"You certainly may venture to hope it; but
my mother's hatred of me is so intense, and my
father's folly about his money is so perfect, that
I think the notion that I possibly some day may
enjoy his wealth, is alone sufficient to make him
loathe me, and I do not anticipate so favourable
an ending of my drama as that which happened
to Count Ulfeld.   In the Montagu as in the

Guelph family, the eldest son is always hated by his family."

"Well, let us change the subject," he said; "and *apropos* of nothing we shall have the Guelphs here to-night, father and son, both followed by some of the basest gold-embroidered knaves on earth, fawning and smiling on the 'fountain of honour,' and ready to sell their souls for a smile or a promise. Who that looks upon such a scene can entertain any feeling but that of scorn for the rogues in purple who call themselves 'most noble,' 'right honourable,' and 'full of grace.' Such titles seem conferred in irony; they are certainly the bitterest sarcasms on their possessors; yet these fellows carry them about as gravely as if they expressed their true inward nature. They always remind me of that right honourable jackdaw that dressed himself in peacock's feathers."

"There is an old saying, Harry, that 'fools are the favourites of fortune;' I think it should rather be that knaves are."

"Fools and knaves, dear Wortley, are convertible terms. I never yet knew a fool who was not a knave also, only that he had not the capacity to carry it out; I never yet knew a knave who was not on the whole an arrant fool. Here comes one who is a beautiful compound of both."

And Lord Hillsborough, the wildest and most scandalous libertine of that day of libertines passed. He was engaged with a couple of pure shepherdesses, one of whom had a pastoral crook and another a sylvan pipe ; Hillsborough himself being attired as Paris on the Dardan Hills, but looking like a bacchanal of Drury Lane. He had pulled his mask off, and was half drunk already. A rabble followed him, listening to brutal wit and ribaldry, only coarser than that of Swift or Rabelais, of whom he seemed compounded.

" I wonder is his wife here ?" said Fielding. " I hope she is."

An elegantly dressed fop now approached us. Bowing to Fielding, he said, in a lisping voice, half song, half recitative—

" Do you know me ? Fal, lal, lal, la."

" I certainly do," said Harry ; " you are Jack Frothwell."

" The same at your service, Mr. Fielding. Damme, I am delighted to see you here. I am looking for the divine Phillis ! Fal, lal, lal, la. And what do you think of my dress ? This pink satin is the heavenliest thing. And this ring I got from the Countess of ——. Fal, lal, lal, la. Damme."

" I think the Countess Fal-lal has shewn exquisite taste in her selection of a lover," answered Fielding ; " you are both well matched, Damme."

" 'Pon my soul, you say truly," answered Jack, "and I'll repeat your compliment to her, the moment I see her ladyship. Fal, lal, lal, la. Have you seen many here to-night that you know ?"

" Oh ! hundreds—England realizes the proud boast of one of the knights of old, all whose sons were brave, all whose daughters were chaste. The superlative degree of both are congregated here to-night."

" Divine England ! divine pleasure ; the first, the only land for the second—the second enjoyed nowhere but in the first. Fal, lal, lal, la. Don't you think that a good observation, Mr. Fielding ?"

" Which ? England, pleasure, or Fal, lal, lal, la ?"

" Nay, if you grow satirical, I must be off. Faith, I see her ladyship yonder. O, Divine ! Fal-lal. Adieu—adieu. I kiss your hands." And the beau went off, like a squib of gun-

powder, muttering his favourite " Fal, lal, lal, la,"
while " damme " softly echoed in the air.

"That man has ten thousand a-year," sighed
Harry, " and you see how he spends it. When
God apportions money, he writes on the label
Detur turpissimo, and consigns it to the Devil to
choose the recipient. In this instance the bequest
has come to its true destination. But you look
as if I were growing personal. Upon my honour,
I never thought of your father when I spoke—
though if I had Fal, lal, lal, la ;" and he mimicked
the absurd beau in a way that compelled laughter.

While we were thus engaged, my old friend
Lord Chesterfield, attired as a Spanish grandee,
passed near ; he wore no mask, and he was
followed by a well-dressed crowd of giddy youths,
who seemed to think him divinity ; and I could
see many a stray glance from bright eyes wafted
towards the strutting little Don. Fielding
looked at me for a moment ; his eyes twinkled
with fun.

" Behold," he whispered, " the glass of
fashion, and the mould of form—Philip Stan-
hope Earl of Chesterfield. He is reputed to be
the finest courtier we have ; look at him and
acknowledge that the eulogy is merited. He
mocks every man, and boasts that he intrigues

with every woman, though his recent affair with
the Duchess of Manchester has not tended much
to his glory as a lady-killer."

" What was that ?"

" Why, just this. Her grace has been married
about nine years, and having no issue, our peer
thought it a pity that the honours of this noble
house should be transferred from the direct line
to a brother. He accordingly waited on her grace
a few mornings since, though he knew but little
of her, having only seen her once or twice at court.
After a few compliments, which no man can pay
with prettier grace, he delicately alluded to the
absence of an heir to this most honourable title ;
informed her that he should be most happy to
form such an acquaintance with her as would
probably produce so desirable a consummation.
The Duchess, who is a namesake of yours, was
silent for sometime ; in fact her indignation
stopped her power of speech, which gave my
lord so much encouragement, that he was proceeding to kiss her hand, when the lady, rising,
thus saluted this well-bred worshipper of the
graces. ‘ Begone, sir, from my presence, nor
ever again dare to enter it—and think yourself
well off that for this affront I do not order my
servants to thrust you headlong out of doors.’
My lord smiled, bowed, and I suppose has come

here unmasked, to exhibit to the world his grand indifference to such trifling accidents, which are unable to disturb his composure even for a moment." *

" I suppose my lady namesake was not so much displeased at the measure as with the man. Had the proposition come from another, who was an Antinous, it would have probably been better received. But this fellow seems an antidote to all love. His short figure, thick make, large rough-featured ugly face, black teeth, and head as big as Polyphemus, are more calculated to frighten the women than to captivate them. Only that he is a great deal uglier and more vulgar-looking, he would have reminded me of little Will, the waiter at the ' Turk's Head.' ' '

" Aye, and he is always prating of ' the graces.' "

" Yet you dedicated to him your ' Don Quixote in England.' "

" Yes, I did, and got twenty guineas for it. What could I do, Wortley? The old general was sending to me every day for a loan, and I could refuse him no longer. It is not every son would do so much for a father—as dedicate to Chesterfield."

---

* This story is repeated also in the " Life of Johnson," by Sir John Hawkins. Page 180.

The music now struck up, and we walked about the rooms. Fielding's fine figure and stalwart proportions attracted the fair sex in crowds. The pretty moths gathered around him as if he were a flaming candle. He reminded me of the Grand Seigneur (my forefather, as some of the wags say), and indeed I think I heard him humming out of Gay's Opera—

Thus I walk like the Turk with my doxies around.

I, though nearly as tall, could of course present no counterpart to his vast attractions. A good deal of his own experience in these matters subsequently appeared in "Tom Jones" and "Amelia"—those glorious novels.

A tall thin figure, with a most affected manner, passed us. He was dressed in the extreme of splendour—but it was an effeminate splendour. It was the luxury of a mannikin aping a fine gentleman. His gait was slow and pompous; but its pomposity made it laughable. I felt an icy chill as he came near. I have always thought there was a vast depth of sagacity in that observation which Shakespere puts into the mouth of one of his witches—

By the pricking of my thumbs,
Something wicked this way comes.

I am never even unconsciously in the presence of

a foe, or a thoroughly bad person, that I do not,
as if by instinct, feel uneasy. The same sense of
oppression, annoyance, and dislike now came
over me.

"Who is this?" I whispered to my companion.

"What," he said, "don't you know him?—

> Narcissus praised with all a parson's power,
> Looked a white lily sunk beneath a shower.

So Pope sang of Lord Hervey, after he had
read Middleton's dedication of Cicero to him."
And then he continued, half audibly, half in an
undertone—

> Let Sporus tremble—What? that thing of silk,
> Sporus that mere white curd of asses' milk?
> Satire or sense alas! can Sporus feel?
> Who breaks a butterfly upon the wheel?
> Eternal smiles his emptiness betray
> As shallow streams run dimpling all the way;
> Whether in florid impotence he speaks,
> And as the prompter breathes, the puppet squeaks,
> Or at the ear of Eve,* familiar toad,
> Half froth, half venom, spits himself abroad.
> Amphibious thing that acting either part,
> The trifling head or the corrupted heart.
> Fop at the toilet, flatterer at the board,
> Now trips a lady, and now struts a lord ;
> Eve's tempter* thus the Rabbins have expressed,
> A cherub's face, a reptile all the rest.

Fielding repeated these terrible verses with so
little heed as to who heard him, that I am satis-

* It was thus that Pope alluded to Lady M. W. and Lord H.

fied " Sporus " himself had the benefit of it all.
He darted a look at us that even under his mask
betrayed rage. " Good Heaven !" I thought,
" can this be Lady Mary's favourite Adonis?"
Fielding divined my thoughts, but he was
too well bred to allude to one of the current
scandals of the day.

"This man," he said, " is another example of
what we have been saying. When he married
Molly Lepell, whom the wags now begin to call
' Old Brimstone,' though it is surely too soon, he
sent her every night to court, to induce old
George the First to take her into keeping—the
doting fool at that time having no less than four
other public mistresses, as well as some half-
dozen on his own private establishment, though
what he wanted them for no one can dream. It
is said that when he is with his mistress he merely
employs himself ' cutting paper.' The Duchess
of Kendal got alarmed, and gave her four thousand pounds to stay away. Our noble friend
accepted the money with great devotion, and
bought a town house and furniture with it, and
our noble lady became a rank Jacobite. So much
for courts. What do you think of the wife?
Wasn't their joint project a notable one? But
she was early schooled into the true value of
money. Her father, old General Lepell, was

colonel of a regiment of horse, and Mary Lepell
regularly drew her pay as one of his cornets;
the thing lasted up to the time when she was appointed Maid of Honour—when it was thought
too scandalous to continue it, and it was transferred to another sister, who I suppose has it still.
My lady is a very nice Latin scholar, and is not
without wit.   What do you think the King
said the other night to her master. 'My Lord
Hervey, you ought not to write verses; it is
beneath your rank.   Leave such work to little
Mr. Pope.'   I suppose this explains the verses—

> And justly Cæsar scorns the poet's lays,
> It is to history he trusts for praise.

And history no doubt will give it.   But hush !
here comes Moll Skerrett—Walpole's lady of the
hareem, daughter of the parish clerk of St.
Andrew's, Holborn.   O, Moll Skerrett! Moll
Skerrett! many ups and downs have I seen in life,
but none more worthy of renown than thine.
Mark my words : Walpole's man (the King) will
make *her* Countess also some day."

The crowd saw not St. Andrews, and heard not
A-men in my lady, but perceived only the quint-
essence of St. James's, and the perfume of the
Treasury—a whole drawing-room full of the
finest people followed her worshipping.   It was
the old story of Vashti.   The jews were not the

only scoundrels that ever lived. They had their imitators in Pall Mall. The noble herd cared not that my lady was Sir Robert's avowed and shameless mistress, and that his wife was living. They only saw the favourite of the all powerful Prime Minister. In her train was Lady Mary, always one of her chief friends and backers. Lord Hervey immediately joined them. My mother appeared in her fancy costume—an Eastern robe and head-dress. It became her well. All the honourable and fashional witlings fluttered about her; all the noblemen and illustrious women dangled after Moll. The Duchess of Kendal, that tall, lean, ill-favoured mawkin, paid court to her; the huge Madam Platen whose two fierce black eyes shone like moons eclipsed, or burnt holes in a blanket, over two continents of painted cheeks, and a whole ocean of neck, did not disdain to flatter the Holborn goddess. The three were, indeed, " birds of a feather," and shed splendid light on court morals. That night, I think, decided me for ever, and gave me a repugnance to society which I have never got over. I am glad of it. Solitude has made me a better man.

"Can this be Lord Cavendish?" whispered Fielding. "Yes, it is he, by Jupiter, and still full of his grand exploit, riding from Hyde Park

Corner to the Lodge at Windsor in an hour and
six minutes—twenty-one miles, for five thousand
pounds !   And here is the fool who lost the
money, Sir Robert Fogg—himself also a horse
fancier.   No wonder it has been said that England is the hell of horses, since they are spurred
to death in this style.   But where is Pulteney
who pinked Lord Hervey in a duel some time
since—and would certainly have sent him across
the Styx, only that his foot slipped just as he was
making the final lunge.   And where is the Duke
of Cumberland, who stands godfather to everyone that asks him, and can give him a good feed ?
But we shall see him with the Prince, unless,
indeed, he follows metal more attractive ; eighty
stone weight of fat and flabbiness.   But what
have we here ?"

And a Mask mounting on a chair, cried out—
" Oyez ! Oyez ! Oyez ! all good people, come
and listen to a right merry ballad, written by the
Virgin Mary, the greatest wit and brightest
nymph that ever celebrated the praise of Bath."
And the silly crowd began to gather at his cry.

I knew the voice ; it was that of Dr. Young.
But the parson did not care where he went, or
what he did, so long as it served his purpose.

When a sufficiently large mob of fashionable
people had assembled round the crier, and silence

had been at length procured, the reverend gentleman read the following ballad, amid great applause. I insert the thing here—first, because
it is not printed in my lady's published works;
and, secondly, because it so vividly reminds me
of the whole folly of the scene that night:—

> To all you ladies now at Bath,
>   And eke yo beaux to you,
> With aching heart and watery eyes,
>   I bid my last adieu.

" You see, gentlemen, what a fine thing it is
to belong to the ancient and honourable order of
beaux; to draw brilliants from the eyes of this
fair and noble lady, must, indeed, be a rare
chance, and such has been that of your Bath
brethren. But let us hope it won't be her last
adieu, and that she will again return to illumi-
nate that Bladudian town, though we can never
see too much of her here." An observation
which elicited general approval from the
crowd.

The reverend gentleman in disguise, read on—

> Farewell you nymphs who waters sip,
>   Fresh reeking from the pumps,
> While music lends her friendly aid,
>   To cheer you from the dumps.

" Aye, faith," says one; " they must have been
in the dumps when Lady Mary was there, for she
carried off all their lovers."

" No," says another, " the reason they were in the dumps was because they drank water instead of ratafia."

> Farewell yo wits who prating stand,
>   And criticise the fair,
> Yourselves the joke of men of sense,
>   Who hate a coxcomb air.

" Gentlemen," says Young, " this observation applies only to the Bath wits—for so I hear they call themselves. They should come and learn of us here in London, who alone have true wit and humour; not of Beau Nash, who is a very dull fellow, indeed."

" There you lie," shouted a mask, " and if I had you in Bath I should order you to be pumped, though you *are* a parson."

" You lie like a knave," said Young, trusting to his disguise; " I'm no parson."

" Ain't *you*, Neddy Young?" asked Nash.

" No, indeed," answered the other, with an unblushing bronze that would have done honour to the court.

" Then I'm sorry to think," retorted Nash, " that there are two of you. I thought the devil could have made only one."

" Hear him—hear Harry Nash," bawled two or three; " demme, he wants to give laws here; but we'll toss him in a blanket if he tries."

" By Gad ! if you do," says Nash, " it will be
the best thing you ever tossed ; but I don't think
you'll try."

" Go on, parson," cried Jack Frothwell; and
Young resumed—

> Farewell to Deards, and all her toys,
>   Which glitter in her shop,
> Deluding traps to girls and boys,
>   The warehouse of the fop.
>
> Lindsay's and Hayes's both farewell !
>   Where in the spacious hall,
> With bounding steps and sprightly air,
>   I've led up many a ball.

" Ah ! you lovely woman," cried one ; " would
to Cupid I had been there to see. These bounding steps and sprightly airs are the very things I
like best of all others in the world."

And here he sighed in a most ludicrous
manner.

> Where Turberville of courteous mien,
>   Was partner in the dance,
> With swimming Hawes, and Brownlow blythe,
>   And Britton, pink of France.

" Three cheers for ' swimming Hawes,' " cried
Jack ; " she is now Lady Vane, and faith, there's
no fish in the sea I'd sooner swim with." This
sally produced great laughter.

> Poor Nash—farewell ! may fortune's smile,
>   Thy drooping soul revive,
> My heart is full—I can no more—
>   John, bid the coachman drive.

"There now, Nash, there's comfort for you," said Young, as he stopped and folded up the paper. "By the Gods, such a wish as that proceeding from so fine a lady must raise you to the seventh heaven of Olympus, if there were such a place at all, which I don't believe there is."

"Aye!" retorted the King of Bath, "but such cursed folly as you have been speaking, sinks me back again into the seventh pit of hell—where I should gladly leave you if I believed there were such a region."

And the crowd separated to seek some other foolery.

"You hear all this," said Fielding to me— "but her ladyship exposes herself to it. When will she learn sense?"

"Aye! when indeed—or respect for her position?"

"Have you read her late verses to Lady Jermyn, Craggs's sister? A receipt to cure the spleen."

I pleaded ignorance, and with perfect sincerity. I was no reader of my mother's writings—they sickened me completely.

"Here they are," said Fielding; "and faith for the sake of the beautiful sex, I am ashamed of them," and he recited—

I, like you, was born a woman ;
　Well I know what vapours mean
The disease alas! is common,
　Single we have all the spleen,
All the morals that they tell us
　Never cured the sorrow yet,
Chuse among the pretty fellows
　One of honour, youth, and wit.
Prithee, bear him every morning
　At the least an hour or two,
Once again at night returning—
　I believe the dose will do.

" Let us change the subject, Harry," I said, " I am tired of it." My cousin was silent. After a pause he asked—

" What do you think of the King of Bath?"

" Nothing," I answered.

" And you are right," he rejoined ; " he is nothing, but out of his nothingness he makes a princely income. He it was who first led the fashion of riding naked on a cow for a wager, which some of our fine gentlemen, Lord Gainsborough among the rest, have mimicked. I have known him in London watch a whole day at a window in the Smyrna Coffee House, in order to receive a bow from a Duke or a Duchess, as they passed, where he was standing, and he would then look round upon the company for admiration and respect."

" I fear the world is full of such."

" Yet," pursued Fielding, " the fellow is a

kind of humourist in his way. He once gave
out publicly that he would drink no wine but
what was strained through his sweetheart's smock,
and I have seen him eat a pair of her shoes tossed
up in a fricassee. And though this savours of
the extreme of madness, there were fifty young
fellows who imitated him in all this. Yet I
admire one part in the fellow, which shows him
not to be entirely lost. He is noted for never
mentioning his father. Dr. Cheyne swears he
never had one. The Duchess of Marlborough
one day said he was like Gil Blas, who was
ashamed of his father. ' No, madam,' he replied ;
' I never mention my father in *this* company, not
because I have any reason to be ashamed of him,
but because he has some reason to be ashamed of
me.' And he bowed to all around. I hardly
think they saw the sarcasm. But whom have we
here ?

" He is the best dressed man in town, Lord
Portmore—with his new wife, the Duchess of
Leeds, whom he has not yet got tired of—" and
Fielding showed me a fine looking figure arrayed
in gold and velvet and a blaze of jewels.

" He certainly does look well ; does his
inner man correspond with this gorgeous outward ?"

" Hear what the Duchess of Queensbury says

of him, and judge for yourself. He was about building a house in their neighbourhood; they proposed him a very fine situation where he might have a splendid view of the sea; but the fine gentleman cried out 'O Christ! the sea looks so fierce it frights me.' Is he not a pretty fellow to be a legislator?

"But who comes here? Antony Henley, one of the most brutal profligates in England, and only inferior to his brother, whom we call 'Surly Bob.' Have you heard of the letter he sent to his constituents last week. They wrote to him to oppose the Excise Bill. This was his answer—

"'Rascals, I received yours, and am surprised at your insolence in troubling me about the excise. You know what I very well know, that I bought you, and by G—, I am determined to sell you. And I know what you perhaps think I do not know, you are now selling yourselves to somebody else. And I know what you do not know, that I am buying another borough. May God's curse light on you all; may your houses be as open and common to all excise officers as your wives and daughters were to me when I stood for your rascally corporation.'

"Now, Wortley, if ever you stand for Huntingdon, you will know how to address your voters;

this indeed may be regarded as a model of composition."

"Nay," said I, "I know something of these matters too, for I had a little to do with the last election for Bilgewater. I think Henley must have been its member, for there is not a line in his letter which is not applicable to that noted constituency."

Henley seeing us looking at him rather keenly, walked unceremoniously up to where we were.

"Hallo! Fielding," he said, "what have you pulled off your mask for? Ain't you afraid of the bailiffs?"

"Why, yes I was," retorted Harry, "but when I saw you walking about so fearlessly, I knew that there were none here, and that I was safe."

"Damn ye," answered Henley, "you're out there—my privilege of Parliament protects me—so you're bitten by G—."

"Well then," added Fielding, "the true reason why I pulled it off was this; I heard you were to be here in a domino like this, and not to be mistaken for the veriest rogue in Parliament, I uncovered my face."

Henley abruptly left us.

"But who is this that trips so nymphlike over

the boards? by her swimming motion I cannot
be mistaken—by the monkey at her side I can
scarcely be deceived. Let me wait till I hear
her voice, and then I shall be more certain."

Fielding put on his mask, and went up to a
lady dressed as Night—a dark lace dress with a
profusion of gold stars, and a veil of the same
costly material floating to the floor. She was
leaning on a gentleman attired as a French
postillion—and he became the character well.
Harry made an elegant bow, and whispered "Do
you know me?" He received an answer in the
negative, but the voice was like the wild soft
strain of a harp—it thrilled through one's very
heart. Fielding again bowed and retired.

"Yes," he whispered to me. "I was right;
it is Lady Vane— the 'swimming Hawes' of your
mother's ballad. She is just married. Her
father is a rich West Indian; he was in the South
Sea swindle, by which he increased his estate
£40,000; and bought a most lovely place,
Purley Hall, near Reading; but ill-gotten gains
seldom prosper; and this old knave having, like
a big rogue, taken a mistress and got a new family,
he brought up this innocent young creature to
town, and published everywhere that she was to
have an immense fortune; five hundred negroes
with silver collars and so forth. This drew all

the young lords and rakes after her; but she ran away with Lord William Hamilton; and old Hawes used this as a pretext not to give her a sixpence—he himself having unknown to her, devised the whole plot of the elopement by bribing her maid, who encouraged her to the step. Poor Lord William was a very honourable fellow, but like all Scotsmen, he had no money; he was disappointed, but what could he do? He died soon after of a fever caught in an election contest, and her father immediately sold her to Lord Vane, the imp by her side, whom she destested, but who it is said settled an immense jointure on her, which I don't think he ever means to pay. But trust me she will soon leave him—or I have no skill in women, or in men either." How this prediction was fulfilled, all the world knows.

Poor Lady Vane! I am truly sorry for her. Dr. Smollett has lately published her life and adventures, and has been much abused for it; but I am heartily glad he has committed them to the press; otherwise she might have floated down to posterity in the same rank with mad Lady Oxford, and still madder Lady Orford, and worst and maddest of all, that wild woman, Charles Townsend's meteoric mother. I followed her with my eyes. I was under a species of fascination for the moment. She half entranced and bound me in her spells. With all her follies there was an amount of *heart* in all she said and did; she was so evidently genuine, frank and good natured, that had I not been all-enthralled to the noblest of women, I fear I should have found myself among this lady's adorers.

A lank lean looking man, something like a horse jockey, now came up to us "Mr. Fielding," said he, " Have you seen my Lady Burlington here?"

" Yes," said Harry, "she has just passed with the Grand Vizier—or one that would be like him."

A peculiar smile, half silly, half spiteful, passed over the other's face, and he left us.

" There is a fellow," said my cousin—"he resigned a place at court some time since, because he would not vote with Walpole,—but his wife, who is openly intriguing with the Duke, as his Grace is evidently amouring with the prim Princess Amelia—would not give up hers, and the fool has nearly made himself ridiculous by losing a post worth £3,000 a year, sooner than sacrifice his patriotism, while he dishonours his family rather than give up the £1,200 which he gets for serving *cette diablesse Madame la princesse,* as the King calls her. How can you account for such things? Does God give the same sort of brains to these creatures that he bestows on ordinary mortals? And here is that blundering blockhead, Lord Falmouth—I know him well though he is disguised as a Spanish Grandee. Avarice and meanness are as proverbial in that family as coarseness and lying in the Stuarts. When this fellow's father was dying there was only his apothecary present. "Watson," said he, "give me a shirt out of that drawer in the corner." The apothecary stared and begged him not to disturb himself—he thought he was raving. 'Pray give it me,' said the dying lord, 'for I understand it is a custom that the shirt one dies in, becomes the perquisite of the layer out; this I have on is a very fine lace one, but that in the drawer is an old ragged one, and good enough for the jade.' And he would not rest and could not die till Watson had changed them."

"Gentlemen," said Jack Frothwell—calling a crowd around him—"I beg pardon, Ladies, my Lords and Gentlemen, who among you can help me to two hundred guineas?"

"Not I," says one, and "Not I," says another, and a third said "I'll see you damned first."

"Ah," says Jack, "I thought how it would be; none of you will own to this robbery."

"What robbery," demanded a hundred voices.

"Why this robbery advertised in all the papers," and Jack read aloud as follows :—

"*Lost or mislaid, one pair of large brilliant diamond earrings with drops, the first water, and one odd night earring, with three brilliant diamonds; three large bars for the breast, set with rose diamonds. If offered to be sold, pawn'd, or valued, pray stop 'em and the party, especially if it be a young lady, and give notice to* Mr. Drummond, *Goldsmith, at Charing Cross, and you shall receive* 200 *Guineas reward for the same.*'

"There now, Ladies," resumed Jack, "you see how it is. Can't you put this sum of money in my way for nothing, and drat me if I won't give half of it to the informer and myself in the bargain, if she's a pretty one?"

"No compounding felonies here," said a mask in the character of Jonathan Wild.

"Oh curse you," cried Jack, "have we a rascally informer among us? Gentleman, here is Wild come back from Hell—faith I didn't think he could get out—but as it is so, let us disperse, or he may take some of us down with him. But hark ye, if the lovely thief comes to my lodgings in Pall Mall any night this week, I shall arrange matters with her agreeably to both parties. I have no doubt she is here, and that if I could penetrate behind yon black silk mask I should see her now, blushing with fear or hope, or love."

" Bravo, bravo Jack," shouted out his companions, and they rushed after a huge figure arrayed in the robes of Lord Chancellor, who was singing an indecent ballad.

" Who is that tall, thin, lathlike man, something like the Monument?" I asked, "who is dressed as Æsculapius?"

" That," said Fielding, scanning him very closely, "is Dr. St. André, who came over to this country a perfect pauper, but by some lucky lines, got himself into notice, and would probably have been appointed sergeant-surgeon to the King himself, only that he made himself the town jest by the rabbit business, which produced so great a noise a few !years ago. He was himself, I believe persuaded that Mary Tofts was the veritable mother of I know not how many of these interesting animals, and he invited Sir Hans Sloane and the chiefs of the Royal Society to be present at the incubation. They went, and were deceived likewise, and the Society was about to adopt her, and identify themselves with the deception, but luckily the cheat was discovered, and the Fellows saved from irremediable disgrace. For they have patronised so many absurdities, that one or two more will squelch them utterly. St. Andrè retired into the country, where he, and the woman who is with him, Lady Betty Molyneux, daughter of the Earl of Essex, contrived to poison her husband, by which the lady came in for thirty thousand pounds, and is now married to St. Andrè. Pope has preserved her in his amber, as ' the poisoning wife.'' They are a very happy nice couple, and do well to figure at this place.''

" Why, Harry,'' I remarked, " you are as good as Asmodeus; you know all these people, as well as if you were their father confessor.''

" Better, my dear Coz, better,'' he answered, "for when you have lived as long as me, and seen as much, you will know that it is only the minor sins that are revealed in confession—the greater never are. But for the honour of the state and our high civilization, this is not the only lady poisoner we have here to-night. Unless I mistake I see Lady Deloraine ;'' and he pointed out a mask who now slowly approached us. She was dressed in Indian costume, and looked magnificent, but I could not see her features. The opportunity, however, was soon afforded. Anthony Henley walked up to her, and without the slightest ceremony pulled off her mask. Her face in-

stantly grew filled with blood; she darted at him
one baleful glance, but in an instant her whole
expression changed.   She absolutely smiled on
him and gave him a cordial welcome.   I could
then observe her; her eyes were round and bright
just like an adder's; they were vividly clear and
still; the lips were thin lines of red; the motion
was soft and gliding.   All poisoners have this
peculiarity.   I happened once to be thrown by
circumstances into the company of the greatest
poisoner of this or any other age.   When he
moved it was with so soft and gentle a step from
place to place that you started to find him beside
or behind you, when you had only a moment before seen him at the other end of the room.   His
voice was low and modulated, but an observant
ear could detect something sibilant in its under
tones.   The whole appearance was remarkably
sleek, smooth and clean ; and so it is with the
most venomous of adders (the puff adder), which
would be miserable if the least speck begrimed
its glittering coat.

"And who is this woman?" I asked Fielding.

"She is bedchamber woman at Court," he
said; "she sings loose songs for the king every
night before he goes to bed, and the woman she
poisoned was a pretty Scotch woman named
McKenzie, who was rather in her way."

Here a middle-sized, ill shaped sort of woman, with fine eyes and thin nose projecting to a point, suddenly pulled off her mask, while she used her fan to cool herself. In doing so she exposed a magnificent pair of diamond ear-rings.

"Are these Jack Frothwell's jewels, I wonder? If so, hadn't we better claim the reward?"

"No," answered my companion, "they are Lord Pomfret's, and are well paid for."

"How do you mean? Is this woman a—"

"Oh! dear no; don't be mistaken; she is no less a personage than Lady Sundon. I happen to know that she got those very ear-rings for procuring the Mastership of the Horse for Pomfret. She does well to wear her bribe in her ears. But I wonder that she has boldness enough to do so."

"Nay; I think she does not only well but wisely. How could you have people know where there is wine to be sold, unless there is a sign hung out?"

"That saying is worthy of your mother, my boy. But Sundon, who is decent in other respects, ought to be above this, for she is now enormously rich. O, England, thou art a glorious land for prime ministers and royal serving women. Walpole came up to town with only eight hundred pounds a year, debts innumerable, and a heap of

brothers, and country cousins and sisters to keep
out of it, and he now owns Houghton, the greatest
house in Norfolk, and with a gallery of paintings
perhaps unequalled in the world.   Lady Sundon
was, like Craggs, a servant at St. James's, and
 aking money from bishops, archbishops, courtiers,
and parsons, she is now worth one hundred
thousand pounds, with probably forty thousand
pounds more in jewels and finery—the gift of the
well discerning, who have quick eyes for that sort
of merit, which can give rewards to its believers."

" Here comes Sewallis Shirley," whispered
Fielding, pointing to a thin well-made man with
blue eyes, but a dissipated air ; " they say he
loves Lady Vane, and if I were my lord I should
beware of him, for he is a dangerous man with
the sex.   And there is Lady Pomfret herself,
Jeffrey's granddaughter—a great crony of your
mamma, who probably had wit enough to make
her husband bribe Lady Sundon.   But who is
this in full canonicals ?   As I live it is Orator
Henley ; but where he has got the money to buy
his ticket I know not, unless some mad wag with
more gold than brains has sent him here to make
us laugh."

The Orator swaggered towards us, and was
evidently pleased at the admiration which he ex-

cited; a crowd of young fellows fresh from Oxford followed him, and wit and puns, and classical allusions were bandied freely about between
them. One of them now pulled forward a chair;
and arranged some benches in a circular shape,
and there being a general call for a sermon, the
reverend gentleman with great meekness mounted
the temporary pulpit, and adjusting his bands and
trying hard to look demurely, began as follows :—

" Beloved brethren, and ye, my sisters, more
beloved still—hearken unto my speech, and give
ear unto my words, for verily they will be of
sweet savour to your worldly souls. Clouds ye
are, without water, carried about of winds; trees
whose fruit withereth without fruit, twice dead,
plucked up by the roots; raging waves of the
sea, foaming out their own shame; wandering
stars to whom is reserved the blackness of darkness for ever. All this ye are naturally, I say;
yet if ye do but follow the holy counsel which I
shall bestow, ye shall ascend with Paul into the
high heaven, which I wish he had described for
the edification of all sinners, like yourselves.
Ask ye where ye shall hear that holy counsel?
In the sacred groves of Academe—I mean Clare
Market, it may be heard; by the classic waters
of the Ilis—I mean, the pump of Clement's Inn,

the words of wisdom may be gleaned. Therefore
do I counsel ye, one and all, repair thither without further delay, and lay up store of that holy
treasure, which shall abide unto you when all
others shall have passed away. But unto those
abandoned ones, who will not listen, woe unto
them, for they have gone in the way of Cain, and
ran greedily after the error of Balaam for reward,
and perished in the gainsaying of Core."

Here a young wag, in a horribly nasal tone,
cried " Ah-men ! "

" We are told by holy Jude, the sanctified
brother of James, the Apostle," resumed Henley,
" that Michael the Archangel disputed with the
devil about the body of Moses (General Epistle,
verse 9); but how he discovered the burial place
of the Hebrew patriarch hath not been revealed,
for he was entombed in great secresy somewhere
in the land of Moab. Many people believe this
to be a literal fact, and the infidels and scoffers
—of whom this wicked city is full—have often
grown irreverent on the subject, even in the presence of these men of God, the Right Reverend
Bishops of the Church that is by law Established.
But it has always appeared to me that holy Jude
merely meant to speak figuratively in that place,
and that he hath bequeathed to us a metaphorical
type, which might often be applied with singular

force to the great variety of things which we daily see around us. For it cannot be seriously contended that the narrative should be taken literally; the dead body of the son of Amram being, as I conceive, of no earthly use whatever to the Prince of the Air, whom some call Lucifer. For to fry it in his fires would avail nothing, the soul suffering not by the dead body's discomfiture; and the soul itself we know he could not get. Therefore I have always regarded the text in question as being one of those grand outbursts of fancy for which the Jewish prophets were famous; and which is capable of being turned to the most useful account in all the transactions of living life."

Here the same wag again groaned out "Ah-men!"

"When I see a Minister of State doubtful whether he shall sell his country to a foreign prince for a bribe of fifty thousand pounds, or whether he shall not rather content himself with the thirty (and security) which he may have by robbing the credulous public at home, methinks I think I see the Devil then contending with the Archangel for the body of Moses.

" When I see a very reverend clergyman, high in the Church, balancing his conscience between his support of public measures, which he knows to be inimical to the country, and his ambition after a mitre, which he is assured is worth ten thousand a year, then methinks I see the Devil awfully contending with the Archangel for the body of Moses.

"When I see a young virgin hesitating between the arms of old age, holding forth in each hand a well-filled casket of gold and jewels, and the seducing smiles of some younger cavalier, to whom she has given what she calls her heart, then methinks I see the Devil wrangling with the Archangel for the body of Moses.

"When I see a merchant great on 'Change, immersed in anxious reflections, whether he shall secure five thousand guineas by some bold fraud in stocks or merchandise, or whether he shall not rather be more safe if he heaps gold on gold by his accustomed quiet driblets of peculation, then methinks I see the Devil stoutly fighting with the Archangel for the body of Moses.

"When I see the blatant patriot, who has entered the House of Commons, sworn to wreak vengeance on the enemies of freedom, secretly selling himself to the First Lord for a place in the Ministry, while with many a pang of anticipation he hears the groans of his deluded countrymen, and is half inclined to wait a little longer—that he may get a higher price, then methinks I see the Devil squabbling with the Archangel for the body of Moses.

" When I see the ermined judge condemning a man to jail whose only crime is that he differs in opinion with the ignorant many who constitute what is called the State, while under his belt he carries the promise of the King that he shall be made a Privy Councillor for his suppleness, then indeed I see the Devil clapper-clawing the Archangel about the body of Moses.

" When I see the skilful doctor listening to his patient's enumeration of symptoms, and prescribing for him the pill, while he pockets the daily fee, yet all the while confessing to his own heart that better than pill or potion would be that hermit abstinence from the bottle or the feast, which is the true source of the disease, but which he nevertheless hints not to the gold bestower, then also I see the Devil brangling with the Archangel for the body of Moses.

" When I see the assembled wisdom of the nation, making the loudest outcries against electoral bribery and corruption, and denouncing it as an iniquity before heaven, while among them they know that some of the most odious bribers and corruptors that ever lived are fat and flourishing, and though they make innumerable false pretences to a virtue which they have not, they take no real pains at all to discourage the villainy against which they declaim, or to expel the bribers whom they abuse—then in truth I see the Devil wrestling hard with the Archangel for the body of Moses.

"In fine, whenever I look abroad upon the vast theatre of society, and see the struggles which in every rank and order hourly do take place between conscience and villainy, the fights that happen between our moral sense, and our own immoral sensualisms; between our conviction of what is true and our devotion to what is false, between our scorn of the beautiful, and our pursuit of the base, then, my brethren, is forcibly brought before me the terrible contest that is always going on between the Devil and the Archangel about the body of Moses."

"Ah-men," groaned the wag who had before officiated, and with a burst of laughter, the congregation left the Orator and ran after a new figure who carried a puppet show. Henley, no way disconcerted, was seen the next minute discussing a bottle with two or three ladies who would never have done for Roman vestals, though I half think they were disguised in that character. And so the scene went on, and the whole of Pandemonium seemed let loose.

CHAPTER XXX.

"And all the devils besought him, saying send us into the swine that we may enter into them. * * * And the unclean spirit went out and entered into the swine."

AND now the Prince of Wales entered, his royal highness Fred (his father called him "Fritz," and his mother "Griff,") a little man of pink complexion, light hair and spindle shanked; with lively eyes, but remarkably awkward and ungraceful. He was attended by his sham court, who in all things set themselves up in pigmy opposition to Walpole and the right honourable lords and ladies who basked in the sovereign presence. There was fat Windham, Pulteney and his wife, Annie Gumley, half vixen, half doxey, and Lord Scarborough, who made a jest

of all religion, and Lady Bolingbrooke, and Bubb
Dodington, and Lyttleton, tall, thin, ugly-faced,
and ill-formed, with a voice like a scritch owl—
the very counterpart of his description in the
ballad—

> But who is dat bestride a pony,
> So long, so lean, so lank, so bony?
> Dat be great Orator Littletony.

"Yonder," says Fielding, "are Rigby and
Winnington; you may know the first by his
matchless impudence of forehead, and the
purpureum lumen of perpetual burgundy which
seems to flash out of every coarse feature. His
father was a South Sea robber; the son is not yet
a senatorial Turpin, but he soon will be ready to
take money and spend it in any baseness.
Winnington, who is member for Droitwich,
seems on the look out for our friend Audrey
Townsend, whose favoured love he boasts himself
to be, though I think she is wild after Harry
Nisbett too, and *he* shares her with half a dozen
stout chairmen of my acquaintance. Both have
come, I suppose, from a cock match. But what
brings old Gibbon here? Are all the South Sea
plunderers here to-night? They should have
poisoned themselves like Craggs. Yonder old
fellow was fined £10,000 for *his* part in the

pillage ; had it been £50,000 it would not have been enough.   Look at him."

I did so ; the perfect image of a baboon he was. Many years afterwards I saw his grandson at Lausanne—he seemed to have been spit out of the old gentleman's mouth.   He has just published the first volume of a very pretty history, but he is a most laughable fellow to see.

Numerous were the illustrious lords and ladies who now attracted attention ; conspicuous among them was Lord Carteret, famous as the greatest humbug of his day, and Lady Archibald Hamilton, who at the age of thirty-five got the place of cofferer to the Prince of Wales, and Surveyor General of the Duchy of Cornwall for her excellent spouse ; the condition which she made with the King for the gift being one of a very plain and simple character.   With her was Scarborough's brother, who was treasurer to the Prince.

But alas ! all their glories seemed but short lived, for scarcely had they entered when the king himself and Madam Walmoden came amid a tremendous clatter, followed by the bowing courtiers ; at whose sublime appearance the rival worshippers of the rising sun looked small indeed. Heidegger at once advanced to the orchestra, and ordered them to play up " God save the

King," which they immediately did, and as that
sacred song arose, the loyal audience seemed
bursting with enthusiasm for the royal mannikin,
who, if he were indeed "the Lord's anointed,"
made one think that God must have been sadly
in want of men when he made a monkey his
representative. For the fellow was so hideous a
dwarf that when poor little Lord Edgcombe was
presented to him at Court, it was said his
Majesty—

> Rejoiced to find within his court
> One shorter than himself.

But here a new, a horrible incident arose. The
Duke of Montagu had long been known on town
for one of the most desperate of wags. He and
some friends had decoyed Heidegger a few nights
before to a noted tavern, where under pretence
of drinking his health they had rendered him so
stupidly intoxicated that they got a plaster cast
of his features, and as they were horribly ugly,
pitted all over with small pox, and full of the
most rugged ups and downs, and crosses and
touches, they had no difficulty in getting a fine
wax mask made, which presented even to the
most skilful eye all the rough lineaments of this
lucky Swiss. It was not difficult to discover in
what dress the master of the ceremonies would
appear on the occasion of the royal visit; and

the Duke had a complete counterpart made in
which he clothed a humourous fellow from
one of the playhouses, who for a bribe of
ten guineas undertook to personate Heidegger
on this occasion. Scarcely therefore had that
accomplished master given the direction which
I have mentioned, and scarcely had the first
bars been played, when the false Heidegger,
taking advantage of the momentary attendance
of the true one on the king, came forward and
very quietly said, " Gentlemen, play *Charlie over
the Water*." The band was rather surprised, but
they could only obey ; so they changed the loyal
note for one that sounded remarkably like trea-
son. All was instantly confusion. Heidegger,
who was following the king, ran back like a mad-
man, and rushing to the master of the band, cried
out, " What for you play Charlie over the Vater ?
Damn you, play God save the King." The band,
in perfect amazement, dropped the Jacobite air,
and struck up the solemn strain. Heidegger
again rushed after the king, doubtless intending
to explain and apologise, when the duke's
Heidegger again came forward and said, " What
for you play dat damned ting ? Did I not tell
you to play Charlie over de water ? You shall
all be dismissed to-morrow, by Gad, for dis ?"

The band could now only conclude that the master of the ceremonies was drunk or mad. They however again struck up the rebellious air, to the horror of all the Whigs and Courtiers, but to the immense delight of all the Tories and Jacobites present. The king himself was now in a rage; the poor Walmoden was white as a sheet, when Heidegger, rushing into his majesty's presence, spluttered out—

"Please, your royal sacred majesty, it is not me—not me. De band is mad; de band is drunk; de band is bribed by some villain—some dirty rascal to do dis. It is not me, majesty; not me—not me."

The false Heidegger as instantly came forward, and pointing to the true Simon Pure, said—

"Please, your majesty, dis fellow is von rogue, imposter, knave, rascal. He it be dat do all dis. He hav de money of de Jacobites. He do this for gilt."

The King burst out laughing; the courtiers at once joined in the royal mirth. Heidegger himself turned pale, and looked as if he saw a ghost. All was confusion, and there would have probably been a general row, had not the Duke himself come forward and humbly begging pardon of the king, explained (in French, for this English

monarch did not know the language of his people)
the joke which he had prepared for the royal
delectation, and all passed off very pleasantly.

"If an angel could come from heaven and see
this mumming, I wonder what he'd think of it,"
said my companion.

"You must be a pretty fellow to make such a
remark as that," said a mask near us, "when
there are so many angels all about you."

"Fallen ones, though," said the dramatist; "I
wonder will they ever get back to heaven."

"Their heaven is here," answered the other.

"Well, I wonder where we shall all be this
time one hundred years. No masking in the
other world, I fear."

"Ah! now you grow profane." And the mask
left us.

"I think I know that woman," said Fielding;
"let us follow her a bit." But the mask eluded
us through the dense crowd; and we stopped to
look a few moments at a table where gaming was
going on at a great rate. Suddenly Fielding
turned away and exclaimed—

"O, ye immortal gods and goddesses; ye who
swelled the hearts of Agamemnon and Pelides
with noble wrath, how heartily I wish that Dick
Savage were here; but he is now, I suppose,
lying in a kennel dead drunk, or fast asleep on

a butcher's bench in Newgate Market. Marry come up, we should have had a glorious scene, to which this of Heidegger is but milk and water."

I stared at this rhapsody. "Why, Hal," I asked, "what's the matter?"

"Matter!" he repeated, "why, matter for fifty dramatic scenes. What a splendid situation —the king present, the heir apparent, all the high nobility of the land. Heidegger and Handel in the full moon glory of their music; in every heart bounding joy; every silver-footed nymph panting for the minuet. Suddenly Dick spies two masked strangers—the one a tall and noble-looking Colonel, the other an ex-contessa, and still beautiful. He rushes towards them, tears open his shirt, and falling on his knees with a passion, cries, "Mother, behold your son!" The Colonel claps his hand to his sword; my lady lifts her mask and looks amazed; the music ceases; the minuet is suspended; the sovereign himself comes forward; when the lady recovers her speech and tragically exclaims, "Begone, impostor!" Dick immediately faints, and there is a grand tableau, worthy of Rich in his best days.

"In the name of common sense, Henry, what is all this about?"

"Why, don't you see Colonel and Mrs. Brett

yonder, whom Savage supposes to be his mother?
And don't you see Miss Brett following, who is
a Court demirep, and whose influence saved the
neck of her half brother when he was sentenced
to be hanged? But who comes here? Sir William Yonge, Member for Honiton, and Tom
Winnington with him."

They sauntered up slowly and unmasked; the
place was now dreadfully hot and close. "We
have had an odd discussion together," says Sir
William Yonge—"Tom and I; nothing less
than whether there is a future; and we want a
parson to settle it for us."

"If you get a parson of the present time to
tell you he will say yes, but laugh at you in his
sleeve if you think him serious," replied Fielding. The pair strolled, or rather reeled and rolled
away.

"There are two beautiful specimens," said
Fielding. "But they merely proclaim what
nearly all feel, but are too timid to say. Lord
Hervey, who is at the head of the wits about
Court, makes no secret of his atheism; he is
Vice-Chamberlain, and sees all the begging
letters which the Queen gets from the parsons to
make them bishops, and he protests that every
one is stuffed with envy, falsehood, detraction of
each other, if rivals; and covert sneers if they

are friends; together with a sum total of un-
charitableness, avarice, and meanness that sickens
him with the whole fraternity. * Now I don't say
that this is true, but Lord Hervey says it is; and
he makes it a rule whenever a Bishop pronounces
the name of God, to laugh in his face as a hypo-
crite. This thing reacts on the whole parlia-
mentary regiment of Sir Robert; and these two
who have just left us are captains in the force;
so that we are prettily ruled and finely fooled,
and think ourselves the most religious people in
the world, with the greatest amount of wickedness practised every day before Heaven and the
Sun."

"You draw a very pleasing picture of things."

"Ah! it's no worse now than it has always been.
Do you think Nineveh and Babylon, were the only
places where they practised vice? Nay, by St.
Ann, we commit more in one day in England
than those stupid Babylonians did in a year."

"Ain't that Grigsby," says Arbuthnot, who
saluted Fielding, "another of the South Sea forty
thieves—Gadslife, but they're all here in honour
of the Royal Family. This fellow was so vain
of his wealth in the glorious days of jobbery,
that he once ordered his coachman to feed his

---

* Anyone who reads the letters to Lord Bute in the manuscript
department of the British Museum, can easily believe this.

horses on gold.   When the bubble exploded, and
all the swindlers were before the House, one,
Moore, moved that this fellow should be allowed
£10,000 out of the spoil.   A wag got up and
said, 'That as Mr. Grigsby was in the habit of
feeding his horse on gold, he had no doubt he
could feed on it himself; he therefore moved that
Mr. Grigsby might be allowed as much gold as
he could eat, and that the rest of his estate might
go to the relief of those whom he had pillaged.'
The House laughed, but they allowed the fellow
£2,000."

While this was going on, Rigby pulled out of
his pockets a bundle of Chinese crackers ; and
assuming his mask, went up to a lady dressed
like a Peruvian vestal, to whom he made a low
bow, and presenting them, said, "Madame, if
you put this to the next sconce, and it burns blue,
you may be sure your lover is faithful."   Luckily
a sconce happened to be near ; and the unconscious
nymph, without a moment's reflection, apply-
ing the first on the string, the whole exploded,
filling the room with smoke and a most unsavoury
smell, in the midst of which Rigby, like an evil
spirit, as suddenly vanished.

A short, stout-made, coarse-looking man, but
with an eye glittering with humour, a true
English terrier face, and a firm mouth, came up.

He shook Fielding by the hand very heartily, saying, " Mr. Fielding, I scarcely expected to see you here, patronising this outlandish French thing."

" Ah! Hogarth," said Harry, " I am delighted to meet you. Surely you may know what has brought me, without suspecting that I had any partiality for the Mounseers and their funny frog-fashions. I have no doubt we have neither of us come to see that ugly owl Heidegger—

Teach kings to fiddle, and make senates dance.

but to sketch characters ; you for the easel, your humble servant for the stage."

" Gad so," said our companion heartily, " you've guessed right. And a pretty lot of long-eared fools, I see—look! I have just taken one on my thumb-nail ;" and he shewed us a laughable sketch of Lord Chesterfield's face, in which " that little monkey full of tricks," as Sir Charles Hanbury Williams called him, was inimitably depicted—the baboon outlines which so many ladies loved, being hit off to perfection.

" I know a woman who would never forgive you, if she saw that," said Fielding, glancing towards a corner of the room where a couple seemed very fond.

" And who may the tasteless jade be ?" asked

Hogarth; " faith, she must be a female ape, I think—though she dresses like one of Eve's sex."

" Why, Lady Fanny Shirley, whom that fellow has flirted with for the last ten years, and after whom he is now dangling in yonder recess," answered the dramatist ; and he pointed them out.

" Oh! by George," shouted Hogarth, " I'll have her also,' and he began to make a humorous sketch of the fair lady.

When it was finished he shewed it to us—the thing was wonderful—worthy of so great a genuis as W. H. certainly was.

" This place is horribly hot," he said, " I wish I could get a pot of honest English porter, and a steak—but this cursed Swiss lets nothing in but his foreign wines, and his French kickshaws, the very look of which makes me sick for the day. How much do they reckon the knave makes by this tom-foolery ?"

" Why, at least £5,000 a-year ; that is by the fair profits, besides what he gets by managing the assignations."

Hogarth sighed. He was then cking out a scanty subsistence for himself, like my poor glorious cousin, and must have found it no easy matter even to spare the money to come here.

He probably had got a pass from Tyers, or some charitable lover of art.

" What's that Brutus said, when he was dying?" he asked.

" O, Virtue! I have long worshipped thee— now I know thee to be but a shadow," responded Fielding.

"Ah! true, true," said the other, with a sad gravity that contrasted strangely with that laughing eye and merry lip. And he repeated with a bluff John Bull sort of accent, that did one good to hearken to it, amid the sighs and simpers of this effeminate crowd.

> As the brute world to Father Adam came
> Requesting with enquiring looks a name,
> To every beast a title he assigned,
> And nominated all the sylvan kind.
> So savage multitudes about me throng—
> Did Adam's power but to me belong!
> Yet though they cheat the world by their disguise,
> They are but asses to the painter's eyes.

And saying this, the splendid little wag moved off in search of new caricatures.

Dodington now sailed up to where we were.

" Ah!" he said, " I think I know you," addressing himself to Fielding, who had put on his mask some time before.

" That is more than I do myself," answered Harry, " though I have been long endeavouring to carry out Solon's advice on that point."

" Your answer convinces me that I am right.
You are Henry Fielding. How is your father?"

" Faith !" said my cousin, " I scarcely know;
he never writes to me but when he wants to borrow money, and then he always tells me he is
dying. I begin to think he must be like
Tithonus."

" And I hope you lend it to him like a dutiful
son."

" I give it when I can, and I lend it when I
cannot ; and I am sorry to say the latter is the
most usual condition with me."

" Every man of talent must be sorry to hear it.
Shall I give you a cheque for £200 ?"

" I should be very glad to get it, but on what
ground ?"

" Why to abuse the Prince, and praise Walpole."

" What ! praise ' that big belly, those swollen
arms, that huge body,' as Queen Caroline calls
him. Mr. Dodington, I did not think you would
insult me so. You know that I am poor; but
have I ever shown myself a rogue ?"

" Oh ! damn it, I thought you had your price,
like all writers; but as you haven't, good-night.
I can buy as good as you any day in Fleet
Street."

" There goes a scoundrel," said Fielding to me,

but loud enough to be heard by Bubb. " His
vanity, insolence, and vulgarity are all insupport-
able. He is the King's pimp, yet he thinks himself
a gentleman ; he is Walpole's butt, yet he fancies
himself a patriot ; he is Bolingbroke's tool, yet
he supposes he is a wit. If a lady but speaks to
him, he repeats among all his friends that he has
seduced her ; and if the King kicks him he falls
down on his knees and begs to kiss his hand for
such a mark of favour. Bridgewater has a member worthy of it."

I could see how nettled he was. To be insulted
by any one is not pleasant ; but to be insulted by
the meanest of mankind, which this Dodington
was, was assuredly a bitter pang. Notwithstanding his philosophy, he was sullen and silent for
three or four minutes. At length he said, as if
involuntarily—

" Why should this flea annoy me ?"

And he recited, in his rich mellow tones-- ·

> When for some time he sat at the Treasury board,
> And the clerks there with titles had tickled his ear,
> From every day hearing himself called a lord,
> He begged of Sir Robert to make him a peer.
>> But in an ill hour,
>> For Walpole looked sour,
> And said it was not in his will or his power.
> Do you think, sir, the King would advance such a scrub,
> Or the peerage debase with the name of a Bubb?

This outburst relieved Fielding ; his rage at

the unceremonious insolence of this fat-faced
fawner on the veriest lap dogs of St. James's,
evaporated, and all was clear again. He laughed
and said—

"Come, let us seek some new game. But before we leave just look at that stiff looking man
following the Duke of Argyle like his shadow;
you have heard of Gyles Earle, member for
Malmesbury, now one of the Board of Green
Cloth—that is he, but I wish you could see his
crabbed face and hog's eyes. He is as covetous
as the Duke himself, and a desperate glutton in
eating oysters, while he starves his unfortunate
servants, and won't pay even his butcher's or his
Billingsgate bills. T'other day, as he was gorg-
ing his favourite food by peckfuls, he said, 'Lord
God what fine things oysters would be if we
could make our servants live on the shells.'"

While we were digesting this joke, a smart
female figure, with the archest eyes in the world
peering through her mask, came hastily up to
where we stood, and tapping Fielding on the
shoulder with a splendid fan, cried out in musical
accents—

"My dear Fielding, I have been looking for
you this hour. Come with me."

"My dearest countess," answered Harry; but
he immediately checked himself, and substituted

for the inadvertent word the more equivocal term
"creature," but not so quickly as to be unnoticed
by me, or a grinning mask close by, who
seemed to contemplate the moving crowd as
Cerberus might look upon the thronging phantoms
hurrying through the gorge of Pluto.

"My dearest creature," says my cousin, "I
am delighted that we have met at last. This is
my cousin, young Wortley Montagu. Wortley,
allow me to introduce you to Mrs. Johnson, of
Bath."

I bowed with great deference, the lady curt-
seyed, and whispered something into my companion's ear. He turned to me.

"Good-night, Wortley," he said ; "I *must* go.
Let me see you in a day or two," and Fielding
and Mrs. Johnson of Bath disappeared through
one of the doors.

The old Cerberus of whom I have spoken came
up.

"So you are young Montagu," she said,
"and a horrid scapegrace too; and that spark's
Fielding, and Mrs. Johnson of Bath is—"

"Aye," said I, "old woman, who is Mrs.
Johnson of Bath?"

"Mrs. Johnson of Bath is no better than she
should be, and Fielding will rue her acquaintance
one of these days. Her maiden name was

Ethelreda, or rather Audrey Harrison, and her
father made his fortune out of the blacks, when
he was Governor of Fort St. George. She is
now the wife of Charles Viscount Townshend, and
a very pretty wife she is. She is squandering
her black blood-money very lavishly, and has a
particular affection for stout young fellows like
your friend."

I heard, and was amazed. Alas, poor Harry!
Had it come to this? Only a few minutes before
he had described this lady in the strangest terms;
and now— Had his necessities then been so
dire? Doubtless. He described all afterwards
in *Tom Jones:* that wondrous work: the most
perfect picture of daily life since Homer sang.

My strange companion resumed.

" But what are *you* doing here? I know your
mother, Jackanapes. Have you come with her?"

" Madam, that you are a woman prevents me
from answering you as I should, but I beg—"

" Pooh, pooh, boy—don't talk to an old woman
like me in your hoity toity style. I am a grandmother—perhaps a great grandmother. I like
your spirit myself, and I know more about you
than you fancy. Lend me your arm—" and she
put forth a hand beautifully white, and loaded
with jewels worthy of a sovereign queen. Every
finger bore a gem worth a king's ransom. I had

never seen or even dreamed of such a sight as this.

I supported her to a seat, and examined her closely. I could perceive that she was what she represented herself to be, indeed, an old woman, but her hair was still beautiful, her eyes were bright, and her hands retained their loveliness. Her figure was bent, but there was an immense spirit evidently in that aged frame. She spoke with an air of command. I felt that I was talking to one who had known and lived with Emperors and Kings. She was attired as Margaret Finch, the Gypsy Queen; and now began to tell strange wonders to gaping enquirers. She seemed to penetrate every disguise, and knew the secret history of all who questioned her. The ordinary rabble who approached her she disdained to answer; but the royal and noble persons who thronged the gay scene were immediately attended to, and I noticed that the majority went away with an air of chagrin. She kept me near her, but yet at a sufficient distance not to overhear all she said, as each new comer came. A wild smile of delight played in her eye as some turned away—a melancholy gleam passed over it as she answered others. I was singularly attracted by this queer being; and was constrained to stay near her, not only be-

cause she told me to do so, but also because I
really could not tear myself away.   I expected
at each new interview something definite and
desperate, which would perhaps require my interference to protect her.

"Here comes Henrietta, Duchess of Marlborough," she said, as a wild looking woman
passed us.   "I wonder does she ever think of
her glorious father, who made her what she is?
Yet I think not, or she would not have disgraced
herself with that blind, gouty, vain coxcomb,
Congreve, the player, or taken the ten thousand
pounds, which he left her by his will, when he
had so many poor relations starving in Stafford-
shire.   I think she is worth a million—so what
she wanted the fellow's pittance for I don't
know.   She has a silver statue of the villain
brought to her dinner table every day—as the
Egyptians had a skeleton—to remind her, I suppose, of hell.   Yet I wish she hadn't connected
their names together on that filthy marble in the
Abbey.   Oh, that John Churchill could come
back to earth but for an hour—then would rare
changes be seen and heard of.   Here is another
Duchess just as mad, Kitty Hyde of Queensbury,
followed by her literary lackey, Jack Gay, who
has grown corpulent on his Beggar's Opera profit,
and his South Sea robberies.   Doesn't this seem

to you the age when rapscallions rise out of the vilest dunghills? We have for our Apollo, little Pope, the linen draper; here is Gay, whose father was a mercer, and who was himself a mercer's shop boy. Mat Prior, a tapster,—and so on for ever. Our great people find their account in patronising these maggots and giving them pensions for unlimited praise. Walpole is supported by some dozens of the vilest wretches that ever crept about the lowest corners of Parnassus. The Tories first called this spawn of vipers into being, and now the Whigs emulate their example. We have for poet-laureat, a common pander to the nobility (I smiled at hearing this allusion to my old friend Colley), and we have for Premier a man who behaves before all as if virtue were a farce, and decency of speech and manner a hypocritical pretence."

In this way the old woman went on blending strange shrewdness with the most cutting sarcasm, and rivetting me by her wit and bitterness —for there was something singularly congenial in our tempers; both being misanthropical, from the best of all reasons, I suppose, a wretched experience of the world. Whatever gaiety I brought with me into the Opera House departed wholly. I looked round and felt as if I could pierce under each disguise—and what I saw there

presented nothing to remove my sadness.   I fell
into a reverie on my own desolate position;
desolate because I would not bind my soul in
fetters, and crawl at the feet of a man who was
a father but in name, and had much less feeling
for me than for one of the guineas that he adored.
My companion observed me.

"Come," said she, "Master Jackanapes, what
are you thinking of?   This is no place for meditation.   You look like Marius amid the ruins of
Carthage."

"And if I do, am I not amid more melancholy
ruins still—the ruins of human souls, utterly
destroyed by vice."

"A parson, a parson," cried a beau near us,
who had overheard my speech—"let us smoke
him and carry him to Mother H's."

"Aye, damme," says Jack Frothwell, who
came up at the time, "I know no fun equal to
singeing a parson's tail. Fal, fal, lal la."

But a movement which I made towards them
with my sword put this gallant company to
instant flight.

"Do you see that man that walks like a tongs—
he is all legs, and scarcely any head.   I know
him through his vain disguise.   The Venetian
Senator's robe was never on a more unsuitable
body.   That is Neddy Harley, son to the falsest

varlet I ever knew. His father, and a slut named Hill (she is now Abigail Masham, and I shouldn't wonder if we saw her here), conspired together to get old Queen Anne wholly into their power, and they did so, by poisoning her mind against her only true friend in the world, the Duchess of Marlborough. They stole in at all hours of the day and night, and when the poor woman was heated with brandy, they got her to pledge herself to the most absurd projects—not the vainest of which was a trick to bring back the Pretender. When the old king was on his death bed at Rome, some of the Jacobites got around him, and made him write a letter to his daughter, praying that if she did not deliver over the throne to her brother, she might die childless, and must expect his bitterest curse. This so frightened Queen Anne, whose nerves were weakened by repeated drams, and was besides so singularly borne out by the successive deaths of all her children, that she was ready to consent to anything, and the Tories here had all prepared even to the proclamation of the Pretender himself in St. Paul's churchyard, when the poor woman was suddenly taken off, and the chief rogues made their escape to France. Had Bolingbroke remained, he must have figured on Tower Hill, as Harley, to save himself, basely

gave up all his papers to the new ministry, and
sacrificed his best friend, Bishop Atterbury, who
was obliged to fly also. But this treachery was
in keeping with all the scoundrel's doings—
though I never will forgive Walpole for not having shipped off Mrs. Abigail to the colonies. She
would have made a good slave-driver, being false,
cruel, and cunning as the snake that deceived
our poor mother in Paradise. But she is now a
peeress—and figures grandly among the Lord's
anointed. Thus is history made. For this sly
worthless, waiting woman elevated Harley to the
government of England, who then devised a
scheme that might have changed the fortune of
the world, and influenced the fate of unborn
generations for the next thousand years; and
Walpole now occupies the same place wholly
through his sister, Dolly Walpole, who was the
first wife of that good-looking fool Townshend,
having by the rarest accident escaped being the
open and avowed mistress of the Marquis of
Wharton. Ah! boy, I could tell you such things.
But the profane many never know these matters,
and think everything ministerial is grand, and
great and noble, and elevated. For my own part,
I believe history is made up of the basest of all
materials, though of course they are finely
tinselled over to deceive the unthinking rabble.

who are all born slaves, and ever keep themselves
so by their ignorance, passion, and prejudice.
There is Fox, whose father was a lackey or a
groom, I don't know which. He spends all his
time at hazard and Mother H's, and is nursed
with every private vice—yet I have no doubt if
he can steal my goose he will one day be Prime
Minister. He certainly tries hard to do it—but
I will prevent him if I can." And to my amazement she went up to the young man, since so
celebrated as Lord Holland, and cried out,
"Charley, Charley—what brings you here—you
should have been 'at the gaming table, or with
the Jews. How is your friend, Mrs. H., and
when were you last in a sponging house?" The
crowd laughed, and one of the beaus coming up
said, "Hey! damme, this is fine—let us tie the
witch to a cucking stool," but a mask habited
like a Bishop, suddenly got up in one of the
corners, and began a sermon in praise of gluttony,
which so tickled the fancy of this fine company,
that they all ran off to hear him, and I could
hear their shouts of laughter, as the fellow
travestied The Sermon on the Mount with the most
blasphemous jokes.

The old woman began to muse.

"Boy," said she, "you ought to be a Poet—
do you remember Dryden's lines?" and with a

melancholy emphasis she whispered into my
ear—

> " When I consider life, 'tis all a cheat,
> Yet fooled with hope, men favour the deceit,
> Trust on and think to-morrow will repay ;
> To-morrow's falser than the former day ;
> Lies more, and when it says we shall be blest
> With some new joy, cuts off what we possest.
> Strange cozenage ! none would live past years again,
> Yet all hope pleasure in what still remain,
> And from the dregs of life think to receive
> What the first sprightly running could not give."

Several persons now came up to my companion,
and taking her for the Sibyl she appeared, requested her to tell their fortunes. She seemed
nothing loth, but first of all requested her hand to
be crossed with gold. There was no difficulty in
this. Among them I recognised Lord Hervey,
Pulteney and Lady Mary herself. Even the
Prince of Wales approached and seemed half
inclined to consult her. But she solicited none.
To Lord Hervey she said, " Ah ! you couldn't sell
your wife—1 pity you; but Walpole wants her,
and he will do as much for you as the King." To
Pulteney, " When you fence with Walpole, aim
at his liver; he has no heart. Don't let him
escape like Sporus." To Young, who ventured to
accost her, she merely said, " Begone, Caiaphas."
To Lady Mary, " Woman, where is thy son ?"
Moll Skerret herself came laughing up, and said,

"Gypsy, you know fortunes—what is mine?"
The old woman fixed a glance of deep hate at her.
"To rise from cinderwench to concubine, and
from concubine to—countess I suppose."

A yell of rage broke out from the virtuous
tribe of flatterers.   One rushed forward, and
would, I think, have struck the old woman, when
I threw myself in front of her ; but ere anything
decisive could occur, some half dozen persons
flung themselves between us, and prevented
violence.   Whether they did so by accident, or
were stationed round her by design, I could not
guess. The lion spirit of the old woman negatives
the last supposition ; but this lucky interposition
makes it not unlikely.   There was a noise; the
great Heidegger himself came forward and inter-
fered ; and even then I feared it would fare but
badly with the Sibyl, for he beckoned to a soldier
who was on duty ; when a person came close and
whispered something into his ear, at which he
trembled, turned pale, and with the most submissive air bowed to the old woman, saying—

"My lords, ladies, and gentlemen, here has
been some mistake ; I can suffer no violence; let
the music play up, and the dances recommence."

The crowd separated, a gaper or two still, including Jack Frothwell, who muttered "damme,"
remained, and the old woman drew me to her side.

" Boy," she said, "you are just beginning your
career; hear the words of one who must soon
leave it. To persons like you earth appears a
sort of paradise—to me it shows itself in the
colours of hell. When I was at your time of
life, I thought all men good and all women true;
I went into the world with a frank open heart and
hand. I would have gone a hundred miles to
serve any one who needed service, and I would
have fearlessly asked the same kindness from
another for myself, so great was my confidence in
human nature. I have seen life in all ranks and
orders; I have mixed in courts and moved in
cottages. There is no phase in human existence
that is to me a sealed book. I have had children
and they have deserted and betrayed me; I have
had friends, and they have abandoned me; I have
had bosom intimates, and they proved false and
hollow; I never knew but one man who was
stedfast to me, and he was—my husband. I
have had everything that man desires or woman
covets, health, power, treasure, fame. Yet with
all these it is my fixed conviction that we are
every one of us in hell at this moment; that this
life is a place of punishment for our crimes; that
it is really and truly no other locality than hell
itself, and we are demons all, who find our joy in
persecuting each other."

"A glorious theory, madam," I said, "to teach to one like me. Yet I confess my own brief experience goes a great way to confirm it."

"When you have lived to my years you will hold it as an article of faith, a great deal more positively than any one of our thirty-nine or forty solemn follies. For these in a great measure have been invented by wicked bishops and doctors to keep themselves aloft, and to bind down the multitude below; but that which I feel, is the spontaneous growth of wisdom itself within the heart, and if the whole world of thinkers were canvassed and polled the great majority of them would confess the truth of what I have said. But amid the world of fools, the world of thinkers is lost. I remember I once asked Lord Shaftesbury what in his opinion was the true religion? He answered, 'Madam, men of sense are all of one religion.' I then pressed him, 'Pray, my lord, what religion may that be?' 'Madam,' he replied, 'men of sense never tell.' Thus he left me to infer that the only religion that can be true is that which is the offshoot of a man's own wisdom, and is not suggested to him by creeds, or liturgies, or prayer books, where we are taught things by rote, as if God were a schoolmaster who could be bribed by our proficiency in learning A B C. This is not so—there

will come a day when you will remember these
words and acknowledge them in your heart to be
true as gospel."

And she left me.   I followed her at some distance, and when I saw her get into a magnificent
chair, with the Churchill arms and a ducal
coronet, I knew that I had been talking to Sarah
Marlborough.

I wandered listlessly about.   The place with all
its crowds now seemed melancholy and miserable.
I sought in vain for Fielding, whose volatile
spirits would, I hoped, rouse me from deep des-
pondency; but though I searched minutely, I
could not discover him.   But two figures in close
conversation now attracted my attention.   They
were so deeply absorbed that surrounding objects
seemed to make no impress on them.   In one I
recognised Lord Hervey ; the other in his outlines, shewed all the daring recklessness of Dom
Balthazar.   He was attired as a bravo—a very
appropriate dress, if it were the same.   I was
impelled towards them, yet I gradually came
near so as not to attract notice.   They were seated
at a small table near one of the pillars. I thought
it no breach of honour to get within earshot.   If
they were plotting against me or Francesca, it
became in truth my duty to be made acquainted
with their devices; but the ever moving crowd

wholly prevented me. I could hear a word now and then from Dom Balthazar, who was evidently under the influence of wine; his companion, more cautious, spoke in so low a tone as to be inaudible to me. There seemed to be some altercation. The lord was evidently angry at the appearance of his confederate in such a place. I could see that the latter chafed under his remonstrances, but he was not a man to yield tamely. At length he said, fiercely—

" I came here because I could find you nowhere else. You have been denied to me at your door twenty times. I cannot and will not go to Spain without money. Money I want; money I'll have. What hinders me this moment from rising up before all this company and telling them that the true owner of certain estates is now a prisoner in—"

My sense of hearing was now wound up to the extreme point, but as the bravo concluded his speech he looked warily about him, and whispered the final word into his companion's ear. The latter started. " Come," said he, " come with me." And they left the place I dared not follow. With an aching heart I left the Opera House. " Yes," I said, " in Spain she is. Akiba was right. The airy vision that I saw did not deceive me. Let me seek her without delay.

Let me at least fly from this land of villains, and in sequestered nature seek with her, its heavenly child, the happiness which belongs not to these worn out and wretched communities. Why do I linger any longer here? I will seek her to the world's end, and if I fail or die in the pursuit, I shall at least have failed nobly, and perish without feeling that I have misused my life."

I scarcely know where I passed that night. I meditated on my proceedings, and arranged my future course. Francesca, if carried to Spain, had without doubt been conveyed through France. But this was a journey which, in my present condition, I could scarcely make. A sea voyage to the Peninsula seemed to me, therefore, the only practical mode of getting there; this would cost me scarcely anything. I hurried to the city, and having parted with my fine clothes to one of that kind and benevolent confraternity who had assisted my cousin Fielding, I found myself with a few guineas in my pocket, and an attire suitable to the condition which I assumed. I made enquiries among the shipping, and soon found one that was ready to sail. She was bound for Bilboa. I entered myself on board as a common sailor, and before night was ploughing the dark waters.

CHAPTER XXXI.

"Beware of false prophets, which come to you in sheep's clothing, but inwardly they are ravening wolves. Ye shall know them
by their fruits. Do men gather grapes from thorns, or figs of
thistles?"

On ! with what fierce delight I was again free. I
turned my back on London—that vast metropolis
of guilt and shame, infamy and falsehood, and
was once more a denizen of open loving nature ;
gazing on her skies, borne over her waters, floating, as it were, like an eagle on her mighty winds.
But for the branded agony on my soul, I should
have been happy ; even as it was, I felt a rapture
such as I had not experienced since my sojourn
among the dark Calorè of the tents. Home,
friends, kindred, all farewell ; I care not if it be
for ever. I am alone on the dark ocean—alone

with heaven and my thoughts; the intrigues,
contamination, vain, insipid joys, and vainer
strifes and enmities of the educated crowd, van-
ishing away like fogs or frenzies, forgotten or
despised by one who longs to be a MAN.   What
though I am poor, a vagabond, and unknown,
still, have I not this divine celestial arch of beauty;
now sapphire blue, now silvered with dappled
cloudlets; now burnished with beaming stars;
now golden with the splendours of the rising or
descending sun; have I not mountain, ocean,
vale, and river; and glorious forest and fragrant
garden, to be the solace of my soul, and to companion it with sublime associations?   And having these, what can there be of merely human
mechanism I need?   And my heart answered
nought, nought; and I was content.

Our ship floated onward before a favouring
breeze; the sun gleamed upon the ocean all
around us, and clothed it with a living light; the
waves rose up, and on their white rolling crests I
saw symbolized that dashing liberty for which I
had pined so long; the sails swelled, the ropes
rattled, we seemed bounding over the mighty
element with pride and joyousness, and the elastic
movement of the vessel communicated a portion
of its own buoyancy to my heart, and made it for
awhile forget.   An angelic vision methought

glittered over the surging prow—more heavenly-
fair unto my soul than to the weary, hopeless
wanderer in the desert, the well-known star that
leads him homeward from despair—the vision of
my lost, my loved Francesca, who, I was persuaded, even now felt as if sympathetically, an
instinctive dream that I was on my way to rescue
her. In the day I saw it like a glittering halo—
in the night also it was there, and it outshone the
stellar glory of the Heavens. " Yes, Francesca,"
I cried out, " I am on my way to free thee—to
break thy chains, and clasp thee to this heart
that beats only for thee. Lift up thy prayers, O
holy one of my hopes, and let them ascend before
the Supreme, that speedily the hour may come
which shall witness once again the blending of
our souls in one."

On, on, and we sped onward, nor did the blessed
wind abate once until we reached that noble cape,
and anchored in the port. What incidents occurred
throughout the voyage—if indeed there were
any—I have long forgotten. I went through the
easy duties of my place—for the wind made the
voyage more like a bird's flight than anything
else that I can think of—I mingled I suppose
with the other sailors, and obeyed the captain's
orders when they were given. But nothing of
these do I recollect. The whole voyage is a

blank on my mind.   I was in the land of dreams
all the while,—and they were dreams brightened
with youthful hope, and smiling expectation.
Whether I slept on deck or below, or how many
days we sailed, or whether we saw other ships, or
what was done or said by anyone, I have wholly
forgotten.   I remember only the aspect of the
ocean, the brightness of the heavens, the grand
loveliness of sea and sky, the arrowlike
motion of our good ship, and the bound of my
heart as I saw the distant Spanish mountains.   I
went on shore. Of the language I knew nothing.
To obtain a knowledge of it was indispensable. I
lost no time, but proceeding to the nearest
convent, I knocked at the gate, and in some way
communicated my wish to see the superior.   He
came—a tall man with a bald brow; austere,
dark, grave, cold, and hard as a stone; selfish-
ness and command graven in every line and
feature.   I accosted him in Latin, and told him
I was an Englishman, ignorant of the language,
but anxious to learn it; a student bent on theological knowledge, but unable at present to pay for
it; a wanderer and an exile with a solemn duty
to perform, but which could hardly be achieved,
unless I were permitted to sojourn there, or in
some similar establishment for a short period.
The abbot listened gravely ; and though I could

perceive that his surprise was great, still only a practised observer like myself could penetrate that brazen mask—his face. He did not speak for some time, but he scanned me with a searching glance—a glance of deep suspicion, though he endeavoured to hide it. At length he seemed satisfied that I had no ill-design. He asked me my name? I told him. My rank?—I told him freely. My religion?—I answered that I had been bred a Protestant, but that I had long had doubts, and here perhaps they could be solved. This last answer decided him. The Church of Rome will run any risk to gain a convert. I was besides an Englishman—and to save the soul of one of that wealthy island has always been a favourite pursuit with the astute soldiers of the Church of Peter. It almost aways brings gold into their coffers—it certainly tends to pave the way for the restoration of that long-lost land to its true and ancient lord—the Pope.

I stayed here six months, during which I learned the language perfectly. How exquisitely beautiful was this monastic solitude—this calm sequestered devotion of the spirit to God—this sublime abnegation of self and the world, and the petty prosaic cares and follies of out-of-door existence; this lonely and august meditation on the Supreme, whose sovereign power was typified in mountain and forest within our view, and who, if ever He visited the souls of mortals, would discover here shrines ready fitted for His reception. Thus it seemed in theory and hope; and for the first week I experienced only piety, solitary thought, purity and devotion—the silver light of philosophic calm. But in a little while the true character of these people was revealed. The fiery passions which are in the hearts of all Spaniards broke forth; the most terrible feud, became displayed. The Abbot was a tyrant whose sway was undisputed and indisputable. The Shah of Persia, the Grand Mogul, owned not more absolute dominion than he. The brethren bowed before him in fear; the slightest infringement of his orders entailed persecution and imprisonment on the unhappy transgressor. The very magnitude of his power destroyed and debased him; it gave full force to all his worst passions, and he surrendered himself wholly to their dominion. His frown was like death; his smile was life to these poor wretches. Thus to win the second, and to avoid the first, became the sole struggle of their minds. They hated each other with an inveterate fury; those who were out of favour, because of envy; those who were in favour, because they dared not do otherwise than hate those whom the Abbot disliked. The whole atmosphere that externally seemed peace, serenity, sunshine, holiness and love, was charged with falsehood, treachery, dark suspicion, base insinuation, terror, anger, and revenge. The air at times has seemed to me as if thronged with invisible serpents exhaling venom. In our chapel, when the organ pealed and the hymns arose, I felt as if I were living in a den of snakes, whose every breath was fire and poison and malignity.

I was put under the tutelage of one Antonio, a middle-aged monk, with fraud and astuteness deeply marked in every lineament. Oil was not more smooth, honey was not more sweet than were the tones of his voice—they trickled softly into the ear like nectar from the cup of Hebe when she served the laughing Gods. But this voice was *not* the echo or the image of the speaker's soul, as most voices are—it was not a true or natural voice, but a false, feigned, and fraudulent one, assumed for a purpose and admirably disguised. There were moments when the real tones penetrated through that deceitful mouth, when he was off his guard as it were; and he either remembered not his part, or was overmastered by some strong passion. Then, indeed, the horrid sound was heard, yet only faintly—but it was for the time the yelp of some savage creature—cruel, cowardly, blood-thirsty, and sneaking; a voice that made your nerves thrill; that jarred against your heart-strings; that gave you a sensation as of something harsh, rough, and cold, against which all your senses had an antipathy. Even he himself seemed startled by it, as if he had heard some demon's whisper, for he immediately looked abashed, and glided, though not without effort, into his usual mellifluous accent, seeking hard to hide his awkwardness and confusion. But on these occasions his eye scanned you with suspicion; you could see its furtive light beneath his downcast modest lids, as if he sought to penetrate your very being and find out whether that tone so marked, yet so unusual, had awakened feelings within you such as he wished to slumber. For a whole hour I have observed him watching me after one of these chance ebullitions of his natural essence; and though I took good care to appear unsuspicious, yet I felt during the whole period as if I were walking in a forest while I knew that a hyena tracked my footsteps.

He took extraordinary pains to indoctrinate me in the language, and spared no labour to convert me to the true faith. He brought before my eyes the long and glorious line of Pontiffs from Peter to Clement, an unbroken succession of Vicars of Jesus, such as no other creed could

boast of. But here my lessons under Akiba
came to my aid; and I at once confuted him by
the far more ancient and illustrious line of the
Grand Lama, which—an elective pontificate—has
continued in unbroken succession for upwards of
four thousand years, and has held unlimited
spiritual sway over the greatest empire that the
world ever saw. Antonio first affected to deny
this fact—but the convent was not without a
library—although it was little resorted to, except
for schoolmen like Sanchez or Aquinas, whose
lives were spent in weaving nets of hell for human
souls—and when I convinced him that I was
right, he merely replied by the old argument
that God permits the Devil to do these things
for the purpose of trying the hearts of men. But
when I told him that in my opinion this was
reducing God to the level of the Devil himself,
he made me no answer, but with a well-masked
scowl, retired to his cell; nor did I again see him
for several days. When he met me, he made no
allusion to our recent controversy, but proceeded
to some other argument; nor did he ever again
cite as confirmatory of the holiness of his church
the historical proof which had been so suddenly
demolished. Had he been a bungler in his art,
he would have harped upon it again, and yet
again, until I should have grown hardened

against him—but he was a more subtle dialecti-
tian ; and I always observed that when he was
thoroughly beaten on any one point he never
again alluded to it—not confessing indeed that
he was so beaten, but hoping that I myself might
in time furnish an argument in his favour, which
did not occur to him at the instant of dispute.

Meanwhile the Abbot affected to regard me as
a prodigy of good sense and learning.   He consulted me on classical lore ; he sought my opinion
on subjects of historical investigation ; he even
professed to ask my advice on abstruse questions
of theology, and insinuated how great and glorious
would be my position before the world if I would
but enter the church and devote myself to her
interests.   Like Dom Balthazar, he struck that
chord in my nature which he fancied beat to
ambition—but like Balthazar, he was wrong, for
I had, and have none.   It has often occurred to
me as strange, that two men of great discern-
ment in mankind should both have so utterly
misjudged me as to mistake for ambition my
lordly feeling of independence—but they certainly
did make this error ;   and no two feelings as it
seems to me are more opposite.   For after the most
intimate knowledge of courts, cabinets, and camps,
I am convinced that what is usually called

ambition is a dirty, mean, sneaking little passion, which has no self-respect at all, but which perpetually debases itself in the mire for the purpose of some wretched gain; despicable in the eyes of the truly great, who are scarcely ever known to the world because they so utterly despise it. The renowned general at whose name the nations are filled with wonder, owes probably his advancement to some courtezan's caprice, at whose feet he has grovelled like a lap dog; the powerful minister who wields an empire and its destinies, has attained his elevation by humouring the foibles of some artful menial, male or female, who has the ear of the Sovereign; and the celebrated statesman has paved the way to eminence by stooping to the filthiest rabble, and sinking below even their level, for the purpose of securing their support. Could we but trace the secret springs by which men of the most illustrious name have risen to the most exalted heights, we should hesitate long before we decided whether the baseness of the individual, or the folly of the multitude who worshipped as a God a very loathsome lickspittle, were the most worthy of surprize. But these springs we never shall have unveiled, and it is only by accident that glimpses of them are seen. And it is with this conviction

that I look upon all history as fable—not more
real than a painting, or a dream, but used by
knaves to enslave asses.

There was a noble hall in the convent paved
with marble, and wainscotted with black oak, on
which were ranged the full length portraits of all
the men who had successively filled the place of
Abbot—dark and fire-eyed men, whose looks
seemed to penetrate beneath their cowls, and to
read the inmost tablet of the heart. They were
in every attitude, from profound study up to rapt
devotion, and there have been nights when as I
paced this place alone, and the broken moonlight
streamed in through the high windows I
have half fancied they were real phantoms congregated together, to devise new schemes to move
the world at their will. In this hall the monks
usually assembled when the pious meditations of
the day were over, and some volumes of legends
were read and commented on by each in turn
under the supervision of the reverend superior.
I had heard and read of the bacchanalian revels
which take place in convents, but here there
was nothing of the kind; all was gloom, asceticism
and repose, but the passions that lay hidden under
this awful stillness were only the more terrible
for being repressed. They were a large community—and properly speaking, I had no right

to be one among them; but an exception was made in my favour; for I have no doubt the Abbot had not failed to ascertain that I was a man of rank, and great expectations; and my flight from home was considered only one of the eccentric aberrations in which the best regulated Englishmen indulge. I was treated no longer like a dependent living almost on alms, but as a visitor who amused his fancy or his leisure by assuming a species of odd disguise; and every little art was brought into play which could either attract my will or secure my judgment. Everything I beheld seemed grave, decorous, holy; and the Abbot himself was represented to me as a sort of sainted being by those who I knew detested him as a fiend.

In my controversial discussions with Antonio, which were sometimes carried on in the presence of some of the other monks, there was one brother Juan, who never ventured to take part in any of them, but who seemed to pay the profoundest attention to all that was said, and to regard myself with great interest. He was a young man, not probably five and twenty, with a mild benign expression, a noble forehead and a proud eye, but the fervour of the last he strove to subdue with all his strength. He was silent, modest and gentle; and I was very much pleased with him.

In a short time a sort of acquaintance sprang up ; my teacher saw that I yearned to the young man, and he gave him permission to come occasionally to my cell and enlighten me on some points of Catholic faith. By degrees our meetings became so frequent that not a day passed in which we did not spend some time together. The more I saw of him, the more I loved him. He appeared to possess all the virtues of a man, and all the sweet softness of a woman. We discoursed on a variety of subjects, and I was amazed to find him sceptical on many points which our reverend Abbot would have regarded as among the main essentials of salvation. He was the younger son of a noble house, and had been thrust into this place solely against his will, to swell the wealth of an elder brother, and add another to the innumerable victims whom the church engages every year in her death-enfolding maw.

Although my senior in years, he seemed to cling to me, as a weaker plant will circle round one that is stronger and more matured. I did not hesitate to admit him into my fullest confidence—to open my heart to him as to a brother ; for although I scorn mankind in the mass, I have never done so in detail, but have ever reposed faith in those whom I believed worthy of it, nor have I always been deceived. I told him all from the beginning, exactly as I have narrated it here; he listened with intense interest, and there were parts of it at which he even wept. More susceptible and passionate in soul than us of northern climes, he was alternately moved with anger, indignation and pity; and he gave full utterance to the promptings of each emotion, as it arose within. I consulted him about the means of finding Francesca—but here we were both wholly at a loss. We could not devise any scheme by which in broad Spain, with its innumerable convents, monasteries, and abbeys, we could with safety say in this or that province she was to be found. To make a pilgrimage from one religious house to another as I had read that the minstrel Blondel did when searching for his Master, Richard Cœur de Lion, over the castellated continent, seemed wholly hopeless, yet what other course remained? or by what other means could she be discovered? And thus might my whole life pass ineffectually, and the close be still clouded by despair. We consulted long and frequently, but without any end gained. Chance alone as it seemed must be relied on—yet what a weak reliance is chance!

Six months had now passed, and I was pressed to make some declaration of my faith. I will not deny that I had seen much which profoundly

moved me. The conduct of my companions was
nothing ; their creed seemed noble and sublime.
A most extraordinary variety of subtle argu
ments had been brought to bear on my understanding, and being young, and of a romantic
temperament, Protestanism appeared to me in
all its chilling and prosaic features, while the
glory of the Roman church, half chivalric, half
celestial, was presented in a glittering light that
excited a powerful interest on my heart. On
my heart, I say—for Popery is a religion of the
senses rather than of the reason ; and it appeals
to and relies on faith, which is always a more
tremendous incentive than mere judgment. But
I noticed that whenever I consulted, or even
hinted to Juan a thought of change, his countenance always fell, and his silence was like an icy
wind on my budding hopes. He longed to
speak, yet he was evidently afraid. His looks
were wary and suspicious ; he seemed to act as
if the very stones had ears. I have often seen
him beckon me to silence, and walk stealthily
towards a picture behind which he looked, as if
he half expected to discover someone hidden
there ; he has done the same in the evening to a
large reading desk, when the dark vesper shadows
fell over the vast hall, and threw its various parts
into blended light and darkness. He has sud-

denly stopped, and listened as if he heard the tread of some advancing footstep, whose owner longed to betray him to destruction. One of the monks suddenly disappeared. Had he escaped? Was he sick? Had he gone on a mission? Had he died? No one knew; no one dared to ask. Even the eye questioned not into the mystery. Everything proceeded as usual. The Abbot looked the same; all the brethren seemed figures of stone on whom no outward circumstance could make the least impression. I was myself filled with a sort of vague awe at this strange incident in our community, the strangest thing of all being that it excited no more observation than if a fly had come and gone.

At length he said—

"Wortley, I can bear this hell no longer. It is slowly killing me. I had rather die at once. I will fly from this place. I will become a soldier, bandit, beggar—anything so long as I can be free. I am surrounded by spies and wretches; my every moment is like Gehenna. All this holiness which is professed here is but hypocrisy of the vilest kind. You have yourself, to some extent, seen it, but never can you dive into its depths like one who has been born and bred in this religion. To you, as a stranger and an infidel, all its finest features are presented; those

which are not so are kept in the back ground,
only your children, if you should abandon your
own faith, will be gradually taught them from
their tender years; to you, to any convert, they
will never be revealed.   There is deep subtlety in
this; but what is there in which the Church of
Rome is not profoundly subtle?   These men
gloss over their vices, but they say what matters
it; we belong to an Infallible Church; we are
the only true believers.   God will depart from
His strict laws for us; He will not mete out to
us His children, as He measures to the heretics.
We, therefore, have a letter of license for our
vices; but woe be unto those who are vicious
but are not Catholic.   On them the vials of
his hottest wrath will be unsparingly poured.
This they do not exactly say, but this is what
we all think and believe.   I can see their strong
desire to make you a convert.   But how can
that religion be good, whose votaries are all
evil?   Let no man persuade you against Jesus
Christ.   He said, *the tree is known by its fruits;*
so it is in all things.   When the believers generally are wicked—as Petro-Paulites usually are
—it is most certain that the creed which they
profess must be false.   You will say this is
true of all religions.   Perhaps it is.   Seek out,
therefore, that religion whose followers on the

whole are the least bad, and cleave to that. It
alone is assuredly the true one—if, indeed,
there be such a thing on earth as true religion.
For if a religion has not force enough to make
its own professors pious, it cannot be a thing
from God. Cast your eyes, then, over all the
earth, and where shall you find any countries
more sunk in debasement than those which
own monastic sway, and bow the knee to the
Vatican ? If the theory which I have broached
be sound, the consequence must be this; avoid
us, we are not of God, but man. *Princeps
noster est Satanas !*

"If I am to wait," I answered, "until I find
a religion which makes perfect men, I must
wait for ever. There is no creed that can perform this."

"That is true; I did not maintain any such
absurdity. I merely said, 'Seek *that* whose
followers are least wicked;' that is about the
superlative point to which fallen human nature
can ascend. Goodness is unattainable by
man. If man could be good, he would not be
man at all, but an angel; he would have no
business on earth; he would be out of his proper
sphere. But no man can be good. All he can
hope at the utmost is to be least vicious. If I
could shew you at a bird's-eye view the habits of

all the men and women of Europe, you would
confess that of all other peoples they are perhaps
the most vicious in existence. Their various
systems must, consequently, be false. Observe,
I do not speak of pure Christianity, for that, as
a system, does not exist. It lives in a burlesque
of that which Jesus really taught. Your form of
it is probably better than ours, but after all, the
difference is only slight. Let us depart together
from this place ; let us abandon Europe for ever ;
let us penetrate to the Orient, which God from
the beginning has made the cradle of all sublime
and holy things—*ex Oriente, Lux ;*—and judge
for ourselves, before we finally decide on a step
that is to regulate our fate for futurity."

"Can it be possible, my friend, that I hear this
from you ?—from you who are a sworn member
of this church and a soldier of this community ?"

" Why should it not be possible ? Why should
it be impossible ? Think you I have lived so
long and dared not to reflect ? Think you that
my daily observation of the men by whom I am
surrounded has not produced seeds of meditation within my mind, and that these seeds have
not produced fruit ? Yes, I am resolved to fly—
if with you, I shall be happy ; if without you,
nevertheless depart I shall ; for now I am in hell,
and have been so for many, many years. If I

remain here I have a home for life; but what a home! My uncle, the Abbot will protect me; will promote me; perhaps even when he departs I may hope to govern this community. But would that make amends for a life misused, and for an existence which is a living lie before my Maker? Wortley, we must part, or go forth together."

"Can you then abandon your uncle? He is a wise man, a powerful man; you say he is kind to you. Perhaps, indeed, since your father cast you in here, your uncle may be your only friend. Do you know what the world really is? Have you considered how precarious is the life of him who wanders penniless?"

"My uncle! Yes, he is wise and powerful. But know you why he is here? Of what use is his wisdom? It is the cunning of the world—no more; and what is that before God? When I look at *him* I am the more positively resolved. If the Church of Rome were true, my uncle should have swung on the gallows; as it is, he is one of her chiefs and generals."

"Has he then committed any crime that you so distrust him, and pronounce so severe a sentence against so near a relation?"

"Listen and decide. My father, as you know, is a great nobleman; my uncle also inherited a

vast estate. He married at an early age the
only daughter of an opulent merchant, who traded
to the East, and received with her an immense
dowry. They lived at Toledo, in a splendid
palace. My uncle was in the habit of spending
a month or two every year at Madrid. Our connections were powerful, and he figured at court;
but he never brought his young wife there, nor
did any of his acquaintances in the capital know
that he was married. Among those houses at
which he visited was that of the Marquis of
Montana. The Marquis had a daughter as beautiful as a young rose. An intimacy soon sprang
up between her and my uncle; it was sanctioned
by the father, and the nuptials were fixed. The
young wife at Toledo wrote frequently to her
husband, but he sent her a variety of excuses.
At length her father wrote to some friends at
Madrid to ascertain what business detained his
son-in-law so long. They inquired. My uncle
was sufficiently eminent in the capital to have his
movements and his projects easily discoverable.
The father-in-law was informed of the coming
nuptials; he told his daughter, who was half
distracted. She wrote a letter to the Marquis of
Montana, and another to the young lady. She
did not upbraid her husband in the least, but
simply informed them of the facts. My uncle

was, of course, expelled the house. He returned
home. His wife was then pregnant. She received him with every demonstration of the most
passionate attachment; she did not once allude
to what had happened, but behaved in every
respect as if he had been the truest of lords. He
received all her love is silence; he sometimes
smiled upon her; she thought all was forgotten.
Her relations vied with each other in giving him
welcome; the most sumptuous feasts and enter-
tainments were given to honour his return. He
went to all, and to every appearance was happy
and contented. When she was about a mouth
before her confinement, he got up one morning
earlier than usual, and told her he was about
to retire to his devotions; he recommended her
also to seek her closet, and offer up prayers to
God for a safe accomplishment of their mutual
hopes. She did so, but in a short time her husband entered. He bore with him various articles
such as are used for the funerals of persons of
rank. Her heart misgave her; she tremblingly
asked him what he designed? ' To murder thee,'
he said. ' Now will I repay thee for all thy
wickedness; now will I have vengeance for the
agonies thou hast made me endure.' In vain she
implored pardon; in vain she intreated forgiveness
for an offence which had proceeded only from

her love. He was inexorable, and bid her prepare. Her maid, who slept in an adjoining room, and overheard all that passed, rushed in and sought to save her. As he lifted the dagger she endeavoured to arrest his hand; but he struck her down, and stabbed his wife to the heart. 'Die both,' he cried out, 'the jealous wife and the eaves-dropping maid.' He lighted the tapers, he darkened the room, he laid his wife upon her bed, and went to her father and mother. 'Come,' said he, ' to a little feast which I have prepared.' They went with him; he led them to the closet door, and, having shown them in, left them and fled. They supposed at first it was some pleasant device; but the expiring maid faintly informed them of all, and died ere she had well concluded the dreadful narrative. My grand uncle is a Cardinal, great at St. Peter's; my uncle is here. The murder was never redressed. Can I be happy under the roof and eye of such a man?"

I was horror-stricken; but before I had time to say a word the Abbot himself appeared in the distance; he moved gravely towards us, and with his usual philosophic calm, "Signor Montagu," said he, "I have marked your intimacy with my nephew; let me have the pleasure of the company of both in my apartment." A cold thrill shot through me; but I knew not how to act. I

looked on Juan.   He was as white as marble.
Could it be that we were overheard ?   It seemed
impossible.   We motioned assent, and followed
the Abbot, who led the way with sweeping robe.
In a few moments we were in his room.   He
ordered wine and fruit; the convent garden was
famous for the latter.   They were soon produced,
and we began to converse.   But a dark chain
seemed thrown over my tongue.   I could not
speak ; I could but listen.   A similar spell was
on Juan ; but the Abbot shone.   Never before
had I seen him so elegant ; never before had his
lip charmed with so much wit, politeness, and
gay elegance.   He was no longer the grave,
austere head of a religious community ; he was
the fine gentleman who had mixed in courts and
camps.   He spoke of his uncle, the Cardinal, of
his power at the Vatican ; his liking for myself ;
and the fine wonders he would do for me if I
enrolled myself among his " sable soldiers," as
he called the monks.   I was infatuated—spell-
bound.   I forgot Francesca ; I forgot everything.
I felt that his was the master mind.   I strove to
resist, to defer compliance, but my mind grew
relaxed ; I could feel its energy slowly melt away
as the Abbott's tongue poured forth its manifold
treasures.   Was it the wine?   Had it been
drugged by one of those powerful soporifics known

to the hierarchy? I had sense enough, however, not to pledge myself at once; in three days I would give him a final answer. We parted; the Abbot kissed his nephew, and embraced myself. He even attended us to the door, and softly bade us " Good night; God bless you both," said he.

When we were alone, Juan grasped my hand convulsively. " Fly," said he, " let us both fly at once. Our interview has been overheard. My uncle knows every word that we have spoken. This feast was but a trick to entrap you. Once you have taken the irrevocable vow you become his, body and soul; he will have an absolute power of life and death over you. *My* fate is sealed. I feel it; I know it. I have his Judas kiss upon my lips, and I know that there is death in that kiss. He would at this moment have ordered me to be immured for life, but that he dreads to lose you. Oh! Wortley, what a pang shot through me this moment. Hold me, hold me. I faint. The wine has overpowered me. I am a poor reveller."

We stole into the garden. By the fair starlight I looked into his face; it was fixed and bloodless. There was a strange wild expression about his eyes, such as I had never seen before. The air revived him a little. We were quite alone. He only of all the monks had a key to this place.

It had been given him as a special favour by the
Abbot. We walked about and concerted our plans.
We crept softly to our cells, and gathered up our
sheets and the few clothes we had; the first we
twisted and tied together until they formed a
rope capable of being thrown up the high wall
which confined the monks within the convent ter-
ritory. We searched in vain for a hook to hold
it at the top, but none was to be found. At last
we wrenched one of the iron bars away from the
window, and with great trouble bent it into a half
anchor shape. Some hours were passed before
this was done. It was now three o'clock, and at
four the convent bell usually rang to call the
monks to their devotions. Juan's excitement
now grew dreadful; he seemed frightfully agitated; he trembled all over; his deadly paleness
increased. At times I could feel it was with difficulty he repressed a scream, for he seemed intensely agonised, but I supposed it was merely
nervousness. At length we got once more into
the garden. We tried to throw up the rope and
hook, but wholly failed, although we used incre-
dible labour. At length I got up into a tree, and
with great difficulty flung the hook. It caught
hold, and the line descended to the ground.
Juan urged me to mount first. I refused, but he
forced me. When I got to the top he told me to

pull hard, and endeavoured to ascend; but was
wholly unable. In vain he put forth his arms;
they would not hold him; they were now too
feeble to support his weight. Securely fastening
the hook to the top of the wall, I descended.
I found him on the ground, nearly fainting; he could scarcely move; he seemed to
me even to breathe with difficulty, he whispered in my ear: "Fly, fly,—I am poisoned;
Oh, fool! why did I trust him? I should have
known better." I tied the sheets securely round
him and again ascended, then putting forth all
my strength, I hauled him up to the top, but
the exertion nearly killed me. When I got him
there I placed him for a few minutes on the broad
ledge, the starlight gleamed with a melancholy
smile over his white features, on which the
death agony was already written. "Fly," said
he, "fly, I say, or you will be discovered—and
then death;—see the sun is already in the East."
I looked, it was so—but I was determined not to
leave him. I untied the sheets and flung them
on the other side of the wall, then securely
binding the hook to the parapet, I lifted the
dying man upon my back, and descended with
him. We got down safely—a little fountain
murmured by. I bore him to it, and bathed his
face; the cold water seemed to revive him. He

opened his poor eyes—their light was fading fast.
I burst into tears.   I pressed, I folded him to my
heart.

"Wortley," said he, "remember my dying
words. Avoid my uncle and his snares. Go to
the East—the sunlight East. See even now the
sun rises. *Ex oriente lux*—so has it ever been—
so shall it ever be. Seek Francesca, and if you
find her, let her pray for me. Pray thou also
for thine unhappy friend. Now leave me. God
bless you—bless you." And he fell back. *Ay
de mi! Ay de mi!* *

He was dead. I laid his limbs at full length
beside that holy stream. I offered up a brief
prayer to God, and kissed his lips already cold.
My heart was full almost to bursting. Here was
my sole friend on earth—except perhaps Manasain.
Well, mine has been a strange existence. Once
again I smoothed his limbs and looked upon his
face. I closed the eyes—those eyes once so soft
with love, and fervour, and enthusiasm. The
early sunbeam had already come forth from
behind the mountains; there was a sacred beauty
in this sylvan place; the birds began to wake and
warble; all nature seemed joyous, bustling, active;
but in my heart was death. My friend alas was

---

* Woe is me. Woe is me.

no more. With difficulty I tore myself away. I
was tossed in a tempest of conflicting thoughts.
Suddenly the convent bell rang out its deathlike
peal, and I fled into the mountains; I found a
cavern, and rushed into its farthest depths. I
flung myself on the ground and slept.

CHAPTER XXXII.

"As if a man did flee from a lion, and a bear met him, or went into a house and leaned his hand on a wall and a serpent bit him."

I CONCEALED myself the whole of the day in the cavern, and ruminated on my condition. What was now to become of me? I was alone in a foreign land, at the mercy I had almost said of a ferocious priest, who from his antecedent history would probably have no scruple in destroying me if he could. It behoved me to be exceedingly cautious. Flight from his vicinity was indispensable, but the method of accomplishing it did not seem so easy. Already I pictured to myself in imagination the bands of military emissaries who were pursuing me. If a leaf trembled on a tree, I thought it was a soldier; if a dog barked I started and supposed it heralded the approach of my captors. I was conscious indeed that I had committed no crime, but I had now seen enough of life to know that innocence is but a poor shield against the malevolence of mankind. Thus the long hours passed, and I was without food in this gloomy hiding place, within a short distance of the convent, and consequently every moment in danger. At length night descended, and I stole forth. How calm and refreshing seemed the mountain-wafted breeze of nature; how much of glorious happy liberty did the open landscape breathe into my soul. For a few moments I felt glad, but the recollection of my wretched condition soon recurred to me, and I determined to lose no time in entering on my flight. There was a clear azure light falling from the heaven, and I could see that the moon would soon rise. I resolved therefore to get forward on my road before this occurred. I proceeded hastily, often looking back, but as it seemed without any reason. I heard no footstep, I perceived no signal of pursuit. The wood through which I took my way was silent as the grave. I began to walk with a stouter step, and a less anxious beating of the pulse.

I wandered thus for a week, concealing myself

during the open gla re of day, and as the evening
hour appeared reco mmencing my journey.   I
subsisted on such wild fruits as I could find, and
on the chance charity of the muleteer or peasant,
who poorer than an Irishman is as stiff and
haughty as a prince.   I picked up a flute which
some traveller had lost, or thrown away, and
often gained a supper and a bed in return for my
musical skill.   Our English airs, of which I
knew a good many, were a perfect novelty to these
people, nor was the flute less so; for Spain is the
land of guitars or castanets.   I saw much to reconcile me to human nature; hospitality, kindness, good feeling, good fellowship, even among
the most humble; the grandees, however, scorned
me, and would give me nothing.   But Spain is a
land of desolation.   Everything is arid, deathlike, melancholy.   The towns and villages are
rapidly decaying; they seem to sink day by day
into the dry and greedy earth.   The people
stately, silent, and desponding, appear to have
resigned themselves up to a proud despair, and
stalk about with a ghostlike solemnity, which to
an Englishman is anything but agreeable to see.
For to our bustling eye of energy and toil this
lounging laziness looks criminal; we immediately
suspect an idle man of being no better than he
should be.   But all Spaniards are so in seeming

if not in reality. Everything is at a stand still; you enter a town and it is a dwelling, not of the living, but of the dead. All the essence of life has gone out of them; their motions are mechanical; there is no vitality in the people or in the land. They are like their own mountains, silent, lonely, and unproductive; they are like their own vegas, dark, solitary and barren. The only living things in Spain are one or two of their rivers, which are rapid enough; and all their women, including duennas, who are as capricious and as bright as their river waves. I had nearly forgotten their goats, which are quite as frisky as their women.

On the ninth day of my flight I found myself in the boundless forests of Almoramia. Here, at all events, I was safe enough. But what a place! North, south, east, west, wherever I looked it was all interminable woodland. Cork, oak, and ilex trees reared their lofty branches; the ash and willow grew in thousands in the marshy parts. I began to fear I should lose my way amid this world of wood. The sun could scarcely penetrate its mighty depths; the widely spreading branches of the cork trees, and the gnarled arms of the oak effectually excluded those scorching beams under which I should have perished during the past week, had I not hidden myself under rocks, and caves, and by the deep and shadowy banks of the rivers. The Guadaranque flowed through this mighty wilderness, but it was an unsafe guide. Nor was it always approachable. It wound under a perfect covering of woodbine, clematis, and other thickly foliaged creepers, and I have more than once almost tumbled headlong into its breast from the deep banks that girdled it in. The open glades that sometimes gleamed like bright islands of verdure reminded me of dear old England; but I had other business on my hands at present than that of sentimental recollection or poetic fancy, and the sight of a wild boar has more than once put all my most romantic reveries to flight. At night the wolves howled horribly; but by this time I could climb a tree almost as nimbly as a squirrel; and when I was thoroughly fatigued I usually selected the softest greenest bough of an oak tree for my pillow; and there ensconced, surrendered myself to sleep, with only the stars, my guardian angel, and Providence to watch over me—no bad sentinels you will probably say.

One night, just as I had got into my perch, I was aroused by a sudden noise, and peering as well as I could into the darkness from my leafy bed-room, I thought I could see a number of figures mounted on mules riding rapidly towards the

very tree on which I was housed. A hundred
thoughts of a pursuing band of soldiers or
alguazils crossed my mind, and I gave myself up
for lost, more particularly as they all dismounted
round the tree where I was hidden, and began to
laugh and talk with the unrestrained freedom of
the camp and guardroom. But in a few moments
my heart was again at rest. These gentlemen
were not government banditti—they were only
robbers on their own account. They had not the
royal license to pillage and maltreat, which is one
of the cherished privileges of the alguazils of
His Most Catholic Majesty. They were merely
a number of jovial gentlemen who were associated
for the same purposes, but without the sign
manual of the sovereign to justify them if they
were detected. They were in all about sixty, and
a terrible cut throat crew they looked ; but I had
more faith in them somehow than I should have
had, had there been the same number of alguazils
with law on their lips and license in their hands
to trample upon every law that hedges round the
rights and privileges of the people. They soon
kindled a fire, unpacked their wallets, and pro-
ducing sundry joints of cold roast kid, a multitude of cooked fowls, and unending baskets of
eggs, cheese, bacon, bread, and garlic, and pigskins filled with wine, prepared a sumptuous

repast, for which I can assure you my mouth
watered and my stomach sadly yearned. The
fact is I had lived upon nothing but bread and
water and a cigar for the last four days of my
pilgrimage, and I was tired of such eremitical,
though heavenly food.

And now when they had feasted like Homer's
heroes, and were filled with food and wine, that
jovial spirit which no Spaniard can thoroughly
hide, and no bandit with a full belly is ever without, broke forth unrestrainedly among these
glorious minions of the moon. Clearing away
their plates and dishes, they drew themselves
closer around the fire; and as the night was
somewhat chill, they largely heaped upon it dry
leaves and branches, and began to smoke and
drink like men who were resolved to be happy.
They stretched themselves at full length on coats
and capes, and junks of cork, and beneath the
glorious green oak trees, formed a group that a
painter would have loved to see, or a poet to
describe. The fire blazed brightly, and its glitter-
sparks ascended almost to the bough on which I
was hidden; through an opening in the leafy
arch overhead, the living stars were seen shining
in the blue ether, and when the voices of the
bandits were hushed, the distant music of the
rolling Guadaranque was softly heard. If I could

have been quite certain that I should remain unobserved by prying eyes, I should have enjoyed
the scene almost as much as themselves; but my
trepidation was not a little increased by my
hunger, which now indeed began sensibly to
remind me, as it did Alexander the Great, that I
was a mere mortal after all. However, I bore
up as well as I could, and as I well knew the
language, I was not a little amused by their conversation. There were some wild wags among
them, and they seemed to enjoy some recent
adventure with more than boyish glee.

"By the Holy Virgin of Toledo," said one,
and he reverently raised his hat, "never did I
think such splendid fun was to be got out of a
rascal monk as we have had this blessed afternoon. Will you hear it my captain?"

The Captain and the rest willingly assented.

"We had not parted an hour, my captain,"
resumed the bandit, "when we overtook one of
those Capuchins who eat up all the food of the
poor, and give them only empty words in return;
so I said to my companion Julian Romea, 'here,
let us have some fun with this fellow,' and faith,
we lost no time in doing so. So seizing him, we
bid him stand and deliver; but the wretch had
nothing—no, not even a maravedi, or if he had,
he must have swallowed his treasure—for nothing

with the holy name of the king could be found in his capacious pouches. Well, this annoyed us— so we gagged him and bound his hands together, and having also tethered his feet with a short rope, so that he could only limp along—not half so well as the Devil on Two Sticks—we tied him up in an old cow's skin which we happened to have, and fastening the horns on to his head, and a couple of sharp bells to these, we dismissed him with our blessing, having just compelled him to give us his benediction; though I think it sounded marvellously like a curse. Oh! what a figure he was! We watched him into the next village, crawling, hobbling, jumping, ringing his bells, and altogether appearing like the devil himself, with a long tail streaming behind him. All the cattle ran away wild; the donkeys brayed with astonishment; the dogs barked and made the most laughable disturbance; the cows cocked up their tails and seemed ready to jump over the moon; the geese gabbled; the cocks and hens made a horrible noise; and the ducks cried quack, quack, while we ourselves were ready to burst. The people in the village came out, but could make nothing of what they saw. At last one bawled out "It is the devil," whereupon they all scampered after their cows; and while the women

screamed, and the children roared, and the asses
capered, the friar himself managed to make a
strange outcry through his gagged mouth, which
completed the scene, and still more frightened
the panic-stricken crowd. Romea laughed so
much that he fell down in the mud, and I had
some difficulty in getting him up. At last the
priest of the village came out with a gun in one
hand, and a crucifix in the other, and when he
came near our friend, he took aim, and would
have probably shot—not him, but a donkey—
when the friar fell flat on his face, and the priest
taking courage, came up, and waving the crucifix
over him, caught hold of one of the horns, which
soon revealed the mystery, and when he had
disgagged his man the whole story was made
clear. But it was too good an opportunity for
the priest to let pass, so he called the people forward and told them he had worked a miracle by
casting the devil out of a holy friar, in proof of
which he showed the cow's hide and horns. Great
was the amazement of the villagers, who soon
assembled in crowds, and our priest cut up the
skin into small shreds, which he sold to the bye-
standers as a charm against all the imps of hell;
but the horns he removed into the chapel, and
there suspended them over the high altar, in
proof of the mighty deed which he had done. So

he and the friar divided the spoil; and we heard him telling the people he had been met on the road by several devils, one of whom had transformed him into a monster; and then he muttered blessings on the priest for having accomplished one of the greatest miracles on record. But I and Romea, having enjoyed the scene, immediately betook ourselves on the journey which you, my captain, ordered us to make, and here are the results thereof."

Whereupon he produced a massive silver goblet, at which the eyes of all glistened with delight; and the captain, with the air of a connoisseur, pronounced it to be a matchless specimen.

Then our friend Romea, rising, sang a ballad of the Cid in a fine, manly voice, which resounded through the forest, and woke up the distant echoes; and fresh logs were piled upon the fire, and the pigskins were again handed round, and all was mirth and jollity.

In the midst of these revels one of the bandits was observed to sigh deeply.

" How now, brother?" said one, " why are you melancholy in the midst of this good cheer?"

" I was thinking of the Holy Virgin of Toledo," answered the bandit, demurely.

" A miracle!—a miracle! " shouted a third; " here is Joaquim becoming religious."

" Aye, faith that will be a miracle," added a fourth, " for I know no man apter in despoiling a fat monk, or rifling a convent cellar."

" Or kissing a young novice," put in a fifth.

" Or pulling the ears of the bishop's pretty housekeeper," said a sixth.

In a word, every one had something to remark upon this new conversion.

Joaquim remained silent until all had had their say ; he then spoke with great gravity.

" By my beard, my brothers, I am, in truth, grown religious ever since I was in the old Cathedral of Toledo, and saw the Holy Virgin decked on last Anunciation day, and I would willingly make the heavenly lady my own if I had the chance to do so, and not envy the Lord Archbishop for the rest of my life ; for her head was covered with a golden crest set so thick with diamonds, emeralds, and pearls, that there was not room to insert one stone, were it but the bigness of a needle's eye ; and on her neck she wore a necklace such as no king or queen of old Castille has ever worn ; but her petticoat—"

" Ah ! I thought you'd come to that," says a sly fellow, with a wink.

" Her petticoat was all adorned, " pursued Joaquim, " with flowers and arabesques of fine

pearls, among which were some as big as an egg,
and these were mixed up with black pearls of so
rare a lustre that each was worth its weight in
gold a thousand times; and stars and suns, and
other matchless devices, all worked with the finest
jewels covered over this sacred petticoat so thickly
that, if I could, I would have sold my soul to
Satan to possess this blessed virgin of my heart.
And now I sigh from the bottom of my bowels
whenever I think of the matchless Mother of
Toledo, and I pray to all the saints that she
were mine."

"Bravo! bravo!" cried half a dozen; "so
much for Joaquim's conversion;" and they drank
his health around.

"Gentlemen," says the Captain, "I have
news for you that will stir your blood, and bring
forth every man's metal. Two hundred of the
king's soldiers are on our track."

There was a melancholy pause. Even these
dare-devils were not particularly anxious to come
to close quarters with well disciplined soldiers.
The Captain waited, but no man spoke.

"How now, gentlemen," said he; "surely we
are not afraid. We have beaten them before.
and shall beat them again like brave men. But
let us take courage. They received their orders
only yesterday at Madrid; so we have the start

of them by several hundred miles, and if we don't like close quarters we can easily beat a retreat."

" Two hundred is a large number," said one.

" The odds are disproportionate," murmured another.

" I don't see what we should gain by fighting," remarked a third.

" Faith, I'd rather seek a convent," sighed forth Joaquim. This sally produced a general laugh. It seemed conceded by all that the better part of valour was discretion, and I could see, that though bold, they were not desperate fools.

" How now, gentlemen braves," said the Captain ; " what is to be done?"

" Why pack up all our winnings, and retreat into Granada," said Julian Romea ; " there is nothing to be gained by fighting, and I have always thought that it is the part of brave men to wait until they are attacked."

This proposal met with general approbation ; the Captain himself applauded it, and it was passed unanimously.

" And now, gentlemen," said he, " let us go to sleep. In the morning, as soon as day dawns, we shall commence our retreat. God assists him who rises early. We have several day's start of the soldiers, and they must be nimble-heeled fellows if they can overtake us, with our light baggage and our merry hearts."

Thus saying, they prepared for repose. This was an easy matter. They spread their valises and saddles under their heads; each man stretched himself at length with his feet turned towards the fires, after having well looked to his arms, primed and loaded his pistols, and seen that they were ready placed at hand, but sheltered nevertheless from the night dew. Julian Romea was chosen as sentinel, and the whole company were fast asleep in five minutes. Julian heaped a new pile of logs on the fire, and sat down by it. But in a little time also he began to nod. I suppose that secret pilgrimage on which he had gone with his companion after their little pleasantry with the friar had taxed his energies to the utmost; for Julian certainly exhibited all the signs of deep fatigue. He wrestled hard, however, with the enemy, and strove to drive off every attack of slumber, but the foe proved too strong for him; and in a little while he was as sound as his companions. He soon passed from a sitting to a recumbent posture, and gave audible tokens that he also was in the Land of Dreams.

I now thought within myself what I had better do? Should I remain in my covert until morning when I should probably be seen and made

quick work of—treated as a spy, and shot, or
stabbed without ceremony; or should I endeavour
to retreat while this lucky spell of sleep was over
Julian; There was immense hazard either way.
I had no doubt that discovery at any time would
be death, and there seemed but faint hope of my
being able to steal away from sixty men, any one
of whom, the dropping of a leaf or broken branch,
the cry of a wolf, or of an owl, might suddenly
wake up while I yet was within their grasp. So
far, I blessed my star that I had escaped unnoticed; but was it wise wholly to rely on their
non-observance of me? The eyes of sixty prying men, keenly suspicious to all appearances,
and made more keen still in consequence of the
information which they had just received from
their Captain, would be soon about the place
where I was hiding, and it seemed impossible I
should escape. On the other hand, cool reason
said, " You have escaped so far—why tempt your
fate by a wild endeavour to break away from this
circle? It is hopeless for you to suppose that
you can elude them if you leave your present
hiding place. In the hurry and bustle of their
quick departure, in saddling their mules and preparing their baggage, they will have quite enough
to occupy their minds, without peering up into
the skies in search of wandering Englishmen,

who are eccentric enough to make their bed-chamber in the boughs. At all events if you are to be caught, it is better to be caught in the morning, when they may probably only make you their prisoner, and carry you off with them into the mountains; whereas if you are now discovered you will be infallibly butchered before you can have time to explain your position and your motives; for sleepy men when suddenly aroused, are about the 'poorest reasoners you can argue with. Lie still, therefore—go to sleep—and put your trust in Providence."

This on the whole seemed wisest, and I prepared to do so. But sleep I could not, though I strove hard enough. An hour thus passed, and the whole band were buried in profound repose. Suddenly I heard a scritch owl cry; something struck me as peculiar in it; my gypsy education had made me well acquainted with the tones of birds, and there seemed to me to be a dash of the unnatural about this such as I had never heard before. " It is a peculiarity in the bird," I thought, and I again endeavoured to fall asleep. But in a little while I heard it again, and the un-usual note jarred upon my ear. To my surprise it was answered from an adjacent tree, and in the answer there was the same peculiarity of tone, " It is some new species," I muttered, and I

looked forth to see them.   But all was darkness.
The cry was now repeated for a third time, and
answered in the same way; the bandits still
slept on, and two men descended almost at the
same instant from a couple of adjacent cork
trees.   They must have stolen into them while
these gentlemen were amusing themselves over
their wine, and they certainly had done so unobserved by me.   I knew at once that they were
soldiers, and probably they belonged to the
King's guard.   After a rapid survey they disappeared together into the woods.

This incident gave me courage.   If these men
can thus effect their purpose, I said, why should
not I?   They have shown me that it was possible;
I were a fool if I did not imitate them.   I crept
noiselessly down, and was already within a few
feet of the ground, when a branch on which I was
supported broke, and I fell on the earth, but
lightly.   No one stirred, and I was congratu-
lating myself that all was right, when the captain suddenly opened his black eyes and fixed
them full upon me; but had I remained still, I
should probably have escaped unobserved, and
the bandit would have supposed he was dreaming.
But seeing him intently looking at the place on
which I stood, and surmising that I was seen, I
put my hand to my lips to indicate silence, and

said " Hold," in tones sufficiently loud for him to
hear, but not audible enough to wake the others.
The captain was a brave man ; he sprang up, but
made no signal.   He came towards me with his
carbine.   He saw that I was unarmed and did
not attempt to fly.   He laid his hand upon me,
and led me away from the group.   When we had
got to some distance he looked at me sternly.
Even in that midnight hour I could see the fixed
fire in his eye, and I could feel the full determination that was in his voice.   His grasp was
like a vice ; but I trembled not in the least ; and
this coolness saved me.

" What mean you ?" he said rapidly.   " What
brings you here ?"

" Release me," I answered, " I am an Englishman.   Your life is in my hands."

" My life," he replied, scornfully.   " Fool, it
is *your* life that is in mine.   With one word from
me your moments are numbered.   Speak instantly.   Tell me who you are, and what brings
you to this place ?"

I recounted briefly as much of my story as was
requisite for him to know.   I then came to that
part which related to himself and the welfare of
his companions.

" You were misled when you supposed that the
soldiers were far off.   They are at this moment

in the neighbourhood. I have seen two of their spies; they are probably now surrounding you in their toils. You must fly instantly, or you are undone."

"Is this true?" he said, slowly, and he was lost in meditation. He roused himself, "Aye! why should it not? It tallies with my dream; meanwhile stay here until I return, nor attempt to escape; if you do a bullet shall stop you."

I pledged my word that I would remain. The captain went and roused his companions. A hurried conversation took place. In five minutes they were preparing for flight; their mules were saddled, and themselves ready. Julian was already a prisoner for sleeping on his post; and I understood he would be tried, and probably shot, unless extenuating circumstances appeared. The men formed into rank, and rode rapidly away in a direction indicated by the captain. The latter remained with me. He was armed to the teeth.

"Senor Englishman," he said, "I am about to test you. Let us climb into the tree where you were concealed, and wait for the soldiers. If they appear you have saved my life, and my soul is yours; if not"—and he stopped.

"What then?" I asked.

"You shall die by my hand," he answered, "for this lie."

He said this with a coolness that convinced me he meant exactly what he said.

I could of course offer no remonstrance. To do so would have aroused his suspicion, and probably led instantly to the consummation which he threatened. I pointed out the tree in silence; he motioned me to ascend, and I did so. He followed and took his place beside me. An hour passed, and all was still. Another hour, and still no signal of surprise. The dawn began faintly to break over the horizon; we could see the light penetrating the branches, and the earliest birds began to waken. Suddenly we heard footsteps —tramp, tramp, tramp—tramp they came. It was the approach of soldiers; we heard the sound from the four quarters of the world at the same moment. All converged towards the point in which we were concealed. The robber drew closer to me.

" You have spoken English truth," he whispered ; " they are here."

And they were. Three hundred soldiers we counted. They carried a piece of artillery with them also. They had evidently calculated on hemming in the foe while he was asleep, and destroying him at their leisure, if resistance were offered. They encircled the place which had been so recently the robbers' bivouac ; but the foe was gone. Their rage no language can describe. The robber laughed within himself. They reconnoitered in all directions, and seemed utterly confused. After an hour they followed in the track of the bandits, but with a tardy motion that offered no likelihood of a successful pursuit.

"Senor Englishman," said the captain, "you have saved us all. Come with me." I obeyed mechanically, and we descended from the tree. In a hidden corner, admirably concealed, we found two swift Andalusian horses, of true Arab blood; mounting one, he motioned me to ascend the other. I did so.

"Now," said he, "ride as if for life."

We did so, and in about two hours came up with the rest of the bandits. By a route only known to themseives, they had effectually baffled the soldiers, and were now pleasantly encamped on the mountains that look over Ronda. We had ridden nearly six-and-twenty miles in that short space, and our horses required respite, though they could have carried us much farther. The mules had accomplished their work leisurely enough, and were now browsing upon what herbage they could find.

A meeting was rapidly summoned. The captain explained to the rest under what circumstances I had become his companion, and numerous and warm were the greetings which I received. Everyone pledged himself to expose his life in my defence; the Southern vivacity broke forth in every word and gesture, and I was amazed to find so many stately Spaniards full of life and motion. One brow only was overcast. This was Julian Romea, who was still in custody, and with his hands bound. I took courage to intercede for him.

"Gentlemen," I said, "there is one man here who is unhappy. I can myself testify to his care and vigilance; but in truth he was overpowred by fatigue, and while he slept I vowed to keep watch in his place. You have seen that I did so, and was no idle substitute. For my sake let him be pardoned."

The request could not well be refused. It was received with unanimous approval, and the captain gave orders for his release. Julian came and thanked me with a noble air, and though he did not use many words, I could see that he felt the full value of my interference on his behalf.

We rested here all day, and at night passed through Ronda. The country through which we rode was grandly picturesque—the very land indeed for robbers. Vast mountains flung their awful shadows over our path; terrific precipices opened wide their jaws before and around us;

woods of oak and cork trees now enveloped us in
shade; anon we were in some steep and rocky
pass, which seemed as if about to topple down on
our devoted heads; in another moment we were
buried in some deep ravine, thickly overgrown
with trees and climbing plants, which made our
journey tedious and laborious. Journeying onwards at night and resting in the daytime, without any adventures worth recording, we at length
approached Granada, reposing at the foot of the
Sierra Nevada, in whose safe recesses we sought
shelter from pursuit. Here the golden Darro,
and the silver bright Genil blend their waters,
and all seems fabled land. We encamped in a
ravine, difficult of approach, even to those who
knew it all their lives, and bade defiance to the
royal troops, which we thought would never
venture within the terrible defiles and passes
of these famous mountains. But we reckoned
without our host.

CHAPTER XXXIII.

"Let his children be fatherless, and his wife a widow; let his children be continually vagabonds, and beg; let them seek their bread also out of their desolate places."

I was soon flung into a new order of existence. A fortnight ago I was a lone recluse in a convent, immersed in studies theological or philosophical; now soaring aloft into the golden empyrean with the dreaming Plato, or bathing my soul in those fountains of light and beauty, the magic dramas of Calderon; now penetrating the deep ocean of metaphysics with Aristotle and Spinosa, or poring into the mystic secrets with which Dante has impregnated his grand poetic trilogy of Hell, Purgatory, and Paradise; now disporting like a summer bird amid the per-

fumed gardens of Theocritus and Moschus, or the
flower-bright haunts of Tasso and Ariosto; now
clothing my soul with the spiritual mail of Origen
—that fine philosophic speculatist of the early
ages, so little known, so splendidly worthy of
being known; and now walking in Paradise with
the majestic thinkers of our own land—Bacon,
and Raleigh, and Hooker, and Barrow, who
seem, like the son of Peleus, to have been fed
from their youth upwards upon the marrow of
lions. And from this glorious converse I was
suddenly snatched—like Orpheus from the presence of his bright Eurydice—to what?—to
be the associate, the friend, the saviour of a
gang of thieves, everyone of whom was stained
with unmentionable crime, and whose career
would probably close with the bullet or the
garotte. I could scarcely follow the sequence of
events by which I, the only son of one of the
most powerful families in England, was thus
made the sport of chance; but I had a happy
indifference to all things from the beginning, and
I could make myself comfortable with a crust
when all other dainties failed.

I took an early opportunity of informing our
captain, whose name I found was Bermudez, that
however flattered I might be by his evident desire
that I should link my fortunes with his band,

and become a robber, I had nevertheless no inclination whatever for the pursuit, and I asked
permission to depart. Bermudez listened to me
with evident reluctance.

"My friend," he said, "leave me not. Thou
hast rendered us a service, such as no man ever
rendered to us before. What is there that thou
mayest not command among us? My life—it is
thine. The lives of all our band—they are thine
also. Tarry therefore until in some way we have
given recompense for that which we never can
repay, but which we shall certainly acknowledge
in the best way we can."

I have always been the most pliable of mankind in matters that are of no consequence. My
Lady Mary was accustomed to tell all her friends
that I was a weak and drivelling booby. Perhaps
she was right, for I have never cared much to battle
about trifles, and as this was really one, I did not
resist my friend's entreaties. What mattered
it to me where, or how I lived?—whether in a
palace or a robber's cave? Both were equally
respectable in my eyes. Had I not had experience
of the first and of its component parts, I possibly
might have doubted, and sacrificed comfort to
ambition. But had I not intimately known the
whole secret history of Carlton House, and St.
James's Palace? had I not seen with my own

eyes that all the fine gentlemen were knaves,
and all the fine ladies were jades? Had I not
witnessed that Walpole himself was only a
Captain Bermudez on a grander scale; and that
our noble senators were only so many robbers,
who grew fat upon the spoils pillaged from the
people, and divided by the minister among his
ablest thieves and counsellors of mischief?

It would therefore have been the meanest
humbug—(yes! that is the proper word)—for me
to talk to Captain Bermudez, in the style of
Captain Grand, or to affect a wondrous
squeamishness as to his life and pursuits which
I own I did not feel. I had seen the Beggar's
Opera, and known and felt its wisdom. I had
fully appreciated the characters of Captain Mac-
heath and Lockitt; and recognized their likeness
to actual living men whom they typified. That
work has been called a burlesque—but it is the
most actual truth ever written; except of course,
the gospel histories of Matthew, Mark, Luke,
and John. Oh! how I laugh when I hear
ignorant fools call it a libel, and interested writers
designate it a caricature. Ah! Messieurs Fools,
ye do but play the game of your masters when
ye so prate; ah! Messieurs Writers, ye do but
serve your own well beloved interests when ye
persuade the fools—your dupes and drudges—

that Johnny Gay was an impudent satirist, who ought to have had his ears cropped, like poor Defoe. Ah! this is right and proper as the world wags. I have no doubt that this veritable history will meet the same fate, and that when all the fools cry out against its bitterness, &c., &c., as false, shallow, and productive of evil, &c., the glorious company of knaves—who belong to the guild of critics—will cry Amen! and lifting up their hands and eyes to Heaven, will cry out " Oh, what wise men these fools are!" So be it; I shall then be a skeleton in my grave, and shall not much care for censure and applause; and whether my book lives or dies, will be equally a matter of indifference to me. As some man in former days said, *Liberavi animam meam ;*—I have given outlet to the feelings of my soul, and having done this I am content to die and be forgotten.

Nevertheless, I was determined not to be a robber, and so I plainly informed Bermudez.

" Captain Bermudez," I said, " let there be no mistake as to our footing—let us perfectly understand each other. I am now willing to depart. I have business in Spain which occupies the dearest thoughts of my soul. I have accidentally fallen in with your gentlemen, and I have accidentally rendered them a slight service.

You are good enough to over-rate that service, but I assure you I regard it only as a trifle." Here Captain Bermudez took off his sombrero and made me a low bow, which I returned as in duty bound—for form and ceremony are everything in Spain. " I repeat, Captain, it was a trifle, and it is not worth thinking of. Of yourself and your companions I say nothing. I believe you are all brave men." Here the Captain again bowed with great solemnity, and I was obliged to go through the humbug of returning it, which greatly disgusted my John Bull-ism. " But I am an English gentleman, and I cannot become a Spanish Caballero." (I used this phrase as the least offensive— cut throat would have been the true word; but expediency! oh, expediency! how necessary thou art in this rascally world). " If you are willing to let me go, I shall be glad; if not I shall remain with you, but only as a visitor. I will have nothing to do with easing monks or merchants of their superfluities. Is this our compact?"

Captain Bermudez seized me by the hand.

" Senor," said he, " nothing was ever farther from my thoughts than that you should be involved with us. I do not ask it. I never supposed it. I have solicited your stay with us only as our honoured guest. If you will abide with us in that capacity, do so, so long as you like. If

not, go; you are free.   But I own I shall be disappointed if you leave me."

Reader! do not condemn me.   I felt the
sympathy of a brother vagabond, with this
vagabond, and so I stayed.   I thank Heaven that
I did so.

Granada, the Moorish city; the enchanted
Alhambra! who has not heard of them? who
has not seen? who has not described?   It will
not do for me to enter on this beaten track.   Yet
will I briefly note their principal features; for
here occurred the crowning incident of my life.
And never do I think of thee, O splendid jewel
of the Snowy Mountains, that I weep not from a
full heart.

Granada is built upon three hills; the first con-
tains the Vermillion Towers; the second, the
sacred Alhambra; the third the Albaycin which
is separated from the rest by a pass blooming
with flowers and shrubs of rarest beauty; the
pomegranate, the rose-bay, the cactus, the
coloquintida, the pistachio.   The silver Darro
flows beneath; rapid as lightning, and many a
lovely garden blooms upon its banks.   It is a
scene of magic.   Spain has nothing like it,
perhaps the world—if we except Damascus.
There is one view of the last named Paradise,
where I have often sat for hours.   It is called, I

think, the Seat of Mohammed. That mighty Conqueror and true Apostle of God rested there for a moment, and exclaimed, *" This is the Paradise of earth!"* And truly said he so. Yet in our own glorious land I have seen a scene almost as lovely and sublime. I mean the Wyndcliffe. The distant Eden of Damascus surprised me not, but made me drunken with a sense of loveliness. But the Wyndcliffe gave me an idea of the sublime and wonderful such as I never felt before. Go and see it, and then seek Damascus if you will. But condemn me not if thou disagreest with me ; for I also have seen many things, and God knows I have no reason to be prejudiced.

O ! Granada, Granada ! never shall I forget thee. When my last hour comes, and my spirit is preparing for that awful and mysterious flight into the Dark or Bright Unknown, still shalt thou be in my thoughts, the next after God, Eternity, and Judgment. For thou hast become a portion of my soul ; and if an earthquake were to swallow thee up to-morrow, then should I know that my hour was come, and I should resign myself to death and oblivion. Thou art a part of my inmost being. There is no Moorish arch within thy walls, there is no flowing fountain, there is no weeping cypress, there is no fallen Mosque that reminds me not of her who is my spirit's twin, and who now lies sepulchred within thy hallowed bounds. I think of thy mighty mountain, peopled with a million fair traditions; and see even now the setting sun upon its silver summits. The rose-light glitters on my aged eyes; the opal-like irradiations gleam from many a cleft and shining peak; there is the deep azure of the blue sea, and the beaming brightness of a silvery ocean mingled into one divine picture, and on the highest point appears, like a diadem of light, the blessed spirit of my lost Francesca; glorious in paradise-lustre, and opening wide her arms to enfold her wanderer. Stay! stay! thou bright vision! Behold my days are numbered; my veins run cold and sluggish; my heart pines and pants after thee, O Beloved One. Long and long hast thou been in Heaven with God—long and long hast thou had the Beatific Vision; and hast communed only with the angels of the Most High. O! Francesca, pray for me to Him; for behold I am a sinner dark with many sins; and I am not worthy to come into thy presence, or to enter under the roof of the Lord.

Where have I been? Where?—whither have I flown? Into what wild vision have I wandered? My pen, my fancy, are vagrants, like myself. They stray into a thousand eccentricities. Let

me bring them back unto the dull and sober path-
way; let me descend again to earth, and plod in
the prosaic.

My interview with Captain Bermudez took
place when we arrived in the Sierra Nevada. I
had lost no time in opening my mind to him. I
had assented to his terms, and was now free to
walk about as I pleased. Until this moment I
had to some extent been watched; but now all
was liberty and trust. On the following morning
I strolled into the Albaycin You may imagine
my surprise when I found myself again among
my old people. The place was full of gypsies.
I was utterly amazed. Here was a community,
nay a very kingdom of the Calorè. I could
scarcely rely on my eyes at first, but in a few
minutes I knew that it was so. Nothing could
equal the surprise, the joy, the wild madness of
these people when I addressed them in the
Zingari language—when I came to them as a
brother, and claimed kindred. I was immediately
brought as it were, in triumphal procession before
their reigning Duke. He was an old man with
a long and flowing beard; but his eye was still
bright, and his brow was unruffled. I spoke to
him in the secret dialect which has a charm for
the gypsy such as no words can describe. I was
the first Englishman he had ever seen—but an

Englishman and a Calorè were two combinations
that he had scarcely ever expected to behold.
Could they have fed me upon gold and pearls,
they would have done so. Young and old
crowded around me with an enthusiastic wildness; the men looked at me with admiration;
the women, old and young, kissed my hands with
a kind of fanaticism.

I passed the night in their caves, and mingled
in their wild gambols. I was happy, for I was
surrounded by happy hearts and smiling faces.
The Duke treated me with distinguished politeness. A courtier of Louis the Fourteenth
could not have been more refined or fastidious in
true courtesy. Goblets of gold and silver which
had been buried in the earth for years; rare
porcelain, which had been hidden in baskets
almost for generations, were produced to grace
their festal banquet; jewels that were as old as
Cleopatra, were worn, and rings of massive gold
that were coeval with the past Pharaohs. Flasks
of wine also were opened that had been buried in
the days of Columbus, and amulets of rare value,
on which were graven words that could make the
Moon diverge from her heavenly course, were
worn round the necks of the aged gypsies. In a
word it was a scene never to be forgotten, nor
have I forgotten it. Thus it was till day-light.

Even then they could not part with me; and I
passed the rest of the day in the Duke's cavern.
In the evening the same scene was renewed. The
vesper star arose and shed her seraph light upon
the scene.   The younger gypsies, crowned with
flowers, danced and sang; the older ones recounted
legends, and the young men chaunted the
glorious soul-inspiring ballads of the land.   All
was beautiful, wild, and full of the spirit of
romance.   Many a sweet smile was cast upon me
from dark eyes, that flashed the soul in light;
many an encouraging look was shed like sun-
beams over me; the blooming virgins came as
near me as they well could, and touched me with
robe and foot, and wondered why I did not recip-
rocate their professed love?

"Ours is a happy life, Senor," said the Duke;
"do you pass it equally well in England?"

I informed him of our employments and our
sports, as I had had experience of both.   He was
anxious to know all that I could tell him of our
island customs.   He had a vague notion of
them, but many of his ideas were wild in the
extreme.

"And have you not a Gypsy Queen?" he
asked.   "Fin! Fin," And he seemed trying to
say the word.

"Margaret Finch," I answered, and I described

the old czarina of Norwood.   Then I told him of
Akiba, and his chequered life, and of the magic
days of King Zandahlo.   They listened and
clapped their hands with wonder and delight.
They were the same wild impressible race, I had
known in my own country.   Indians in all
their traits and habits—Indians to the back-bone
—the Aborigines who founded Egypt and raised
the statue of the black Memnon, children of the
mighty, when we poor Saxons were painted sav-
ages, and when at the bidding of the glorious
hierarchs of Boodh and Brahm (when those great
creeds were one) they reared Stonehenge and
Ambersbury, and piled on high the astounding
tolmen that even now strike wonder into our so-
called engineers.

"This also," said an old gypsy, "is an enchanted place.   Wherever we look we see traces
of the Magi and their art, and find memorials of
our own people.   It was they—not the Moors—
who built the Alhambra; but the Spaniards are all
liars, and the Moorish writers are not much
better."

I smiled at this; but where is the good of dis-
pelling a grand dream?   I have no doubt the old
man and his people believed it, and I left them
in their faith.   It is commonly said that the
Gitanos have no traditions, but this is nonsense.

There is no tribe without traditions; and these wild wanderers have thousands of them. They are all, it is true, discordant with each other, but what of that? Consult the historians of all people, and see what a sad chaos they fall into, when they treat of the origin of nations and peoples. Why should our people be wiser than Livy or Geoffrey of Monmouth? Why expect more from them than from William of Malmesbury or the Edda of Sœmund? Nay, is not Hume himself a farago of nonsense and lies?

They led me into the Alhambra, the palace of their sires. The moon now shone in all her glory over the scene, tinting every line with silver, burnishing every leafy tree and mouldering battlement with her soft radiant colours. We went into the palace of Charles the Fifth, which that gloomy conqueror hoped would survive the splendour of the Moorish princes, but vainly; for the modern building is little better than a ruin already, while the fairy-like arches of the Moor seem destined to defy time itself. I was disappointed in the size of the place. Like most persons who have read or heard of it, my imagination had run loose, and I pictured to myself something grand, extended, and Titanesque. But it is not so. Everything may be said to be on a small scale; but then, how beautiful are the proportions. Probably this very symmetry makes things look smaller than they are; as in St. Peter's, a saint, six feet high, appears no bigger than a little boy. We lingered in the Court of Lions; we lounged through the long arcades, and marked the light and shadow in this holy silent hour, and listened to the plaintive music of the fountains that sparkle with a kind of spiritual airy brilliancy in the descending moonbeam. We lingered in the Hall of the Two Sisters, and from the Golden Saloon looked on the dimly lighted City at our feet, and the dark valley of the winding Darro.

All who are acquainted with the Spanish annals, know of the terrible decree which was issued at this period by the Holy Office of the Inquisition. The gitanos had now grown into so vast a population, that the attention of the ruling powers of Satanas had been particularly called to them. They were to be counted by thousands all throughout Spain, and Granada was their head quarters. Here they were in immense numbers. All the efforts of the Priests to convert them to the Church of Rome had failed; all the legislative measures of the Cortes had been unable to extirpate them from the land. True to the traditions of their eastern blood, it was found impossible to work any change upon them.

Neither time, nor climate, nor example operated in the least. As the sun of Africa made them no blacker, so the temperature of Europe made them no whiter; so also was it with their minds and customs. All the other great conquering nations had absorbed into themselves the inferior tribes whom they had subdued, or had been absorbed by them when the vanquished were really the superiors. The Persians became Greeks; the Romans also yielded to their subjects, and had adopted the tones and habits of the Hellenians; the Franks became Gauls; the Normans absorbed the Saxon tribes, and the Cymri, who were a superior race, absorbed the Mantchous, who were their masters in battle. But the Gypsies were still unchanged. They neither amalgamated with the people with whom they lived, nor would they become identified with them in any one particular. They were a nation apart and alone.

Some of the more zealous priests had taken occasion to get hold of many of the younger gypsies, almost in their infancy, and to breed them up in the Papal faith; but when they reached the age of puberty the gypsy blood broke forth; everything that had been instilled into them was forgotten, or despised, and they fled to the camp of their tribe; wild as Arabs, untameable as hyenas. What, then, was to be done with these Bohemians, Heathens, Tartars, Charami, Pharaoites, and Gitanos—for by all these titles they were known? The Church was sorely puzzled; but the Church is subtle—there is no difficulty which they cannot solve, or which they do not strive to solve. They deserve credit intellectually, but what do they deserve morally? Let Time declare; I won't. They met in secret solemn conclave, and voted that it was a sin, a blasphemy against the Redeemer, that so many immortal souls should perish in their obstinacy; and therefore they passed a law that all the young gypsies should be forcibly removed from the contagion of their parents' example, brought within the pale of the infallible Church of Heaven, and saved—whether they would or not. For this purpose they invoked the aid of the civil power; and a secret ordinance issued from the king, authorising and commanding the aid of all his military officers to the servants of the Sacred Inquisition, for the purpose of carrying out his project, holy in the eyes of God and Heaven. And the three hundred soldiers of the king's guard who left Madrid were part and parcel of this contrivance, though Captain Bermudez had heard otherwise.

One night, about a week after our arrival at Granada, I strolled with the captain into the

gypsy locality. As usual, they were delighted to
see me, and they received my companion with the
warmest cordiality. We gathered about a large
fire, and song and anecdote went round with
light hilarity. Bermudez told us of Rodrigo
Diaz de Bevar, surnamed the Cid, the mighty
hero of the land; how, when his father was
smitten by the Count of Gormaz in the very
presence of the king, and he called his sons together for vengeance, all of them were craven
cowards, except the youngest, who vowed that
he would revenge in blood the insult offered to
his ancient house. Wherefore took he the rusty
sword of the bold bastard Madurra, which he
found in his father's armoury, and went forth in
search of the fierce Count. And when he saw
the Count he challenged him to deadly combat;
but the Count despised his youth, and called him
page, and threatened him with the whip. Whereupon the bold Rodrigo rushed upon him with
his drawn sword, and a dreadful fight ensued;
and he cut off the Count's head, and carried it to
his father, who was overjoyed at his son's bravery,
and placed him before all his other sons at the
head of his table in token of superiority. Then
Ximerra, the daughter of Count Gormaz, once,
and twice, and thrice, and twenty times, besought the king to wreak vengeance upon the

young man ; but King Ferdinand consented not,
for he feared his people, who were all enamoured
with the youthful knight and his bold exploit ; and
it were as much as his crown were worth to offer
violence to that chivalric head.   And Ximerra,
in the lapse of days, herself softened towards
Rodrigo ; and, as he had made her an orphan,
besought the king that he would command him
to protect her ; whereupon she became his wife,
and he loved her as his own soul unto his dying
day.   And after these things the Cid went forth
and fought the Moors at Estremadura, and won
to his own share two hundred horses, and a hundred thousand golden marks ; but none of these
did he retain, but gave them all among his men.
And when the haughty Emperor of Germany pro-
claimed war against the Sovereign of Castille, because he alone of the kings in Christendom refused
to give him tribute, then did my Cid go forth, and
with eight thousand men he crushed the army of
the Emperor on the plains of France.   Nor did
he cease to harass him until he begged the Pope
to interfere, and save him from all further
molestation.   And after these things my Cid was
banished ; but still he fought against the Moors,
and having won two mighty fortresses, he sent
the spoil to King Alfonso, who now sat upon the
proud Castilian throne ; and many other mighty

achievements did my Cid perform until the king restored him to his favour, and the court was once again brightened by his presence. Then did my Cid again wend out and vanquish many Moorish armies, until the whole earth rang with his renown; and no knight whatever could be found to charge against him in mortal combat; and the haughty Persian Soldan sent him an ambassador in token of his great deeds; whereupon my Cid said unto him—"Welcome thou unto my city of Valencia; were thy master a Christian with great joy would I go to his land and visit him." And the Paynim prince returned home, marvelling much at the wealth and power and glorious valour of my lord the Cid. And when my Cid was dying Saint Peter himself appeared before him, and welcomed him to paradise; and my Cid was pleased; and because the Pagan Moors then besieged Valencia, he ordered his corpse to be set on horseback, and to charge the enemy with his old and conquering banner, the which indeed was done; and when the Paynims saw the stately form of the dead Cid, as his horse was led into the vanguard of the fight, behold they were stricken dead aghast, and fled in pale terror. Then was the sainted body of my Cid buried in the Chapel of San Pedro de Cardina, and many a miracle was wrought before his tomb.

All this Bermudez told us in recitative; and there was a strange charm in the wild strain, which produced a marvellous effect on his listeners. We were in the midst of these amusements, when all the watch dogs set up a fierce and simultaneous barking. Some of the gypsies went out to see what was the matter, and returnd with fear and trembling. As a body, the gypsies are sad cowards; and they will endure almost anything with impunity. But when they are urged on to combat by others, then indeed they fight like so many devils. It happened now, however, that they were wholly panic-stricken. The scouts who had gone forth reported that we were surrounded by at least a thousand men, consisting of soldiers of the royal guard, and officials of the Holy Inquisition. And soon the women's screams informed us that the horrid work of spoliation had commenced. From every cave and corner resounded wild and melancholy shrieks. The grief and fury of the Gitanos knew no bounds. They raved like mad things; but the soldiers and familiars of the Inquisition executed their office without stay or compunction. All the children were gathered together, hastily aroused from their sleep, and naked as they were born, and were driven like so many goats into one place. In vain their mothers besought these hardened

wretches to let them have a last kiss or embrace
of these lost ones. Every request of that nature
was sternly refused; and the gypsy mothers were
in despair. When every tent and cave was
thoroughly despoiled of all the young gitanos of
either sex, and under ten years old, some of the
soldiers and familiars advanced towards us. I
need not say that both Bermudez and myself
had done all we could to animate the Zingari to
defend their children; but a torpor of terror
seemed to have thoroughly cowed them; and
they remained inactive, drooping and afraid,
setting up only fierce and angry cries which had
no effect upon the spoilers, except to increase
their passions into fury, and to induce them to
maltreat the poor creatures whom they had so
rudely seized. Bermudez, seeing them coming,
stood firm; nor did he blench in the least. A
person in command addressed him.

"And you, Sir Gypsy, how dare you kick
against the king's edict? Were I not disposed
to mercy, I should shoot you like a wolf."

"As you please, Sir Soldier," replied Bermudez, "but I only did what was my duty—to
protest against this hellish act."

"And who the devil may you be?" asked the
other, "that you dare address me in this language?"

"That matters not," answered Bermudez,

turning away; " you shall perhaps know at some other time."

One of the familiars now came forward, and looked carefully at the captain. After scrutinizing him some moments, he turned and whispered to the officer in command. The latter started, and cried out—

" Ah ! sayst thou so indeed ? This must be looked to. Soldiers, seize this man." And in a moment Bermudez was seized and bound.

" I am told," said his captor, " that you are the notorious bandit, Bermudez."

" Whosoever I am," replied the other, " I am not likely, after this insult, to give you any information."

" Lead him away," said the officer, " bind his hands and legs, and take care that he escapes not. Let him have a guard of six soldiers, and I swear by Heaven that if he eludes them they shall be shot." And it was done as he commanded. He then turned to me.

" And who may you be, young sir ?" he questioned.

" You have no right to ask me," I replied. " I am an Englishman travelling in this country for my own pleasure."

" And what brings you, Senor Englishman, among thieves and gypsies ?"

" That, Captain, is my own affair—not yours.'

" Let me see your passport," said he.

I told him that I had none.

" It seems to me," he said, " that it will be my duty to apprehend you."

One of the familiars again came forward; he was the same fellow who had already pointed out Bermudez, and he seemed to know everything. He held a paper in his hand; he looked at it and me attentively, comparing my personal appearance with what was there written. He then spoke apart to the officer, and showed him the paper. After some whispering the familiar came forward.

" Is your name Montagu?" he said.

I was so suddenly questioned that without thinking I answered—

" Yes."

" Then," said he, " you will come with us."

And I was obliged to go. The following chapter will explain why.

CHAPTER XXXIV.

"As troops of robbers wait for a man, so the company of
priests murder in the way."

No. I.

In the Royal Palace of the Inquisition of
Seville, on the 10th day of August, 1734, present,
the Inquisitor Dr. Domingo Abbad Y Huerta,
officiating alone in his morning audience, having
examined the information received against
Edward Wortley Montagu, native of London in
England, ordered that the above-named person
be arrested and confined in the secret prison of
this Palace of the Inquisition for the purpose of
accomplishing fully the ends of justice, and that

his trial be instituted in form, for which end let
the necessary steps be taken.

Before me,

MATTHEO MAGRE,
Secretary.

To FRANCISCO COLL, COMMISSARY,

1. On the receipt of this you will
proceed to take prisoner on the part of this Holy
Office, Edward Wortley Montagu, a native of
London. He is a tall, long-faced person, with a
commanding brow, pale, with a dark but slight
beard, piercing eyes, and good presence; he
speaks Spanish well, and is supposed to be wandering through the country parts of this province
in a disguise; having secured him and divested
him of every kind of offensive weapon you will
dispatch him under good attendance to this Holy
Office by the hands of the Familiars, in such a
manner that he cannot escape; taking measures
in all the places through which he may pass to
let it be known he is apprehended by this Inquisition.

2. Also, if occasion should offer, you will seize
so much of his property as shall be sufficient for
his maintenance, which you will transmit by
those who have him in custody.

3. The prisoner being taken, you will inspect

his person and his lodgings, in order to secure a
book about the size of the hand, in which it is
confidently believed there are certain prayers and
superstitious matters. This book you will dispatch to us.

4. Also all papers and instruments found upon
him, as well as those which may be found in his
baggage, are to be seized. Care should be taken
that he may have no time to conceal anything.

5. You will then transport him to this city
which he will enter at dusk, just before the gates
are shut. You will enter at the Gate of St.
James's and present the accompanying passport
of the Governor to the officer of the Guard.
God preserve you.

6. This letter is to be returned with a statement
of all that may have been done agreeably to the
above orders. With respect to which we trust in
the guidance of our Lord.

By order of this Holy Office,

DOCTOR DOMINGO, ABBAD Y HUERTA,
MATTHEO MAGRE, Secretary.

No. II.

In the Royal Palace of this Inquisition of
Seville, on the 10th day of September, 1734, in
the morning, the Inquisitor, Doctor Domingo
Abbad Y Huerta, being at his morning audience

appeared according to summons, Padre Juan
Baptista Lopez and Padre Augustin de Vinaros,
and swore fairly to declare the truth.   And first,
Padre Francisco Liges, Chief Abbot.

Questioned—If he knew or conjectured the
cause of his being summoned to appear.

Answered—That he neither knew nor conjectured.

Questioned—If he knew or had heard that any
person had spoken or done anything which was
      appeared contrary to our Holy Catholic
Faith and evangelical doctrine preached and
taught by the Holy Catholic Roman Church, or
against the just and free exercise of the Holy
Office.

Answered—That about eight months since, or
thereabouts, the deponent being moved by charity
did take in and receive into the Monastery of
Mercy, at Biscay, one Edward Wortley Montagu,
in the hope of baptising him into the holy bosom
of the sacred Catholic Church, the said E. W.
M. then and there professing an ardent desire
to know the true doctrines of the Faith.   And
the deponent from that time until the fraudulent
flight of the said E. W. M. did teach him all the
said truths and doctrines as well as he could.
And the deponent verily believed that the said
E. W. M. was then a sincere and worthy believer

in the truths and doctrines. But on the eve of
St. Epimachus last, the deponent happening by
chance to enter the cell of E. W. M. found him
seated at a table with some bacon before him,
but when or how procured the deponent doth not
know. And the deponent then and there informed
the said E. W. M. that it was now the eve of a
most holy festival, and that it was positively forbidden by the church that any such food or any
flesh meat whatever should be eaten. The said
E. W. M. answered that he meant to eat notwithstanding, and the deponent asked him
whether he had a license so to do, or any infirmity; to which the said E. W. M. answered,
mockingly, "I have a license from myself, and a
sad infirmity called appetite," and thereupon
proceeded to eat the said meat. This is the truth
according to the oath of the witness, and being
read in his presence, is declared by him to be
correctly recorded, and was thereupon signed with
his name in his own hand. The deponent further
states that he does not make this declaration out
of malice; and secresy being enjoined upon him
he promised to observe it.

And second, Padre Antonio Mira being questioned, &c.,

Answered that he supposed it to be for
the purpose of ascertaining whether a certain

Edward Wortley Montagu had done ought which
was or appeared to be contrary to our Holy
Catholic Faith, and evangelical doctrine, concerning which this deponent testified that about
four months since, being in the cell of the said
E. W. M., this deponent heard him say that he was
as great as God, and that he had a book, which
being put into the fire along with a crucifix, would
remain unhurt, while the crucifix would be consumed, which words being uttered with much
earnestness by him, the deponent was greatly
shocked and frightened, and advised him to
abstain from such speeches, as they were scandalous; and should they come to the knowledge
of the Inquisition, would bring punishment upon
him. But the said E. W. M. repeated his asser-
tions several times; but at length desisted, and
appeared somewhat alarmed at the rebukes which
this deponent gave him, and turned pale. The
book was a small book, about the size of the
hand, but thick, and was read by the said
E. W. M. in great secrecy, as if he were at
prayer. The above is the truth, according to the
oath of the deponent; and being read in his
presence, is declared by him to be correctly
recorded, and signed with his own hand. He
further states that he does not make this declara-

tion out of malice, and promises to observe secrecy.

And third, Padre Juan Baptista Lopez being questioned, &c.,

Answered that he supposed it to be for the purpose of ascertaining the truth respecting the life and conduct of a certain Edward Wortley Montagu, concerning which this deponent testifies that during the whole period of his sojourn in the Monastery of Mercy, the said E. W. M., though often requested, did not once confess himself; but on being rebuked, and advised to confess, he broke out into blasphemies against God and his Saints, with such violence, that he appeared more like a demoniac than anything else. It being suggested to him that God did not prosper him, because he did not attend mass, or wear a rosary, nor hear sermons, nor confess, but swore, and blasphemed; and that if the Holy Inquisition knew of it, he would be apprehended, he replied that the Devil must help him; that he did not care for the Inquisition, and would not confess, and that God gave him nothing which the Devil would not give. The deponent had asked him why he did not confess, observing that to kneel at the feet of a confessor and relate his sins was to relate them to God; and the said

E. W. M. replied that this was all babble, and
he believed just as he pleased. Someone asking
him if he was not afraid of dying, he replied that
if he knew there was a tavern in the other world
he should wish to die immediately. He declared it
was nonsense to relate one's sins to a confessor,
and that a man should tell of nothing but what
he pleased. At one time he went to bed after
tiring himself with swearing, and told the convent next day that a woman, a monkey, and a
young man then in the house, had appeared to
him in bed, scratched his face all over, and
thrown him down stairs. The deponent believed
that this had been done by the Devil, from his
mentioning him so often.

The deponent further declared that on making
a full confession last month of all his sins, and
his own negligence in denouncing the said
E. W. M., he was directed to give information of
the whole to this Holy Office, and was refused
absolution unless he complied, and that there
were many more things to be told, which he
could not recollect, as they happened long since.

The above is the truth according to the oath of
the deponent, and is stated by him, not out of
malice, but solely to discharge his conscience. It
was read to him, and he declared it to be faithfully recorded, and signed it with his proper name.

And fourth, Padre Augustin de Vinaros being questioned, &c.,

Answered that he supposed it was for the purpose of giving information to the Holy Office respecting a certain E. W. M. On the evening of the last day in May, this person, being in company of the deponent declared in conversation with the deponent, that he possessed the faculty of discovering the thief when a thing was stolen. This he had performed in the following manner. The deponent a long while ago had lost a certain rosary, and suspected four or five persons of the theft. E. W. M. said he would discover the thief. He then wrote the names of all the persons suspected, upon separate pieces of paper, and threw them into the fire. Those which contained the names of the innocent were consumed, but that containing the name of the one against whom this deponent had the strongest suspicion, remained. Nobody was able to take this out of the fire except E. W. M. The paper was kept from consuming by the power of the words *Christo Señor Nuestro*, uttered by him ; and it was drawn out from among the coals by the help of this expression 1, *Ego Sum* ; 2, *Factus est homo* ; 3, *Consummatum est.* Besides this, he said, he knew another way of practising his divination ; and this was, to collect the ashes made by the

papers, and rub them on the back of his hand,
where they would leave marked the name of the
thief. This deponent thereupon rebuked the said
E. W. M., who replied that what he had said and
done he would say and do even before the Inquisition. Proceeding in conversation with the
deponent, he told him that he had some instruments in his pockets which were useful for many
things. He then drew from his right pocket a
paper folded up, and containing two or three coils
of something which the deponent did not see dis-
tinctly on account of the darkness, but felt and
handled them. The deponent asked the said
E. W. M. where he had obtained the above knowledge. He replied that he had got it by studying
a Book of Magic which he possessed; that he had
learned from this the secret of making himself
invisible, and also to render a man invulnerable
to thrusts with a sword. The said E. W. M.
came to the cell of this deponent next day, and
after some conversation gave him a slip of parchment almost a finger's breadth wide, and above a
span long; this was slit through the middle
lengthwise, and had written on it the following
words:—*Ego + sum. Ecce + homo + Consummatum est +*. This was rolled up in lead
with a small piece of bone, and the said E. W.
M. told the deponent to wear it in the shape of a

cross next to his skin, near the heart, and it would shield him effectually from all thrusts with a sword. It was exhibited by the deponent.

The said E. W. M. also gave this deponent another slip of parchment of half a finger in breadth and two yards long. At one extremity was drawn with ink a leg and foot, and at the other a heart with a cross above it. Other figures and letters were drawn in different parts. With this he proceeded to take divers measurements upon the body of the deponent, as from one shoulder to the other, from the shoulder to the chin and nose, &c. This he informed him would secure him from being wounded, if he used it in the following manner. He was to rub it with the wax which dropped from the tapers during the celebration of mass. This was to be done on nine several days during mass, keeping it under his cloak, and taking care that no one saw him. Afterwards it was to be worn in the shape of a cross next the skin near the heart. He gave him at the same time three bits of parchment, each about three fingers' breadth long, and one wide. Two of these contained each two lines of writing, and the other three. These were severally numbered on the back 1, 2, 3. To these was added another very small, also written over. He informed him that by the help of these he could perform any kind of divination; and that if he wore the thinnest of these parchments upon his left little finger under a white stone set in a ring, he would be directed by it in the following manner. Whenever the stone turned red, he might play at any game which was going on, except dice or *quillas*, and be sure to gain; but if the stone turned black, he would lose by playing. Before any such use, however, was made of the parchments, he was directed to put them in the shoe of his left foot near the ankle, and to sprinkle them with the water used by the priest at mass. These parchments were also exhibited. The deponent requested the said E. W. M. to shew him the Book of Magic, but he declined, alleging that the deponent could not read or understand it.

This deponent further says, that in consequence of these statements of the prisoner, the deponent one day assembed certain monks in his cell, among whom was the person whom this deponent violently suspected of having stolen the rosary aforesaid. The prisoner then said that each one present must put his finger into a cup of water, and that the water would blacken the finger of the thief; and he shewed them a cup containing a quantity of clear water. They all agreed to the proposal and the room was shut up, so as to exclude every ray of light. When the windows were again opened, they found every man's finger black but that of one. The prisoner perceiving this, and observing the agitation which he manifested, exclaimed to him, " You are the thief," and the said person in his fright confessed the robbery. And the deponent believes that this was indeed done by the power of Satan, and no other.

Questioned, if he knew or had heard that the said E. W. M. had any temporary insanity, or was given to wine.

Answered, that he knew not. He averred that the whole of the declaration was the truth, and not uttered by him from malice or ill-feeling, but solely in obedience to his conscience and oath. Secrecy was promised by him, and he added his signature.

No. III.

FIRST AUDIENCE.

In the Royal Palace of the Inquisition of Seville, on the 10th day of October, 1734, Doctor Domingo Abbad Y Huerta being at his morning audience, ordered the prisoner to be brought from his cell, who, being produced, was sworn to declare the truth on the present as well as on all other occasions till the decision of his trial. He was also sworn to observe secrecy with respect to everything which he might see, hear, or learn, and everything which should befal him.

Questioned.   What was his name, age, occupation, birthplace, residence, and the period of his arrestation by the Holy Office.

Answered, that his name was Edward Wortley Montagu aged twenty-two, of no occupation, native of London, in England, and that he was arrested six weeks ago by the Commissaries of the Holy Office in the ravine of Los Molinos. Questioned, who was his father, grandfather, paternal and maternal, and wife? who were his uncles, brothers, and children? what were their occupations, birthplaces, and residences? [*Here follows an account in answer to these questions, which I suppress.*]

Questioned.   What was the origin and descent of his ancestors, and collateral relatives, and whether anyone of them had been punished, or put under penance by the Holy Office of the Inquisition? [*The answer to these questions follow here, but are not material—wherefore I suppress them.*]

Questioned, if he could read or write, or had studied much, and in what science or faculty?

Answered that he could read and write, but

had not studied much in any particular science.

Questioned, if he had any dealings with persons of equivocal faith?

Answered—that he had lived for some time among the Gitanos.

Questioned, what were the events of his life? [*The answers to this the reader may surmise, wherefore I suppress them as superfluous.*]

Questioned, if he knew or conjectured the cause of his imprisonment?

Answered, that he knew not, nor could conjecture, unless it was for this, that he had fled from the Monastery of Mercy, at Biscay.

The prisoner was then informed that in this Holy Office it was not customary to imprison any person without sufficient information, that he had committed or had been seen, to have committed some act which was, or appeared to be, contrary to our Holy Catholic Faith and Evangelical doctrine, which is taught and professed by our Holy Mother Roman Catholic Church, or against the proper and free jurisdiction of the Holy Office; for which reason he was to understand that it was in consequence of some such information that he had been apprehended, and on this account he was exhorted on the part of God our Lord, and

his glorious and blessed Mother the Virgin
Mary, to bethink himself well and confess the
whole truth. Whereupon he was remanded to
prison.

No. IV.

SECOND AUDIENCE.

In the Royal Palace of the Inquisition of
Seville, on the 10th day of November, 1734.
Doctor Domingo Abbad Y Huerta, and Dr.
Bernardo Luis Cotoner being at their morning audience, ordered the prisoner to be brought
from his cell, which being done, and the prisoner
present he was—

Questioned, if he remembered anything relating to his affairs which he was bound to state,
according to his conscience?

Answered, that he had nothing more to
say.

The prisoner was then informed that he had
been already in a former audience exhorted in
the name of our Lord and his glorious and blessed
Mother the Virgin Mary, to bethink himself well
and unburthen his conscience by declaring the
whole truth respecting all which he had done,
said, seen, or heard, offensive against God, or
contrary in reality or appearance to His Holy

Catholic Faith, and Evangelical Doctrine, taught and professed by the Holy Mother Roman Catholic Church, or against the proper and free jurisdiction of the Holy Office, without testifying anything false. By following this direction he would have his trial despatched with all possible brevity and mercy; but if not, justice should be executed upon him.

Answered, that he had nothing more to say. He was then admonished, and remanded to prison.

No. V.

THIRD AUDIENCE.

In the Royal Palace of the Inquisition at Seville, on the 10th day of December, 1734. The Inquisitors, Dr. Domingo Abbad Y Huerta, Dr. Bernardo Luis Cotoner, and Joseph de Otero Y Corsio, being at their morning audience, ordered the prisoner to be brought from his cell, which being done, and the prisoner present, he was—

Questioned, if he remembered anything relating to his affair, which he was bound by his conscience to declare?

Answered, that he had nothing more to say.

The prisoner was then notified that the Promoter Fiscal of this Holy Office had an accusation to bring against him, before which he would do well to declare the whole truth, as he had already been admonished, in which case he would more fully experience the mercy which the Holy Office extends to those who confess freely; otherwise the Fiscal would attend and proceed to the accusation; and justice be executed.

Answered, that he had nothing more to say.

Straightway appeared Dr. Francisco Gregorio, Promoter Fiscal of this Holy Office, and presented the accusation signed by himself, against the said E. W. M., making oath that it was not done out of malice; which accusation was as follows :—

ACCUSATION.

I, Doctor Francisco Gregorio, Fiscal of this Holy Office, appear before your Excellencies, and accuse criminally Edward Wortley Montagu, a native of London in England, resident in this principality, attached to the secret prison of the Inquisition, and now present, stating that the said person being a baptized and confirmed Christian, and enjoying the graces and benefits which such persons do, and ought to enjoy, not having the fear of God before his eyes, but regardless of his

own conscience, and the justice administered by
your Excellencies, has committed offences against
our Holy Faith, by saying and performing things
which savour of the heretic Luther, and by utter-
ing superstitious and blasphemous speeches, and
compacting with the Devil, and by blaspheming
and denying God our Lord, seeking favour and
help from devils, and by professing and practising
various necromantical arts with insult to the
Holy sacrifice of the Mass, its sacred ceremonies
and the Holy Cross, and doing other things in the
manner following : —

1. The said prisoner being in a certain Monastery in the province of Biscay, did procure a dish
of bacon, and being reminded to take heed for it
was a fast, and such food was forbidden, did
nevertheless proceed to eat the same, and mocked
and derided the person who had so warned him.

2. Furthermore, the said prisoner being of a
nation infected with heresy, it is presumed that
he has on many other occasions eaten flesh on
forbidden days, after the manner of the sect of
Luther, and committed many other offences
against our Holy Faith; besides knowing that
others have committed the same offences, and the
said prisoner having been admonished by your
Excellencies to declare the truth, has not done it,
but has perjured himself.

3. The said prisoner likewise declared that he possessed a Book, which if it were thrown into a fire along with a crucifix would remain unhurt, while the crucifix would be consumed.

4. From the above it is to be presumed that the said prisoner has uttered many other superstitious and blasphemous speeches, and done many other things appertaining to the Devil; also that he is cognizant of the commission by others of many such crimes, the whole of which he has maliciously concealed.

5. The said prisoner while he resided in the Monastery aforesaid, could not be persuaded to confess, although he received many admonitions to that effect, but remained careless of the salvation of his soul. And the said prisoner being rebuked therefore, blasphemed God and the Saints with such fury and malice that be appeared like a demoniac. Being threatened with a punishment from the Inquisition, he replied that he did not care for the Inquisition, and that he would not confess; also that he wanted nothing from God which the Devil could not give him.

6. He says that he does not fear God, and that if he knew there was a tavern in the other world, he should not care if he died.

7. He said that a man ought not to tell his

sins to the confessor; and that it was nonsense for a man to tell anything but what he pleased.

8. Furthermore, it is to be supposed that the prisoner has committed many other such offences against our holy Catholic Faith, and uttered other blasphemies and heretical speeches, as well as known that other persons have done the same, all which he conceals like a bad Christian.

9. The said prisoner on a time specified, declared that he was able when anything was stolen to discover the thief, and in proof of this assertion wrote the names of certain other persons suspected of a theft on papers, and putting the papers into the fire, repeated the words *Ego sum*; *Factus est homo*; *Consummatum est*. The papers were consumed except that bearing the name of the thief. No one but the said prisoner could take this paper out of the fire.

10. Furthermore, he asserted that he could execute the above purpose by rubbing the ashes of the papers upon his hand, where it would leave impressed the name of the thief.

11. Continuing the conversation, he declared that he possessed certain instruments of use in various ways; and in fact showed something folded up, which he took out of his pocket. And on being asked whence he obtained the know-

ledge of these arts, he replied that he learned them from a Book of Magic in his possession, which enabled him to do whatever he pleased.   I request that he may be questioned with respect to this Book of Magic, as well as the contents of the above-mentioned envelope.

12. He told this person that he could learn from the same Book to make himself invisible, as well as invulnerable to the thrust of a sword ; and used various other damnable speeches and devices, which I am prepared to prove.

13. He furthermore, by the help of a certain damnable device with water, and the assistance of Satan, discovered a theft which had been some-time previously committed in the said Monastery.

14. For which reasons I request and supplicate your Excellencies to admit my charges as proved, or such a portion of the same as shall suffice for the ends of justice, in a definitive sentence, or whatever measure may be taken, and to declare my accusation fully proved ; and the said E. W. M. guilty of the above-named abominable offences ; condemning him to the heaviest punishments by law thereto affixed, and executing them upon his person and goods ; by turning him over to the secular arm of justice as a punishment to himself and a terror to others.   And I request that if

necessary he may be put to the torture, and that the same be continued and repeated till he confess the whole truth of himself and others.

15. And I formally swear that I do not present this accusation out of malice; but solely to accomplish the ends of justice, which I request at the hands of your Excellencies.

MATTHEO MAGRE,
Secretary.

The accusation having been presented and read, the said E. W. M. was formally sworn to declare the truth in answer to every interrogation relating thereto. The accusation being read over, article by article, he aswered as follows :—

1. To the first article he confessed that it was true that he had eaten the bacon, but he had a license from the Abbot to do so, he being an Englishman and a visitor in the Monastery of Biscay; and being excused by him from conforming to the rules and customs of the said Monastery, so far as relates to food.

2. To the second article, he said that being an Englishman he had always eaten meat in his own country whenever he pleased, as he lawfully might do.

3. To the third article, he said that it was wholly false and untrue.

4. To the fourth article, he said that it was untrue.

5. To the fifth article, he said that he did not confess, being an Englishman and Protestant, and that he was entertained in the same Monastery with full knowledge of his country and religion. The remaining portion of this article he delared to be wholly false and untrue.

6. To the sixth article he said it was false.

7. To the seventh article he said it was false.

8. To the eighth article, he said it was false.

9. To the ninth article, he said it was wholly false and untrue. He confessed that he had said he knew a gypsy who pretended to have this power, but he never professed it himself.

10. To the tenth article he gave the same answer.

11. To the eleventh article he said it was wholly false.

12. To the twelfth article he said that part of it was false and part of it was true. The true part of it was this. A certain monk in the Monastery had lost a rosary, and violently suspected another monk of the theft. The prisoner, at his request, desired him to ask the suspected person, together with four or five others, into his cell on a certain day. He did so, and the object of the meeting was then explained. The prisoner produced the

water and declared it would blacken the finger of the thief. He then darkened the room, and introduced a quantity of ink into the water, for the purpose of discovering the said theft, as he supposed the thief would be the only person of the party who would not dip his finger in the water. They all dipped except one, and all had their fingers blacked; the thief had wet his finger in his mouth, and it was not blackened. Then the prisoner knew that this one alone of all the others had been afraid to dip his finger in the water, whereupon he at once accused him of the theft, and he confessed it. But there was no witchcraft or sorcery; it was only an ingenious device to discover a rogue. He added that although he were put to the torture he could say nothing more.

The above having been read to the prisoner, was declared by him to be correctly recorded, and the truth according to the oath which he had sworn.

Signed by him,
Edward Wortley Montagu,

Mattheo Magre,
Secretary.

The Inquisitors then ordered him a copy of the accusation, that he might within three days make arrangements for his trial by conferring and agreeing with one of the lawyers who are counsel for those persons tried by the Holy Office, namely Dr. Magrina, priest, and Father Geronymo Vidal, Jesuit; giving the prisoner liberty to make choice of either. The prisoner made choice of Dr. Magrina, on which the Inquisitors ordered him to be summoned. The audience then closed, and the prisoner being admonished, was remanded to prison.

Before us,

> DR. DOMINGO ABBAD Y HUERTA,
> DR. BERNARDO LUIS COTONER,
> DR. JOSEPH DE OTERO Y. COSSIO.

No. VI.

AUDIENCE FOR COMMUNICATION OF THE ACCUSA-
TION AND EVIDENCE.

In the Royal Palace of the Inquisition at Seville, on the 10th day of January, 1735, the Inquisitor, Dr. Domingo Abbad Y Huerta, being at his morning audience, ordered the above-named E. W. M. to be brought from prison, which be-ing done, and the prisoner present, he was—

Questioned, if he remembered anything which he was bound to declare according to the oath he had sworn ?

Answered, that he had nothing more to say.

The prisoner was then informed that Dr. Francisco Magrina, whom he had selected for his counsel, was present, with whom he might confer, and make arrangements for his defence.

Dr. Francisco Magrina was then sworn in *verbo sacerdotis*, to defend well and faithfully the said E. W. M. : to inform him if his case was not on the side of justice : to do everything which a good advocate is bound to do, and to preserve secrecy throughout.

Then were produced and read the several examinations of the said E. W. M. made from the 10th day of October, 1734, to the present time with the accusation, and the answers of the prisoner. These he examined, and conferred with the prisoner respecting his case, counselling him as to the best defence which could be made, to confess the whole truth; and if he had been guilty of any offence, to beg for pardon, by which means he might obtain mercy.

The said E. W. M. replied that he had already declared the whole truth, as appeared by his confession; that beyond this he denied everything contained in the accusation, and in consequence begged to be acquitted and set at liberty.

The Inquisition then ordered a copy of the above to be given to the Promoter Fiscal of the

Holy Office, who requested that they might proceed to the proofs. The Inquisitor replied that the cause should be judged definitely, and the proofs on both sides received *salvo jure impertinentium et non admittendorum* according to the style of the Holy Office; and the same was notified to both parties.

The Promoter Fiscal then declared that he reproduced the testimony which had been received and registered against the said E. W. M. in this Holy Office, which testimony he desired might be examined and ratified in form; and also that all other necessary investigations might be made and the testimony published; whereupon the audience closed, and the prisoner being admonished to bethink himself well, and declare the truth, was remanded to prison.

MATTHEO MAGRE,
Secretary.

No. VII.

AUDIENCE FOR THE PUBLICATION OF THE
TESTIMONY.

In the Royal Palace of the Inquisition at Seville, on the 10th day of February, 1735. The Inquisitor, Dr. Domingo Abbad Y Huerta, being at his morning audience, ordered the above

F. W. M. to be brought from the secret prison, which being done and the prisoner present, he was

Questioned, if he remembered anything, which he was bound to declare, according to the oath he had sworn?

Answered, that he had nothing more to say.

The prisoner was then informed that the Promoter Fiscal of the Holy Office had requested a publication of the testimony against him, before which it would be well for him to declare the whole truth, as this would cause him to experience more benignity and mercy.

Answered, that he had nothing more to say.

Straightway appeared the Promoter Fiscal, and requested publication of the testimony against the said F. W. M. according to the style of the Holy Office. The Inquisitor ordered the publication to be made concealing the names of the witnesses, and other circumstances which might cause their persons to be known, according to the order and style of the Holy Office; which was done in the manner following:—

Publication of the testimony against Edward Wortley Montagu, native of London, England.

A certain witness sworn and qualified in the proper time and manner, in the town of   , on a certain day of the month of September, in the year 1734, declares, &c.   [*Here follows the testimony of the first witness before given.*]

Another witness sworn and qualified in the proper time and manner, declares, &c.   [*Here follows the testimony of the second witness.*]

Another witness, &c.   [*All the other testimony repeated.*]

The Inquisitor then ordered the prisoner to make arrangements for his defence ; and admonished him and remanded him to prison.

No. VIII.

AUDIENCE TO COMMUNICATE THE PUBLICATION.

In the Royal Palace of the Inquisition of Seville, on the 10th day of March, 1735, the Inquisitor, Dr. Domingo Abbad Y Huerta, being at his morning audience, ordered the above E. W. M. to be brought from prison, which being done, and the prisoner present, he was

Questioned, if he remembered anything which he was bound to declare in discharge of his conscience, according to the oath he had sworn?

Answered, that he had nothing more to say.

The prisoner was then informed that Dr. Francisco Magrina, his counsel was present, with whom he might communicate, and take measures for his defence.   The publication of the testimony against the prisoner was then read to the said Dr. Francisco Magrina, who proceeded to confer with the prisoner about his defence. Having done this, he received from the hands of the prisoner a sheet of paper, upon which he drew up articles of defence, which were then read to the prisoner, and he declared that he made a formal presentation of the same.   Here follows the defence.

DEFENCE.

Although Edward Wortley Montagu has no necessity for any defence against the charges brought against him by the Promoter Fiscal of this Holy Office, nevertheless for greater security, and with an express declaration that his impeachment of the testimony of the witnesses against him is not occasioned by a desire to injure them, but solely to defend himself, he states the following :—

1st. He confesses that he has committed an offence against the rules of the Church, but denies that he ought to receive any punishment for the same ; which is the truth, because

2nd. Although it be the fact that he ate the meat on the feast in question, yet it is not the fact that he did it through malice or with any desire to transgress the ordinances of the Church, but he supposed that he lawfully might do so, having a license from the Abbot ; which declaration is the truth.

3rd. It is not true that he was informed that he ought not to eat the meat, yet he who says he so informed him, suffered him to eat it notwithstanding; which is the truth.

4th. The third and fourth accusations are not corroborated by any witness, and are utterly false; which declaration is the truth.

5th. The sixth, seventh, eighth, and part of the ninth accusation are not corroborated by any witness, and are wholly false; which declaration is the truth.

6th. The eleventh and twelfth accusations are also false *in toto*, and are not corroborated; which declaration is the truth.

7th. These things that he has confessed to are harmless; which is the truth.

8th. Single witnesses to such grave accusations are not deserving of credit, insomuch as *non det fides testibus singularibus*; which is the truth.

9th. The prisoner suspects that the witnesses against him are acting maliciously, and under the command of their superior; which is the truth.

10th. On the above accounts the said E. W. M. ought to be acquitted by your Excellency, and released from prison, experiencing justice at your hands; *vel alias omni meliori modo quod de jure sibi adaptari valeat; et verum.*

11th. *Ponit quod, omnia et singula, sunt vera;*

super quilus jus dici et justitiam ministrari postulat; et verum.

F. MAGRINA.

This being presented to the Inquisitor was by him ordered to be put on file. Whereupon the prisoner, being admonished, was remanded to prison.

Before me,

MATTHEO MAGRE,
Secretary.

No. IX.

SENTENCE.

In the Royal Palace of the Inquisition of Seville, on the 12th day of March, 1735, at the afternoon audience for the determination of causes : present, the Inquisitors Dr. Domingo Abbad Y Huerta, Dr. Bernardo Luis Cotoner, Dr. Joseph de Otero Y Cossio. Having examined the proceedings of the cause against Edward Wortley Montagu, now in the secret prison of this Holy Office, ordered unanimously, that he is to be confined for life in the said prison.

Before me,

MATTHEO MAGRE,
Secretary.

CHAPTER XXXV.

" And when thou art spoiled, what wilt thou do? Though thou clothest thyself with crimson, though thou deckest thee with ornaments of gold, though thou rentest thy face with painting, in vain shalt thou make thyself fair ; thy lovers will despise, they will seek thy life."

I HAVE plunged the reader so abruptly into the heart of the Inquisition that I suppose he will scarcely be prepared for it, nor would he be less surprised by the pile of legal documents—not the least value of which is that they are perfectly genuine—with which I suddenly surrounded him, and left him puzzled doubtless not a little at their professional jargon and pedantic forms. I will now endeavour to help him out of the maze into which I so unceremoniously thrust him, and when he reads or re-reads the preceding chapter, by the light of this, I have no fear but that he will more thoroughly understand the nature of the mysterious tribunal of which I was now the victim, than ever has been understood by Englishmen, or even foreigners, before. For in no work that I know of is there so complete, so circumstantial, and so accurate a narrative of the legal process of this ecclesiastical star chamber as in the present; and as every step in the proceedings is here minutely traced, the world can judge of that institution on grounds more authentic and distinct than have ever before been presented to its eye. Circumstances, which I shall probably at a future time disclose, put me in possession of these documents, and I have no scruple in making them public—not out of any hatred to the Church of Rome or its establishments, but simply as historical memoranda, well worthy the attention of the philosopher of every creed and kingdom, and valuable to all who make religious systems the subject of speculation or enquiry.

The reader already knows how suddenly I was snatched away from the dreamy vagabond sort of state in which I found myself at Granada. Though I am not usually cold-blooded, or quakerlike when wrongs are offered to me, I knew at once that resistance was hopeless; and I trusted rather to the goodness of my cause than the

vigour of my muscles. For I had no terror of
any dangerous result. The charge was heresy—
this the semblance of my captors at once signified,
a charge which I dismissed with scorn, and which
I had no doubt I could easily repel. Had they
been alguazils, and had I been apprehended for
murder, or some other offence against the criminal
laws, such as my monks might easily have invented, I should probably have been not a little
nervous; but to an accusation of heretical opinion,
I was conscious that I was in no way liable; and
therefore I bore my fetters without complaint.
Strange and absurd it will appear that I reasoned
so. I ought to have known that if they were
capable of inventing a criminal charge against
me, they were equally capable of sustaining one
whose basis should be heresy—but in the confusion of the moment, I did not reason so, but in
the other and foolish manner that I have mentioned; and I went my way with a cheerfulness
of demeanour which seemed to surprise the grave
and black-robed lictors of the church.

I was carried into a gloomy building as large
as a barrack, with vast silent courtyards, dark
porticos, and frowning arches; and through stone
corridors, along which our steps were painfully
and sadly echoed. On each side I saw small and
iron-studded doors, leading to cells innumerable;

but every door was firmly chained and locked, and double barred with massive bars. I was then led into a sort of dungeon, and having been stripped, I was clothed in a long sad coloured doublet, and a man, who seemed a clerk, entered in a book an inventory of all my clothes, telling me at the same time, that I was now in the Holy Inquisition, and that there was nothing lost there, but that everything should be restored to me when I went out, were it even of the value of the hundredth part of a farthing. I asked him why I was brought here, and demanded the name of my accuser; but he answered—

"Sir, you must observe a strict silence here, and ask no questions whatever; you must be as still as if you were dead: and indeed while you remain within these walls, you are truly dead to all corporeal things; you must not speak, nor whistle, nor make the least noise that can be heard by any; and if you hear anybody cry or make a noise, you must still be silent, upon pain of two hundred lashes. Your properest course will be to recline upon this mattress all the day until you are released, and thus you will escape all censure." I told him I could not always recline there; whereupon he added, "Well, you may indeed walk; but it must be softly, so that no one shall be disturbed in the least. This place is the Place of Silence." He then departed with the apparitors, and I was left alone.

This was a new scene in my eventful drama, which I now began to contemplate with feelings anything but satisfactory. So long as I was in the open air, cheered by the sun, and breathed upon by the free wind, I could look forward without dismay to the prison which I approached, for it seemed to me that after all it would be but a temporary residence; but the scene had now become changed, and the prospect was anything but agreeable. I had so long been a happy denizen of Nature, and had been so used to trip over her hills and dales, like some wild free creature of the forest, that I cared but little for what ordinary men consider the worst privations. My clothes, my lodgings, or my food, were the least of all things in my thought—but liberty was a priceless gem, to which nothing else could be compared; and of this it now seemed that I was likely to be deprived, for some unknown period, and for some unknown offence. In place of the glorious forest, or the sublime lonely mountain, I was in a little cell of ten or twelve feet in extent; and so dimly lighted by one small grated window, that if you had a book, you could with difficulty read its pages. I was surrounded by a horrible silence, which ate into the

very essence of life, and made me most intensely
sad; I missed the rustle of the trees, and the
song of birds; the merry music of the rivulet,
and the sense of heavenly freedom, which above
all other sensations is perhaps the most rapturous
to the soul and heart of man.

The food with which they supplied me was
frugal and monastic, or rather anti-monastic—for
in our convent we fed luxuriously on all the
dainties that can gratify hunger and thirst. A
little wine and bread and half a dozen walnuts
was all that the Holy Office supplied daily to its
prisoners; but as we had no exercise, our appetites
were not great, and we remained in health on this
slight refection. A week passed in solitude,
during which I saw no one but my keeper. At
the end of that time he hurried one morning
rapidly into my cell, and told me to make ready
to go out. I hailed this as a sign of freedom,
and with boyish gladness asked him whither?
He answered, "You must go to audience."
"What!" I asked, "to the king?" "No,"
said he, "but to my lords of the Holy Office."
This reply damped all my courage. However I
prepared myself, and was conducted to the place.

It was a large oblong chamber, not very well
lighted. On the wall at the extreme end were,
on the right, the Papal arms, the mitre and

cross keys, finely carved and gilt, and on the left
the royal arms of Spain, under a naked sword.
In the centre was a collossal carving, represent-
ing the crucifixion, and as it was finely painted,
and all the deathliness and horror of the event
were plainly represented, it struck the eye with
a vividness that is but seldom felt at mere pic-
torial images. In front of this, before a long
table, was a chair, in which sat an Inquisitor,
and near him was a small crucifixion, placed
upright, so as to be ever in his eye, doubtless
that he might be filled only with the most holy
thoughts. At the end of this table was a little
bench, at which I sat, and near, at a small table
at my right, was a Secretary, who made minutes
of all that took place.

The Inquisitor himself, whose name I afterwards learned was Dr. Domingo, Abbad Y
Huerta, was a middle-aged man, of a saturnine
expression, a large and somewhat coarse mouth,
a broad forehead, well developed, and a piercing
gaze in his eyes, which had, at times, something
sinister, and which seemed to search you through
and through, though he never looked me once
fully in the face during the whole investigation.
There was an air of command in his features,
habitual to one who had long exercised power of
life and death, and his voice was clear, cold,

harsh, and imperious. I was informed by the
apparitor, that I was now having my first
audience, and I was accordingly questioned
in the manner set out in the legal document
which is so headed. I observed that however
carefully the Secretary wrote down all my answers, there was an air of incredulity about
both himself and the Inquisitor, as if they noted
what they heard, as a matter of course, without
according the slightest particle of faith in its
truth, or being in any way affected whether it
made for or against me. However I answered
frankly and sincerely, for I was in no fear at all;
and though I had seen something of the interior
of religious life, the parting benediction or advice
with which the Inquisitor dismissed me, seemed
so sincere and well intended, that had I really
anything to confess against myself, I should have
been tempted to do so. But I had nothing to
charge myself with, and therefore I was obliged
to appear contumacious to my judges—if, indeed,
the Inquisitor ever condescended to think at all
about me.

The next day I asked my keeper how long I
should be kept in prison? I told him that I
was wholly ignorant what charge of heresy or
disbelief could be brought against me, and that
it was useless for the Inquisitor to endeavour to

extort a confession of that of which I was wholly
innocent. He told me not to be afraid; that the
inquisitor was a most holy and just man; and
that all he did was intended for my benefit,
spiritual and earthly; that if I answered freely
to the questions put, I should receive the highest
marks of favour and respect—the Inquisition never
exercising its sovereign powers except over those
who were so obstinately wicked, that they were
insensible either to prayers or commands. He
told me he had known persons to be confined
there ten, twenty, and even thirty years, for
refusing to make that full and open confession
which the Church sought simply for their own
benefit, but that nothing could be more honourable or expeditious than their mode of adminis-
tering justice, when the accused dealt fairly with
them.

A day or two after this I received a visit from
one of the reverend Doctors of the place, accompanied by his secretary, who, with an air of
intense kindness, asked me whether I was well?
whether my keeper was kind to me? whether
my food, my bed, and lodging were pleasant and
agreeable? whether I had any complaint to
make? for if I had it should be speedily inquired
into and redressed—and, finally, if there was
anything appertaining to my spiritual welfare to

which the Holy Office could in the least contribute, —I had but to name it, and it should be at once looked to; for the Church regarded with maternal love all its children, however erring, and never was filled with more heavenly joy than when she could see them repent and live.

To all these fine speeches I simply answered that I had committed no offence deserving spiritual chastisement; and that further, the loss of my liberty was the greatest punishment which could be imposed upon me. Wherefore I besought him that I might have a speedy trial, for I had no doubt I could make manifest my innocence the moment I saw my accuser. The reverend doctor parted from me with a " God bless you, my son," which might have melted the heart of a stone, and in sooth I suppose it would have melted mine into water, had I not been thoroughly on my guard. Despite the vigilance of my jailor, I noted a hundred symptoms that I was in a place of torture. I could hear at midnight long and dismal groans, whose dying echoes were dreadful to the ear; in the day when I was meditating, a shrill scream as if produced by a paroxysm of the direst anguish seemed to echo through my cell, as if conveyed by some strange passage with which the dungeon of the sufferer communicated with mine. The keeper stole often outside my door to see whether he could hear me say anything, and to discover no doubt also whether I was communicating with the tenants of the next cells, or plotting against the ordinances of the place.   Once when I asked him about Captain Bermudez, he   smiled   significantly, shrugged his shoulders, and signified   that I was doing myself no good by enquiring after such a reprobate.   To my enquiry as to what had become of the children of the Gitanos, he flew into a passion, and ordered me to mind my own business, or he would report me to his superiors.

In another month I was again summoned by an apparitor to the Second Audience, when another holy Doctor appeared on the tribunal. This audience ended as unsatisfactorily as the first, and I was sternly remanded to my cell.

The Third Audience was on the following month, and on this occasion there were three Inquisitors ; the particulars of it are set forth in the legal instrument, and it certainly tried my patience to the utmost to hear such false charges. On this occasion I was furnished with the depositions, and the accusation against me; but the names were carefully suppressed.   I became possessed of the authentic documents afterwards in a manner that will be explained.   The countenances of the Inquisitors had now grown dark

and angry; and that accent of benevolence
which on their first or second appearances they
had used, was now changed into one of harsh
and imperious terror, in which was developed
the true nature of the men; hard, cold, cruel
as steel. However, I did not heed them much,
being convinced in my own mind (against all
reason and experience as I now know), that
nothing really could be done to me, as I was
innocent. Some other formal audiences being
had, which are mentioned in the document, I was
visited by my counsel Dr. Magrina, who told me
that God was the first Inquisitor, for he had
questioned Adam and Eve in the garden, &c.,
which precedent clearly proved the heavenly
origin of the Holy Office, and the sublime nature
of the duties imposed on its ministers. He used
a great many sophistical arguments to induce me
to make full confession, and appeared wholly to
mock my protestations of innocence. However,
he maintained appearances as well as he could,
and he often spoke to me on other matters, on
which we could converse freely without suspicion.
He was pleased to say he felt the deepest interest
in my welfare, and that if I would but embrace
the pure and holy faith of the Catholic Church, I
might be immediately appointed to a most
honourable and confidential office in England

on behalf of the rightful heir to the Throne. My connections and opportunities were hinted at, my supposed knowledge of the court, and court intrigues would be beneficial to the illustrious family most deeply interested, and I might be dismissed at once with every token of dignity, if I did but prove the sincerity of my heart, and the falseness of the accusation, by consenting to be baptised in the Holy Catholic Faith. My answer to this impertinence may be surmised. I had not abjured slavery to a parent in order to assume it under a priest.

At last the final hearing came on. The defence of Dr. Magrina, I suppose, was in the usual style of these proceedings. The result the reader knows. But to me the sentence came like a sentence of death, and I was filled with horror. I am certain I should have infinitely preferred the stake itself, to perpetual imprisonment in this odious place.

CHAPTER XXXVI.

"Then they cried unto the Lord in their trouble, and He saved them out of their distresses. He brought them out of darkness, and the shadow of death, and broke their bonds asunder."

But a power was working outside the walls of this Royal Palace of the Inquisition, on which its sacred governors never calculated. The recent foray on the Gitanos, and the abduction of upwards of two hundred of their young ones, had driven this people into frenzy, which would have evaporated in mere talk (for the Gitano race are the most timid of all the people under the sun), had not the accidental arrest of Captain Bermudez supplied flame to what was already full ready to blaze forth. The gallant Captain had ostensibly done nothing to subject himself to the spiritual interference of the Holy Office.   His crimes were, it was thought, altogether of a secular nature; and it was always the spirit of the Inquisition to meddle with nothing but their own affairs, and to let the municipal power exercise the laws upon those delinquents who had transgressed in worldly matters; reserving to themselves the whole jurisdiction over those who had violated conscience by some speech, or thought, or act, which was not directly cognizable by the civil courts.   But it would seem that this was not so; and that the Holy Office had received an accusation against the Captain of some spiritual transgression.   I believe it was the abduction in early life of a novice, or a nun—for which they were now resolved to wreak full satisfaction on his head.   Accordingly, although a band of soldiers had been despatched from Madrid for the sole purpose of securing him and destroying his companions, the Holy Office with that air of superiority over the civil tribunals which they always exhibited, and never failed to carry into practise where they could, claimed full power over Captain Bermudez; and the soldiers of the king, after several ineffectual attempts to get into the stronghold of the bandits, were obliged to return the way they came—the gypsy Duke hinting pretty freely that their commandant had

received a large sum of money as a peace offer-
ing—the vulgar would call it a bribe—from
Julian Romea, who acted as a kind of confidential clerk to Captain Bermudez. The bandits,
therefore, being wholly unmolested, soon con-
cocted measures with the Gitanos for a general
attack on the Royal Palace. They waited for
fully seven months, until all measures of precau-
tion had been laid aside and the soldiers were
safely barracked in the capital. Numerous
meetings took place, and the Gitanos were
rapidly instructed in the use of the trabucho and
the pistol, though I believe nothing short of the
terrible outrage perpetrated on them could have
induced those people to lay aside their peaceful,
timid habits, and enter on a course which must,
necessarily, terminate in carnage. During these
proceedings Dom Balthazar arrived from a distant quarter, no one knew where, but everyone
recognised his right to command. Balthazar, as
we have seen, was no craven. On the contrary,
he was a man fully equal to any emergency of
this nature. His recognised position among the
Gitanos entitled him to counsel, and even to command; and the gypsy Duke willingly surrendered
up to another the leadership of an enterprise
which was wholly repugnant to all his former
instincts and habits.

Of the bandits, the one selected to fill the
Captain's place was an arch, but bold wag, who
rejoiced in the nickname of St. Joseph.   He had
been a student for the priesthood, but having
got a young Jewess in the family-way, he fled
into the mountains, and joined himself to some
noble spirits, who with true cosmopolitan philosophy, waged war alike upon Christian and
Hebrew.   The incidents in which he had been
engaged, and his own profane comparisons of
himself to the venerable sage, had gotten him
the name in which he now rejoiced; and he was
well and widely known for his unrelenting pillage
of all holy ministers of religion, whom he usually
shaved, or experimented upon in a manner
absurdly ludicrous to all who could dissociate
religious duties from the order of the priesthood,
and who did not quite hold that every monk was
a deity or an archangel.   Priests and Jews were
the chief game he hunted; and as luck would
have it, he had had remarkable success in the
chase.   His bags were full of reliques, scapula-
ries, holy beads, cassocks, and other paraphernalia
of priests; and though he had a large collection
of breviaries, the only portion of them which he
ever read were the legends of the saints, on which
he bestowed unlimited jokes, and which he said
were far pleasanter than the miracles of Ovid.

But the other consecrated trappings were subjected to unmerciful profanation. He would
dress himself as a priest, and, entering a village,
confess all the young women of the place, and
return to his companions primed and loaded with
extraordinary anecdotes, which he recited with
an air so comical and waggish, that none, even
of the most pious robbers, who prayed three
times daily to the Blessed Virgin, could abstain
from laughter. But with all this, the fellow,
like Mercutio, was as brave as a lion.

Seven months passed, as I have said, before
the banditti or the Gitanos took any steps in
their meditated siege. They now put themselves
under the leadership of Balthazar and St. Joseph,
and the event was fixed for the first dark night.
They had an emissary within the Palace, in the
shape of a turnkey, who was a Gitano by blood,
and whose fidelity the robbers ensured by the
promise of a purse of gold if he would open the
gates and admit them. This fellow was soon
persuaded. He had originally been a robber
himself, but a priest whom he had eased of some
doubloons, wrought a miraculous conversion in
him, and after a probation of piety and religious
exercises, he was made an officer of the Inquisition, where he had, up to the present period,
performed his duties with fidelity enough. But

the fame of Captain Bermudez was so widely
spread through the provinces that our new convert felt not a little inclined to seek adventures
with him, and the old vagrant humour breaking
forth, when the Captain himself was incarcerated,
he determined to confer on him such a service as
would ensure enrolment in his band and thorough
reliance on his future trustworthiness. He got
into communication therefore with the Captain,
and an amicable negotiation was entered into
between Bermudez, Balthazar, St. Joseph, and
Sylvetti (so was the officer called), which was
satisfactory to all parties, and resulted in the
arrangement which I have mentioned. The
guard over Captain Bermudez was to be knocked
on the head, the Captain himself was to be let
loose, and taken into the quarters were the young
Gitanos were huddled up, and where a party of
the gang were to meet him, and, furnishing the
urchins with torches and flambeaux, were to fire
the Palace, and in the general confusion sack it
of all it contained, and liberate the imprisoned
heretics, out of whom they anticipated some fresh
and desperate recruits to their ranks.

Everything succeeded miraculously. A saint's
night was chosen for the siege, when half the
officers were drunk ; for though the Spaniards are
a sober people, there are certain holy seasons

when indulgence is permitted; and the festival of a Saint is one of these. Sylvetti manfully carried out his project; and Captain Bermudez, to his unmitigated delight, found himself a free man—as free at least as he could be within the walls of a prison, though unconfined within any cell. He proceeded at once to the quarter indicated. Sylvetti opened the door, and let in the rabble; they entered silently, and then barred the huge doors. And now a terrible struggle arose. There were at least a hundred officers and warders within this vast place, and they were all well armed. The encounter was terrible, but numbers prevailed; and the Gitanos once heated by the sight of blood, and the certainty of conquest, grew perfectly wild and furious. Fire was applied in a hundred places at the same instant to the Palace; the most fearful hand-to-hand encounters took place; the work of pillage commenced; and though there was not much to seize, still to the Gitanos, almost everything was valuable, though the gentlemen of Captain Bermudez cared only for gold cups, or silver crucifixes. They got a few of these in the great chapel, and managed to sack some rich vestments, one of which gorgeously worked in gold St. Joseph wisely secured for himself; and having carefully packed up all that they intended to take away, they were preparing for their departure like men entirely satisfied with their night's work.   But Captain Bermudez had not forgotten what he owed to me. It suddenly occurred to him that I also was in the Inquisition, and as he knew it would be impossible to find me, he proposed a general and instant liberation of all the prisoners—a part of the original plan which in the hurry and confusion had been well nigh forgotten.

It so happened that I was among the very first on whom the Captain himself accidentally dropped. I had heard the horrible uproar, but could form no conception as to its cause; but when the place began to fill with smoke, and the groans of the dying and wounded, mingled with the shouts, the blasphemies, and the execrations of the exultant victors began to swell into a tempest, coupled with the shrill screams of the children, who scarcely knew whether they were in the hands of friends or foes, I began to get alarmed for my own safety, and to regard the chances of being roasted alive as not the least remote from possibility.   I kicked against my prison door, and did all I could to make myself heard—but I did not know that my worthy keeper was then lying within a few yards of me with his throat cut from ear to ear, and his pockets rifled of the few silver coins which they contained. And now on all sides arose a terrible chorus of cries; the shriek of despair, the shout of vengeance, the accent of supplication, the howl of frenzy—for there were several in this odious place whom their wrongs had driven into madness. Hastily, at the head of a few chosen men, all of whom had keys, came Captain Bermudez along the arcades. I could hear each cell unlocked, and I was in an agony of expectation until my turn also came, for I could see a red glare now imaged in the sky which told me that this mighty prison was on fire. The Captain saw me, but could scarcely believe his eyes—so great was the change which a few short months had wrought in my appearance; nor was it until the torches shone full over me, that he was quite certain who it was. For my part I did not leave him long in doubt; for I rushed upon him and clasped his hand with thanks for my deliverance; a greeting which the worthy Spaniard received with his accustomed gravity.

"Come along, Senor," said he, "and join us in liberating the rest."

I gladly did so, and we went wildly from cell to cell. The vast quadrangles were now one vast Babel of confusion; in every place were men and women dressed and undressed, who added to the

tumult by their tears, their terrors, their amazement, and their joy. The subterranean dungeons
were every moment disgorging fresh victims;
there was feeble querulous weather-beaten old
age, and youth in all its brightness dimmed in
the very vigour of its hopes. In one cell we
found a Jew nearly eighty years of age, with long
gray neglected beard and haggard eyes, who told
us he had been taken away from home and wife
and children fifty years before, and locked up in
this hell ever since; enduring a living death, for
he had never heard the least tidings of his family
from that time to the present. The old man was
like a mummy; it could be just said that he lived,
but nothing more. He was like a toad disentombed
from a hard rock, where he had lain buried for ten
thousand years; the sight and hope of freedom
was too much for him. He told his tale feebly,
gasped for air at the end of it, and fell down expiring in a few moments. In another place we
found a priest, who had been originally immersed
for some slight ecclesiastical offence; but when
he was searched in the prison, a copy of Spinosa
was found in his pocket; and for this frightful
crime, he was sentenced to a dungeon for life. He
was a tall and noble looking man; his eyes were
full of philosophic calm and dignity; he seemed
to treat all things as the result of destiny; and

when we told him that he was free, and the
manner in which it had been brought about, he
mildly reproved Bermudez for so wicked a contrivance as an attack on the citadel of the Holy
Office, and asked him how he hoped to obtain the
intercession of the Virgin for his participation in
this blasphemous outrage upon the sacred temple
of her best beloved ministers? So great is the
force of custom on the mind, that I have no doubt
this man would subsequently surrender, and
willingly submit himself, to his allotted punishment.

And now a loud cry of the wildest exultation
was heard. We turned to the corner from whence
it came, and as we had nearly emptied the whole
prison by this, I accompanied Captain Bermudez
to the place from whence the noise proceeded.

"It is time," he said, "to prepare for flight,
if we remain much longer we may be suprised."

We found ourselves among the Gitanos, who
were dancing wildly like so many mad people—
their joy knew no bounds. They had found an
Englishwoman who knew their language, and
there were loud plaudits. What icy chill was it
that suddenly ran through my heart? I rushed
into the middle of the crowd. The gypsies made
way at once when they saw who I was; nay,
they began to congratulate me on the joy I should

feel at being thus a party in the liberation of my countrywoman. She was lying on the ground, tenderly supported by some of the Gitanos; her hair was loose upon her shoulders, and her appearance fair, but fragile in the extreme. Her eyes were closed; but as I looked at her for a moment she opened them, and with a bound, a superhuman exertion, she rose and flung herself in my arms.

" O, Wortley," she said, " are you indeed come at last ?"

I was overpowered. Could this be Francesca? Could this be my innocent and noble wife? It was so. The sudden surprise had bereft me, as it were, of my reason; but I knew that it was she, and I folded her to my heart.

" She is my wife," I said to the people; and many of them melted into tears. She meanwhile lay upon my heart bereft of sense and motion. Captain Bermudez instantly ordered a mattress to be brought forth, and when she was laid on it he gave her over to the charge of the gypsies and ordered a retreat. I walked by her side, holding her hand and wondering what new revelation was now to come. Even at the moment I could not convince myself but that I was playing a part only in an incoherent dream.

With some difficulty we made our way from

the burning palace. The whole city was now aroused; the guards and the authorities were there; but seeing a determined force of sixty men armed with knives and pistols, and upwards of six hundred of the Gitanos bearing sledge hammers, pikes, guns, and swords, as they guarded their liberated offspring, who clung to them with eager limbs; observing, too, that we were momentarily reinforced from the Albaycin by crowds of the female gypsies, who gathered around us with frantic cries of joy, almost all being armed with daggers, or other implements of offence; and that among those whom we had liberated, there was a large number prepared to fight desperately for freedom should any attempt be made on the part of the magistrates to detain them by force, they thought that moderation was the safest course; and indeed there were hundreds among the assembled citizens who could not but sympathise with the energetic means to which the Gitanos resorted; and few saw with sorrow the downfall of so horrible an institution as that which was now surrounded by the flames. Any notion of attack upon us, therefore, if ever it was entertained, was abandoned when our numbers were discovered, and our resolution to defend ourselves to the last extremity could be traced in our determined, silent, dogged bearing. The crowd

opened a passage for us ; we passed in silence,
but with vigilant eyes. I think I saw a movement made at one place towards Captain Bermudez by some of the magistrates ; but that
worthy, with a pair of pistols in his hand, looked
stedfastly at the approaching party, and without
wasting many words, signified to them that an
attempt on him must be the prelude at all events
to their own destruction, and to the most deadly
civil com motion that Spain had known since
the days of the Moors. Our march was rapid
and terrible ; the few villages we passed through
were evidently cowed and overawed by the imposing fierceness of our appearance ; miles seemed
nothing to us in our excited condition.

CHAPTER XXXVII.

"My God my God, why hast thou forsaken me? why art thou so far from helping me. O, my God! I cry in the daytime, but thou hearest not; and in the night season I am not silent."

WE now mounted upward by the winding road of the Alhambra. The moon was bright in heaven; the snowy mountain peaks of the Sierra Nevada were one sheet of glittering crystal. The lonely Tower of Comares rose before us still and stately; the hills and valleys rich with fig and pomegranite lay in deep repose and shadow; but here and there we could see the soft moonlight imaged on many a fairy stream that flowed in silver from the emerald glens and gorges of the Alpuxarras. I was once again happy—or at all events indulging in a happy dream. Beside me, with her hand clasped in mine, was my own

beloved Francesca beautiful as ever, though faint
and thin ; while in her eyes which now beamed on
me with enthusiastic fondness, I read a world of
love, as pure as snow; as undying as ever animated the heart of woman.   We did not speak,
for I could see how feeble she was, and I was
satisfied to hold and press her hand, knowing
that in each mute caress she understood the
whole of what my spirit felt.   And now we had
passed that Moorish palace, and were ascending
the higher eminence on which the gypsy tribes
have made their dwelling for so many centuries,
burrowing in the rocks and caves, and nestling
amid fruits and flowers, with an Arab independence of the mere superfluities of life, which in
my judgment is the surest proof of high organi-
zation.   Of two men—one of whom is content
with a handful of dates, while the other can do
nothing without a beefsteak, the first is certainly
the greater.   Suddenly there was a loud disturbance in our rear; and a tall horseman rode up,
mounted on a powerful mule. Our eyes met. We
both knew each other at a glance, though we had
not met for some time.   It was Dom Balthazar.
Looking at the litter and at myself, he rudely
demanded—

    " What means this ? and what brings this man
here ?"

I returned him a look of hate and scorn, but I disdained to answer. In a rough voice he called out to the bearers of the litter to halt, and they did so.

" Drag away that man," he said, pointing to me.

But now Captain Bermudez came forward.

" My friend," he said, " I don't know who you are, or what you want, but you had better go home, and become sober. You have no business with us."

"And who may you be ?" asked Balthazar, with an angry gesture of hatred and rage.

" I am called Bermudez," answered the other ; " who are you ?"

" Whoever I am, it matters not to you," replied Balthazar. "I am in command of my brethren here, and this woman is my wife."

" Scoundrel !" I said, darting towards him, " how darest thou to say this ? Thou the refuse and scum of mortals !"

He looked at me with a cold hate ; and drawing his dagger, came to meet me. Bermudez flung himself between us.

" Sènor," said he to me, " are you mad that you mind this varlet ? You who have but just recovered your wife, and such a wife, ought not to be moved by this fellow."

" I tell you she is my wife," roared Balthazar,

and he made towards the litter. As he did so, Francesca rose; she seemed imbued with new strength.

" Begone," she said, " torment me not. Are not all my woes and troubles from thee ? What have I done that thou shouldst persecute me longer? Now I am with him again, and all thy malice shall be defeated."

She looked at me with all her innocent and loving heart in her eyes. She breathed her spirit into myself.

" Yes," said I, " Francesca, fear him not. But my hour is come, and I shall have vengeance on this villain."

" Sayest thou so," he said, urging his mule still towards me as I supposed, and almost trampling down Bermudez in his way. The Gitanos seemed half disposed to aid him; they looked threateningly at me and the Captain, and one or two of them drew forth their long knives.

" No man shall lift his hand against Dom Balthazar," said one; " we all owe him fealty, and he has but to say the word and we shall obey him."

" True, my brother," he cried out, " but this is a traitor knave who has broken every law of the tribe, and deserves death. The woman is my wife, and I shall have her, or know why, in his heart's blood."

The gypsies were about to deliver over the litter and its burthen to Dom Balthazar, when Francesca sprang out of it, and placed herself beside me.

"Good people!" she exclaimed, "it is false—all false! here only is my husband," and she hung on my neck; "that man has always been my deadly foe."

"It must be true," said Bermudez; "men come forward and arrest this scoundrel," and he called to St. Joseph, who was laughing beside him, in his usual wild way, and caring little what took place, so long as there were blows and fun.

A deadly fight appeared imminent. The Gitanos were evidently disposed to believe Dom Balthazar in preference to me, when the latter rode right against me, and lifting his dagger, aimed, I know not at which, but Francesca flung herself before me, and received the blow in her bosom.

Who can describe the yell of fierce revenge with which this diabolical villain at length accomplished the purpose of his soul? He raised his dagger, recking with her blood, and shaking it in the air, kissed it, and ere I could

recover from my stupor he was gone. Several of
the gypsies pursued him ; but he warned them
off with some mysterous gibberish, which seemed
to awe them all. The bandits then took the
chase, but all traces of Dom Balthazar were lost.
For my part I was transfixed with deadly horror.
I flung myself on the earth beside her, and
groaned aloud. Some women now ran up to us ;
we gently lifted her on the rude litter, and bore
her to the Albaycin—there was no other refuge
for either her or me. She was placed in a cave
which belonged to the Duke himself. It was
trellised with myrtle, orange, and other oriferous
trees ; eglantine, clematis, and the wild vine lent
their sweet shades over and about it. The Gitanos
seemed to have forgotten their own troubles in
this dread catastrophe of one so young, so innocent, so beautiful; and though the parents pressed
their rescued babes to their hearts, and covered
them with kisses and endearments, yet still I
could detect many an anxious, pitying glance
upon her who had but a moment ago shone like
some lovely lily of the stream, but who now, with
broken stalk and drooping head, was passing
away into the dark oblivion that is in death. The
blood had ceased to flow, for they had bound up
the wound ; but when the leech of eighty years,
who knew the force of every healing herb and

drug saw her, he shook his head and intimated that all was over.

"O, my own, my loved, my long lost, lately found, Francesca," I exclaimed, "art thou indeeed leaving me for ever? For this have I endured sleepless nights and days of agony? for this have I abandoned home, and friends, and all that reconciles to hated life? Thou who art the spirit of my own soul, art passing away; thou knowest me not, thou canst not give me sign or token that in thy heart I still am loved; neither canst thou open wide the mystery that has so long concealed thee from thy husband-lover. Oh, wake! wake! look upon me once again before thou departest for ever; let those sacred eyes shine upon me, and speak; let me know what thou hast endured, that if I live I may at least avenge thy wrongs. Ah, poor child! a sad and wretched destiny has thine been. Torn in earliest youth from all that could make thee happy, thou wert brought up alone, and far away from all the sweetest sympathies of life. For a brief space thou hadst a dream of light and beauty —for a brief space the hallowed paradise of love was opened unto thee, and we did walk together in its gardens; but a hand and sword of fire expelled us, and since then our wanderings have been wide and many. For me the glory of my youth and hope is gone; for thee thy life is ebbing fast, and thou knowest not that I am beside thee. Speak, speak! wake! or I shall go mad—if indeed I am not already so with many woes—but this, the darkest of them all," and I flung myself on the earth beside Francesca, hopeless, nerveless, and heart-broken.

In an hour my sweet wife revived, in an hour the soft and star-like light of those heavenly eyes was again cast upon her husband-lover. But death was in their mild beam. Her hours were numbered ; before the Morning Star glittered on high, she would be far away—far, far away in the Unknown and Silent Regions, whither I could not go. While she was here, she was mine, and no man, no power could come between her and me ; in a few fleeting minutes I should no longer have dominion over her. She would be the inhabitant of another realm—the subject of another sceptre, the lonely denizen of another sphere, into which no mortal foot could enter. She stretched forth her feeble hand, and touched my brow, and head, and cheek. The magic of her touch penetrated me, as the touch of Alla penetrated his apostle, Ahmed, the Ambassador of the Most High. It ran through my being. It was like the hand of Death—but the hand of Death guided by undying Love.

"Oh, Francesca! Oh, my wife? is it thus that we meet again—meeting but to be separated for ever? Thou knowest my agony; yet see it not, but pass in peace."

"Wortley," she said, "my own love, better is it that I should die at once, than live longer to be the sport of chance. From my childhood upward, what have I known but wretchedness? I am one of those doomed to be unlucky—nay, look not so, for there are many who are fated to be unhappy. Well did the Wise Man of the Hebrew people say, 'The race is not to the swift; nor the battle to the strong.' Every day I have lived I have felt this to be the truth. I am the daughter of ill-luck. It is better that I should pass away."

"O, Francesca sayst thou so? Is this the justice of Heaven—to give to one the happiness which it witholds from others?"

"I know not," she answered; "I cannot penetrate the secret ordinances of God. I believe, I know that He is Most Just. But I know also that some are fortunate, and others are unfortunate; that there are many who pine and toil, and are unhappy all their lives, while they possess the noblest attributes of mankind; while there are others who reach the proudest heights of mortal glory, yet are the lowest and most vicious of human beings. But God judges not as we judge. He alone is Wise and All-knowing—but we are only poor blind moles, who see nothing truly. Glad, therefore, am I, that I am passing away—for I am of the unlucky ; nor can I bring to others that which I possess not myself. But thou, mine own, shalt be soon separated from her, who gave thee no enjoyment."

" O, Francesca, say not so. Thou wert my joy, my life, my heaven on earth. Thou also didst first reconcile me to existence; thou alone didst first teach me to believe in a God of Justice. Until I knew thee, I was as one who wanders in a desert, who had no thought of God or the Future. But when I learned thy gentle virtues, then was I convinced that it was not chance, but a Supreme superior Power that made thee what thou art; the type of all that is pure, holy, sacred, and exalted; and knowing thee, I first began to know what God was and is."

She paused, and seemed buried in thought. Perhaps it was weakness.

" Wortley," she said, " I am dying. In an hour I shall be no more. The dagger has pierced me to the heart. We shall be separated soon for ever."

" Oh ! not for ever," I cried, " say not, that it is for ever."

She faintly smiled. "No," she answered, "not for ever—we shall meet again above. But hearken now to what I say. Thou wouldst know my history since we met; in brief have it, for I cannot hold out long."

I begged her to hoard her strength; I endeavoured to cheer, to comfort her, to give her hope; all my exertions were vain.

"I am dying," she said, "dying fast. I feel my strength momentarily going. The gate that lets my spirit out is open. Hearken to me before I die."

"Thou rememberest our last parting—alas! we dreamed not, that it was our last. I sat up for thee late that night. I counted the slow hours. I had got for thee the little supper which thou wert wont to have; I prepared it as of old with my own hands, and sat by the fire, murmuring the old ballads which we loved so well. The hours passed, but thou didst not come. I heard St. Paul's strike twelve—the long funereal sound went into my soul like a death knell. Never before hadst thou been absent from me so long— never before had I so waited for thee in vain. The fire was dying out, but I heaped fresh logs on, and strove to sing, and strove to while away the lonely moments over the songs of Tasso; but an unknown gloom seized me. I could no

longer read or sing, or do otherwise than think ;
and all my thoughts were now grown dark and
melancholy. One o'clock, and thou wert not
returned. The sound entered my heart like a
knife. Two—three—struck, and then I thought
thou hadst gone home with one of thy friends,
and so I considered no more about it, but retired
to bed. To bed—but not to sleep. I tossed all
the remainder of the night uneasily on my pillow.
In the morning I was up by six. He will return
early to breakfast, I said, and I prepared all for
thee. The little bird sang in his cage; the little
geraniums put forth their flowers ; but bird and
blossom were unheeded when thou wert away.
Six—seven—eight—nine—ten—eleven—twelve.
Oh! weary, weary, were those long hours! I
now began to get alarmed. It was evident that
something unusual must have happened. Thou
wert not wont to leave thy poor bird thus for any
length of time—thy poor lonely bird, Francesca,
that always pined when thou wert away. I strove
again to divert my thoughts by reading—but I
could not. I seemed encircled by a dark cloud ;
my eyes saw blood; my heart felt instinctively
that there was something nigh which would appal
me. I strove to eat a morsel of breakfast, but it
was like a lump of fire in my throat. I could not
swallow, so I went into a corner and cried. Yes,

Wortley, I cried for a whole hour. This relieved
me. At the end of that time, I heard a knock
at my door. Judge of my delight, my rapture,
when it was a message from thee—a message from
my own loved one, who had not forgotten me.

"Thou hadst been to Twickenham—thou hadst
sought and seen thy father. Thou hadst confessed all—he had forgiven his prodigal son, and
all was well. Thy mother had joined her tears
with his and thine; never was there a more happy
union. It wanted only my presence to make all
perfect. I was to come at once. Thou didst
apologize for not hastening to accompany me,
but thy father could not bear to part with thee—
to leave his sight after so long an absence was
more than he could endure. Fancy my joy.
Conceive the heart-felt transport of my soul.
Nay, Wortley, my own darling love, blame me
not that I believed this tale. I was so sad, so
excited at thine absence, that I would have believed
anything that purported to come from thee. In
a few minutes I was ready. A hackney coach
was at the door. I kissed the bed where thou
hadst slept; the glass that thou hadst touched.
I am going to him, I said; we shall be happy
and united for evermore. Away, wild thoughts!
torment me not; with Wortley's love, my life is
heaven; earth a paradise."

" I gave my glad news to the woman of the house, and descended the stairs. The carriage was empty, but there was a man with the driver. The latter touched his hat. 'He is a friend, my lady,' he said, 'who has asked me to give him a lift on the road. May I do so? If not he shall go down.'

"I was so happy myself that I could not deny anything that another needed. 'By all means,' I said, 'I shall be glad to serve him in his necessity. Drive on.'

"We went on rapidly. I did not know the road to Twickenham, nor did I suspect anything. I lay back in the coach immersed in happy golden dreams. I was to see my husband; to embrace my new parents; to take a recognised place in society. For thy sake, my Wortley, I was pleased. I cared not for the change on my own account; I was happy with thee in a garret, or anywhere; I required not anything but thy heart. That was my world; it was for that alone I lived. We stopped at a house on a lone heath. It was a large house, but there was an air of desolation about it. I had heard of thy father's parsimony, and I supposed this desolate wild place was in accordance with it. But I wondered as we drove up the bare avenue that led to it that I saw thee not. I hoped for thy welcome presence. I

thought thou would'st rush to meet me; but thy
friendly eye and smile greeted not thy fond wife.
Presently, I thought, presently I shall be in his
arms and shall forget all. We stopped at the
door, and the man who had come with the driver
dismounted and knocked. It seemed a long
while before it was opened. I was amazed to
hear the sound of bolts and locks. It was slowly
unbarred; it seemed a massive door, and moved
heavily on its hinges. A servant came out
and bowed. I descended and entered. As I did
so the man said, 'This is the mad lady,' and
disappeared. The door closed on me, and I found
myself in a vast and cheerless hall."

Here she paused; exhaustion seemed to come
upon her; she was half fainting; when one of
the Gitanos gave her a cordial which revived her.
She endeavoured to collect her thoughts; but I
could see the damp dews of death upon that
sainted brow. Oh, how I cursed my fate! I
writhed in agony, but I repressed my feelings and
was still. I wonder my heart did not burst in
twain. Would to God that it had.

"My own Wortley," she said, "I have but
little to add. I was a prisoner. I was locked
up and treated as an insane person. When I
spoke of you I was laughed at. When I endeavoured to interest the woman who waited on

me with some allusions to the past I was treated
as a hopeless lunatic who was not to be noticed
or listened to; but every word was to be regarded
as an idle raving. I would willingly shut it out
from memory. To me it seemed an age; but I
know not whether it was weeks or months. It
was all oblivion and death so long as I had not
thee. What weary days and nights I passed.
What dreary hours did I go through. What
spheres of lonely desolate thought. I sighed only
for thee. I thought only of thee. I suppose I
was punished because I never thought of God.
But thou wert my God. Alas! I ought not to
have made any mortal so. Yet even still as I
tread the dark bridge that leads to Eternity, I
see thee—only thee. Thou art my only star, my
only hope, my only heaven. Ah! me. What
speak I? God forgive me, but Wortley, thou art
my very soul for ever and ever."

O God of Light and Truth, where art Thou?
Art Thou indeed a living Power? How can I
endure this fearful memory? How can I go on
and again harrow up my soul by retracing this
scene of agony? I have sought Thee, O Mighty
One. I have bowed myself, I have humbled me
before Thee. But where art thou? I have not
seen Thee. I have not recognised Thine Almighty
hand. Still vice is conquering; still virtue is

perishing. The mighty triumph; the lowly are trampled; the evil are exultant; the virtuous are beaten down to the dust. Where art Thou? Thou heedest not! Thou comest not from Thy Heavenly Throne to set all things right. What shall I say of Thee? Alas! I know not. Thou art Unerring Wisdom, Holiness, Truth, Justice, and Perfection. To doubt this were to doubt and disbelieve all things. No, I will not. Pardon my involuntary thoughts. I humble myself before Thee. I fling myself prostrate. Wretched worm that I am, let me submit. Let me yield in all things unto Thee. For Thou art the most sure and perfect Justice. Thou wert not God if thou wert not. But Thou art. Francesca's form has passed away, but her pure immaculate spirit is in Thy hands. Crowned with ambrosial light, she has long forgotten what she has endured. Thou, O Heavenly One, has taken her to Thyself. Her past sufferings are but a dream. Her present life is with Thee in the Paradise of the Blessed.

She revived again, and resumed, but her voice was now more faint and sad than ever. The dark enemy of life had made rapid approach within the last few minutes.

" One night, midnight it must have been, I was suddenly called up and forced to dress. My clothes were huddled on; my trunk packed with the little that it contained; and I was put into a carriage. A man was inside, but I noted him not. We drove off rapidly. We drove for several hours until the stars sank one by one out of the heaven, and the morning dawned, bleak, cold, and gloomy. I was utterly weak and nerveless. A feather would have knocked me down. I now scanned my companion. He had remained silent all the night, muffled up in a large cloak, but it seemed he did so rather for warmth, than to conceal himself; for I could observe no attempt to screen his face. Thou wilt wonder who he was. It was Dom Balthazar. (A cold pang shot through my soul, but I remained outwardly unmoved.) I looked at him long and earnestly before I could be positive that it was he. At length he looked at me steadfastly, saying—

" ' Do you know me ?'

" ' Yes,' I said, ' you are Balthazar, the gypsy.'

" ' The same,' he answered, ' hast anything to say to me ?'

" ' Why am I here ? Where is my husband ?'

" ' These are questions I cannot answer now. But you are going to your husband. He has left England in search of you. I only heard so last night. The moment I did, I resolved to place you in his hands, without further delay.'

"'Balthazar,' I said, 'this is a lie. You do not mean to take me to my husband.'"

"He swore that he was telling me the truth; he swore it with such awful oaths that I half believed him. Alas! what will not powerful hope persuade the heart? Even when we sink into the abyss of waters, and all around is tempest, we do not quite despair of succour. I remained silent in meditation. The man also spoke not. We changed horses, and got to the river side; I suppose it was somewhere below London. I was now passive in his hands. As we approached the place, he drew a pistol and said—

"'You know me; I shall have no noise made. Your true policy is to be silent; if not you shall. I will do you no hurt unless you compel me—but if you do, I shall shoot you on the instant; and I have prepared measures so that it will appear you did it yourself.'

"I was terrified by his threats. I have since known that they were foolish; and that I ought to have despised them and called out at all hazards—but, dear Wortley, all my courage was gone. I had had neither food nor sleep. I was beside a reckless, deadly villain, who I knew would stop at nothing to gain his ends. I hoped to find someone in the ship who would defend

me from him. I went on board, or rather I was
taken on board, for I was so weak that I could
hardly walk. I was carried down into a cabin,
and left alone with a woman; but I fainted, and
when I recovered I was in bed.

"I remember but little more. A long time
passed—a long and gloomy time. I took no
heed of it. Whether it was days, or months, or
years, it was all the same to me. I was in a
convent. I was surrounded by women who besought me to take the veil, and spoke smooth
words. But I distrusted all their arts. Instinct
whispered to me that they were my foes, and I
hearkened not to them. They told me that thou
hadst perished at sea, and that it was thy dying
command that I should take the veil; I believed
them not. I had now become so suspicious in
all things, that I trusted no one. Hour by hour
this wretched importunity continued; my life
was all miserable. At length I said, ' Why
should I be a nun? I have no faith in your
religion; I have a religion of my own. Your
creed is all show; my creed is of the heart within.' What more I said, I know not, but I was
soon after taken to the Holy Office—as it is
called. I had spoken blasphemy; those to whom
I had spoken it revealed it in confession, as they
were bound to do. The Inquisition never par-

dons words like these ; I was brought before
them, and mildly questioned. But thou knowest
their manner—the mildness of the dove—the
poison of the serpent. I answered little ; I
learned that I was condemned. I found by their
questions and by the papers which they sent me
in my cell, that I was unknown ; I had been
given over to them under a false name. Had
they known who I was, I suppose they would
have sent me elsewhere ; they would scarcely
have risked placing me so near thee. I bless
God that they did so, for to die thus in thine
arms, my husband, is the sole pleasure I have
had for years. Oh! better is it so to pass
away, than to have lived a prisoner in a cell
alone."

Again she fainted ; again the woman gave her
that vivifying cordial, and she strove to sit up,
but she could not. She opened her eyes, but
saw me not.

"Wortley, my husband, where art thou ?" she
said, "I cannot see thee."

"I am here, Francesca ; here by thy side ;"
and I guided her hand to my face.

"O my husband! bless thee, bless thee ; But
the last minute is come. Would that I could see
thee once again."

She stroked my face with her poor feeble hand,

as well as she could, and fell back heavily on my
arm.   I laid her gently down on the bed.   All the
women were dissolved in tears.   Her eyes were
closed.   We thought her gone for ever.   But it
was not so.   She opened them in a little time,
and looked at me.   A holy and immortal light
beamed out of them.

"God be blessed," she murmured, "He has
heard my prayer.   My husband, I see thee ; kiss
me once more—thou knowest not how I have
loved thee," and a smile came over that innocent
face.

I bent to kiss her ; and as I pressed my lips to
hers, her spirit parted.   A bright and heavenly
splendour illuminated her face for a moment.   It
was like the Aurora light of the northern heaven.
It gleamed and was gone.   She was no more on
earth.   She was in the Infinite and Eternal.

What more occurred I know not.   I fell down
stricken to the heart.   When I regained my
sense, they told me that she had been buried a
week.   And it was so.   Fare thee well, Francesca—mine own—my holy one—but not for
ever.   In another Land of Beauty we shall
meet.

CHAPTER XXXVIII.

"Therefore I shall be unto them as a lion, as a leopard by the way will I observe them. I will meet them as a bear that is bereaved of her whelps, and will rend the caul of their hearts; and then will I devour them like a lion."

AND now there remained but one duty, and that was vengeance. This I had sworn to have, and I did not like to break a vow which I had once made. I enquired for Dom Balthazar; to my amazement I found that he had not left Granada. I had supposed that he was far away, and that I should have had great difficulty in tracking him; but here he was within my reach, apparently determined to fight it out whenever I felt inclined to give him the opportunity. But single combat with this wretch was not what he merited. I resolved to kill him unrelentingly the first moment

I could do so.   On further enquiry I found, however, that although he had not indeed left
Granada, he was concealed in the Sierra Nevada,
and was in hourly communication with the
Gitanos.   Some business of the last importance
detained him, it was said : he was hastening to
conclude it by every means ; and I was assured
by my informant—one of the band on whom I
could rely—that he was in agony of fear lest he
should fall in with me, for his conscience, perhaps
his instinct told him, that when we next met, one
or both of us must fall, and that our encounter
was to be war to the knife.   I communicated
with Bermudez, and sought his advice and
assistance.   That grave commander mused and
hesitated.

" My friend," he said, " that you are right in
killing Dom Balthazar cannot admit of any
doubt.   All the Vatican priests will absolve you,
and even the Holy Office will give you absolution
for so virtuous a deed.   But there are two ways
of killing a man—one is that in which whilst
you destroy him you perish yourself; the other
is that in which while he perishes, you yourself
get off scot free.   If you are for the first of these
you will have no trouble; you have only to denounce him to the police as a murderer, and he
will be garrotted, but you will be again locked up

for life in the Inquisition, or probably put to
death for having been mixed up in our little siege
of Troy. For my own part I don't approve of
the first mode at all; but I prefer the second
course, which is the pleasantest in the end."

"Captain," I answered, "I have no desire to
bring myself within the hands of the priests
again, and time presses. We must all depart
from this place, and speedily, or the whole
country will be upon us for our late affair. But
justice imperatively demands that the man shall
die; and if I cannot myself find him, I must
then denounce the murder to the authorities; so
that I destroy him, I disregard what happens to
myself. There are some things for which I wish
to live, and I will live if I can; but be it life, or
be it death, Balthazar must perish. We two
cannot live on the same earth."

"I think," replied the Captain, "that it is
always better to live than to go into the grave.
It is a cold and lonely place; or if you have
companions they are but a poor set of worms. I
applaud your resolution to keep yourself in a
whole skin; and I equally think that Balthazar
must die. Indeed, it is now come to this that
one of you must cease to live for the security of
the other. Neither of you can sleep in peace.
The next question is, how he must die? I know

a friend who, for a small consideration, will stab
him when you say the word. Nay, for one like
me, he will do it out of pure pleasure."

"That would not do at all," I answered; "I
mean to stab him myself."

Captain Bermudez opened his eyes and laughed.
He shook my hand.

"By the Holy Virgin! you are right," he said.
"How came I not to think of it? Body o' me,
but I grow as dull as a monk."

And the gallant fellow laughed again, and
rubbed his great hands, and flung his arms around
me, and kissed me on either cheek.

Disengaging myself from his embrace, I enquired —

"Can you bring me to the place where he is
concealed? That is all I want."

"I do not know that I can," he rejoined.
"The Sierra Nevada is no small mountain, and it
is full of nooks, and corners, and caverns since
the hiding days of the Moors; so that you might
search for a hundred years and not find your man.
But fortune always leaves a door open. I will
put one of my best scouts upon his scent, and if
the wit of man can find him, he shall be found.
Confide in me, Senor, and all will be well. To
an old dog you need not say *tus, tus.* We shall
ourselves leave this place in a few days to let our

recent little pleasantry blow over; but here, there, and everywhere, you may command us."

I thanked the Captain, and waited eagerly for our next meeting. He came to me on the following day about sunset. His eyes sparkled; I knew that he was successful.

" Senor," he said, " I have found your man; he is hidden in the Mulhacen. From all I can discover he leaves Granada in a day or two, never to return. He intends, we are told to sail over to Africa. Now, therefore, is your time, or never. You can have two of my men as guides, and my best mules or horses for your expedition. But you had best set out to-night."

I thanked him with all my heart, and immediately got ready. I borrowed a pair of pistols and a dagger, of finest keenest steel, from Bermudez, and wrapping myself up in a large cloak I started with my companion for the bandits' quarters. We reached them about nine o'clock, and Bermudez added to the scout, who had discovered the retreat of Balthazar, our old friend Julian Romea, who willingly joined me in my holy expedition. They put up a quantity of provisions, and we proceeded on our way at midnight. We took several mules, and three noble Andalusian steeds.

I was now going on the most just and honour-

able expedition that ever man had taken. The
career of Balthazar seemed to have been that of
a villain from his cradle. By his own account he
had dealt in blood and murder ever since he could
do anything. Poison and the knife were familiar
to him. He was in truth a wild beast let loose
upon society. He had come in my path and
crossed me from the basest and most mercenary
motives; he had vowed enmity against me without a single act of provocation, and he had carried
out that enmity by driving me from the gypsies
where I had so long been domesticated, by plotting against my Francesca; by forcing us to
flight; by procuring my own confinement and
her abduction; and finally by his cruel murder of
my innocent wife in my very presence. My own
fate would doubtless follow, unless I purged the
earth of such a wretch. His destruction, therefore, became my duty. I thought of Akiba, and
the similarity between this portion of our lives,
and though my moral feeling made me admire
that astonishing sacrifice of himself to duty,
which Manasam's life had developed, my judgment and my heart rebelled against any consideration operating in this case on the side of
mercy. "Is not revenge the law of nature?" I
asked. And I thought of the swallows and spar-
rows which I had seen and noted so many years

before, when the guilty were punished even to the death, by the instinctive justice that was in the very birds. " Had Manasam been a man," I said, " he should have smitten his brother to the heart, if in truth he knew that his brother was a party to that foul and cruel wrong." He should have acted like the wise and learned Akiba, who destroyed all his foes, and in their blood appeared the spirit of the murdered.

My companion, Julian, strove to amuse me, or to lead me into conversation, but I was too much absorbed in thoughts like these to attend to him, or to answer his remarks. The moon shone above us an orb of silver splendour, and lighted up the whole mountain with a soft and gorgeous loveliness ; but a sad and melancholy halo seemed to wrap all things, and when I gazed upwards to the stars they seemed to gleam over me with a cold reproachful glance, which penetrated to my heart. But when I looked before me, I knew that in the mountain dwelt that fierce, relentless tiger who had destroyed my hopes of earthly happiness for ever, I was resolved that no feeling of pity, or compunction should stay my hand until it was red with his life blood. We passed over the smaller hills, that seemed like seas suddenly petrified ; and reached a gentle slope, which is the first table land. We rested our mules beside

a little spring whose waters sparkled like
diamonds over the green grass; and as the sun
now began to rise, we could now clearly see the
distant peak of Mulhacen where I knew my
enemy was sleeping. How calm and holy it
looked; the abode of innocence itself could not
be more still. While we refreshed ourselves, a
huge viper stole out of some adjacent brush-
wood; he fixed his dark eyes upon us and hissed
fiercely; a greeting which our guide repaid by
thrusting him through the stomach with a sword-
stick. And here a curious incident occurred. A
little bird no bigger than my finger had watched
our proceedings very attentively. No sooner was
the viper disabled, than it flew up with the
feathers of its neck standing on end; its eye was
all fire; it flapped its wings and piped a strange
and shrill note of exultation. Every time that
any portion of the venemous beast writhed convulsively, the bird shrunk back in deadly fear;
soon however it returned to the charge, and
pecked the viper with its beak, after which it
would rise into the air three or four feet, chirping
loudly again and again. I do not know what
the serpent could have done in its lifetime to the
little bird, or what was the feeling of hatred we
had gratified by killing the viper; but it is

certain that I never beheld such an amount of delight in anything before.

"It is a good omen," said my companion, and I hailed it as such. We mounted our mules and proceeded onward in silence.

The sun had now fully risen and revealed to us the wild and ragged aspect of the mountain. We could no longer see the summit, for each separate table land hid all that was above it; but we could form an idea of the vast extent over which we traversed. On every side were awful chasms, deep down into the base of the mountain. I looked into them and longed to fling my foe head-long from their tops; and so suspend him half alive on one of the naked crags that rose up out of the bottom, until he was devoured by snakes, or cats, or vultures. We crossed a pass scarcely two feet wide, on either side of which yawned one of these frightful abysses, but I scarcely saw them. On and onward seemed to be the only thought in my heart, and I believe I should have walked with naked foot over a red-hot plank of iron spikes, without feeling pain, if I had but beheld Dom Balthazar at the other end, so ardent was my thirst for vengeance. The eagles rose and screamed above our heads. I hailed the tutelary birds with joy, and in their shrill clang

I recognised as it were, a voice from heaven urging me to go on, on.

We were here met by a caravan of donkey drivers, descending from the higher points of the mountain with their panniers of snow. We stopped and questioned them. My guide was the spokesman. Lifting his sombrero, and bowing profoundly, he asked whether they had met any-one that morning on the upper hills? They answered no, but on the day before they had seen a tall, dark man with a great beard, who seemed watching the distant city with a large glass, and was so intent that he did not even see them pass. We bade them good-bye, and rode on. This was Balthazar; I knew him by the descrip-tion. He was then evidently alarmed. Probably he was even now on the alert. Speed was necessary—in rapidity of movement was my only chance. We urged on our mules more quickly than ever. The Andalusian horses which up to this were led by a youth belonging to the band were tethered here, so that we might have them fresh for our return. The boy stayed with them to watch.

The snowy region now appeared. We had got to traverse a terrible wild of rocks and precipices, flung as it were by the careless hand of some Titan upon the ascending slopes. It was as if a thousand Stonehenges were here all massed into one confused ruin. We saw innumerable snakes and vipers, and disturbed a vast variety of birds, whose shrill and angry cries disconcerted us a good deal. They protested against our intrusion on their domains. They seemed to hate the face of man. Had they but known his heart as intimately as I have, they would have had bitter reason to loathe his presence.

From this place we could see an immense rock, that rose towering to the right. My guide pointed it out.

"In yonder nook," he said, "the man you seek abides. But if you speak, let it be in whispers. The thin air carries the voice far, and your approach may be known before you are quite ready. With a good rifle from yonder elevation, the gypsy thief might easily shoot you to the heart. And he always goes armed."

With what a fierce exulting joy I fixed my eyes upon the accursed dwelling of my foe. In an hour we should be there; in an hour I should grapple with the destroyer of Francesca, and rid the world of his presence for ever. Oh! that I had done it on that well remembered night, when his life was in my hands, and a touch of the trigger would have prevented all these miseries I had undergone; would have preserved the life

that was dearer to me than mine own ; and given
me happiness for all the future. But it was not
to be ; and it was now too late to repine. We
dismounted again under the covert of some of the
vast firs with which the place was filled ; our
mules were sadly tired ; we ourselves also were in
need of refreshment and we were quite sure that
if Balthazar had not already escaped, and were
in the mountain, he could not now elude us.
We let our mules browse freely, and gave ourselves up to the necessary indulgence of food
and rest. The sun was now in his zenith ; all
was still and bright ; but the mountain air cooled
the beams that otherwise would have struck
death. We bathed our feet and brows in a
gushing tarn and were again ready for the
saddle.

"It seems to me," said Julian, "that the
greatest caution is now requisite. If we proceed
further at present, we shall one and all of us be
picked off by this fellow's bullets, as easily as a
child may fling a stone against a wall. With
the elevation that he commands, and the front
we shall present, escape would be hopeless, and
from what we while ago heard, it is evident that
the gypsy will not be caught napping. Indeed,
I should not wonder if he has already discovered
our approach with his telescope, and only waits

until we are within a safe distance for his rifle, to rid himself of all further apprehension, or pursuit. What say you, Senor?"

There was no disputing the sagacity of my companion's remark. To wait was evidently the wisest and safest course for ourselves ; but was it certain that while we were so dilatory, the foe, supposing that he had discovered our pursuit, would not make off by some other route, and rid us of all further trouble about him. Besides, I was now in a state of wild and savage excitement. I felt as a hound feels when he scents the track of the game. I longed to see his blood, to dabble my hands in it, to see it flow on the stones. I was become a perfect wild beast in my thirst for vengeance. While my judgment, therefore, for a moment approved of the counsel of Julian, my passions stood up against it, and after a brief pause I decided to proceed.

"Julian," I said, "I must go on. I should drop dead if I were to remain here inactive until evening; the very anxiety of the delay would kill me. Whatever be the risk I shall proceed. I feel a presentiment that I shall not die, but that he will fall. Meanwhile, my friend, now that I have my eye upon this tiger's den, suffer me to proceed alone. I shall rejoin you when all is over."

Julian shook his head.

"No," said he, "I will not consent to this. How know we that Balthazar has not friends with him who would overpower you with their numbers, and murder you in cold blood. And you are as yet only twenty-two. I pledge my honour to you, that if he should be alone, I will not interfere with your just revenge; it shall be a fair combat between man and man. But if he has companions, I and my brother here will aid you to the last gasp, and it shall not be one life that they shall take, but three."

He said this with such a determined resolution, that I saw it would be useless to argue him out of it; I seized him by the hand and thanked him. We said no more, but got into our saddles and proceeded.

I felt at this moment as if every nerve were iron. I sat upon my mule, stiff as a statue of cold steel. I could not feel my heart beat, or my pulse throb, so calm and passionless was my condition. I went upon this, the final stage of the hunt, as a judge goes upon the judgment seat to condemn some hideous criminal to death for murder. It was not as if I were going to rid a human being of life; but to trample out the existence of some noxious and pestiferous beast, the foe alike of God and

man, whom it was a positive blessing to the earth
to slay. I could now no longer judge of time or
space. I knew not whether I rode or walked; I
only found that I was impelled along towards the
lair where my foe was harboured.

From this reverie I was aroused by a sudden
cry from my companion, and looking up I saw
Dom Balthazar, who was standing with his back
against a steep precipice, and almost before I
had seen him, my hat was pierced by a bullet,
and in a moment after, my mule fell dead beneath me from a second shot. Julian instantly
dismounted to give me up the mule which he
himself had ridden, but before he could do so,
the creature reared on its haunches, and fell shot
through the very brain. Balthazar again aimed
at us a fourth time; but Julian now fired, and
this or something else unnerved him for the
moment, for his shot passed harmlessly over our
heads, and he retreated behind his rock, apparently for the purpose of loading again. We now
lost no time, but charged up the slope. To our
surprise, no fifth shot was fired, but when we
reached the place we saw Balthazar already half
a mile off, mounted on a splendid mule and fully
armed. The creature seemed to know the road
well, and went forward with a sure foot ;
but as it was necessary for his rider to

get into the route by which we had ourselves
ascended, he came gradually nearer, and
nearer to us, as he made the circuit, and when he
was within pistol range, I fired, but missed, and
the mule alone was hit.   She reared, and threw
him, and then fell; but he was evidently unhurt,
and he stopped to unstrap the carbines from her
side.   We now rushed down upon him, and were
so close that he lost his coolness, and he ran off,
leaving his fire-arms behind him, but still
formidable with a sword and dagger.   He
descended the mountain with the speed of a
hunted deer.   We pursued him, but not with
equal quickness, for we were a good deal fatigued
by our long journey.   Quick and quick, almost
as the very thought, he rushed headlong, leaping
wildly over all impending obstacles, and we could
see he distanced us considerably.   At length he
got to the place where we had left the Andalusian steeds tethered.   Balthazar immediately
perceived the value of this discovery.   Striking
down with a terrible blow the boy who attempted
to prevent him seizing the horses, he unsheathed
his sword, and having hamstrung two of these
splendid creatures, he mounted the third, and
disappeared almost in the twinkle of an eye.
Here was a catastrophe wholly unexpected—the
very means we had provided for our safety being

used against us by this vigilant knave. One
mule only remained, and this I mounted, determined to overtake him or perish. Lashing the
beast into a fury, we went along with a terrific
speed, such as I had never before seen put forth
by such a creature—but I had made it mad, and
it scarcely knew what it did, or whither it was
borne. I myself was perfectly insane. We
crossed fearful chasms, and rattled down the
steep mountain side, as you may see the burning
lava dash, when all Mount Etna is in flame, and
the moon is red as blood. Fire flashed out of
every flint—dust and smoke were mingled ;
through stream and underwood we rushed. The
whole scene before me seemed to wave and roll
and whirl. The distant Vega stretched out like
one vast boiling ocean, and was now near, now
afar off; now clothed in blackness, now mantling
with sunny light. I saw a hundred mocking
fiends between myself and Balthazar ; a hundred
figures seemed to rise out of the very stones, and
laugh me to scorn, and struggle to impede my
wild pursuit. Methought also that I heard
borne backward by the breeze, the disdainful
shouts of my foe, as he urged on his fiery courser,
and bade defiance to all my threats.

But now hope arose within my heart. We
were approaching the place where Captain Ber-

mudez and his friends were lodged, and I doubted
not that a bullet from some friendly hand would
stop the course, either of the horse or his rider.
My mule was now getting beat; the steed of
Arab blood had distanced her, and albeit occasionally I caught a glimpse of Balthazar, I was
guided in my pursuit rather by the thunder of his
flying courser than by any other indication that I
was on the right track. But though I could see
from afar off that we were right in the bandit's
course, no sign of stoppage was presented. On
the contrary, Balthazar appeared at the extreme
end, having safely passed through the bandit's
bivouac. I urged my wearied mule more and
more, but more and more she faltered in the race.
At length as I galloped madly down a narrow
bridle road, through which I could still hear the
far retreating echoes of the Andalusian's hoofs
and iron shoes, the mule staggered, groaned, and
would have fallen headlong had I not supported
her with a tight rein, and checked her terrible
course. But scarcely had I stayed her, and dismounted, when she fell dead before me; her
heart was broken in the fearful race. I lost no
time in pressing onward. The first person I saw
was Captain Bermudez. In a few moments I
told him all. He chafed furiously over his hamstrung steeds; nor was he less enraged about that

which Balthazar was so unceremoniously using;
but he ordered out the finest stallion he possessed,
and forcing some wine down my throat, he
mounted me again, and bade me God speed!

"I would have shot the fellow as he passed,"
he said, "but I know revenge is sweet, and I
would not deprive you of the heavenly morsel,"
and I was glad he would not.

And now I was mounted like a king. Never
was a nobler steed than that which my friend
Bermudez owned. His Arab blood was imaged
in his eye, so bright, so calm, so noble, yet so full
of orient fire. He might have carried Mohammed
when that Mighty Prophet bore at Bedir the
thunders of the God of Truth; and gave the
first blow to that wide spread atheism of the
East, which had so long developed itself in idol
worship and sorcery. Such a steed was Pegasus,
when with wings flashing ten thousand splendours, he soared in heaven; and every tenant of
Olympus envied his haughty rider; such a steed
was the bull-headed horse that carried Alexander
to conquest, and bore him safely through a
thousand perils. He was dark as night; his
coat was smooth and glossy, as opal or venetian
glass; his arched neck was like the horse
in Job clothed and girt with thunders;
his haughty nostrils breathed ethereal flame.

Nay, by the Gods, I do not exaggerate. No praise can be too great for me to give this splendid animal. I have loved and honoured the horse ever since that day for his sake; and I never until then appreciated the deep wisdom of Swift's adventurous traveller, who like Ulysses, though he had seen and known the customs of so many strange people, yet found all the virtues under heaven only in the horse. In a few words Bermudez told him what I meant—that I was following a fiend, and must perish, or destroy him; and he patted his neck, and pinched his ears, and bade him be my friend in all I did. And well, oh noble Selim, didst thou understand thy master's word. He pawed proudly ere I mounted him; he turned upon me his eyes, of full and bright intelligence, and when I was seated on his back, he moved forward with a stately grace, that passed almost from a trot into the speed of a lightning flash. But a moment since I was with the bandits—and now where were they?

On, on, and we were at Albaycin. The perforated caverns of the Gitanos crowned with Indian fig trees, and shrubs of emerald green passed before my eyes like a quickly moving panorama. I had a short glimpse of hundreds and hundreds of dark-eyed children rolling

before their mother's doors, or crowning each
other with flowers; but like a flashing meteor, I
was there and gone, and though my brethren
rushed in crowds to see me, attracted by the
thundering noise of my horse's hoofs, I can only
recollect all that then occurred like a nightmare
dream. I had now wholly lost sight of Dom
Balthazar, but some of the Gitanos had pointed
out the road that he had taken, and it was that
precisely which I supposed he would pursue. It
was in the direction of San Roque, from which,
as I supposed, he might possibly obtain a passage on board ship; and thus effectually baffle
me for the present. And now I had got outside
Granada, and was in the glorious Vega, over
which I passed like fire, enquiring of every pas-
senger whether a flying horseman was in front,
and receiving satisfactory proof in every answer
that I had followed the right course, and must
soon overtake my man. The crops were in full
perfection, and might have easily afforded him
a hiding place, for they were full seven feet high;
but I was so careful in my enquiries, and the
answers to all tallied so well, that I had no
doubt he was still in the high road a-head; and
he had already slacked his horse's speed, so confident was he that my mule had failed, or
speedily must do so. And now I passed La

Mala, and over that wretched road and gloomy
country which lies between that and Huelma,
passed in less than twenty minutes, cheering my
noble steed, and patting him on neck and head,
until I felt that in every nerve and vein he fully
sympathised with his rider.

Yes, by Alla ! it was a glorious hunt. I
likened myself to an avenging Angel pursuing
some odious demon. My brain swam with hot
excitement—a thousand glorious purple flashing
thoughts darted across it, as I beheld the earth
and heaven, the mountain and the river, dance
as it were before me, or commingle into one
mighty chaos, through which I saw only one
distinct being, and that the object of my pursuit.
The splendid epic recollections of the past rose
before me, and I was by turns every god and
hero I had heard or read of, from the Orient
Rustam to the Western Rinaldo. Now I was
Jove, following the Titans with avenging thun-
derbolts, and hurling the awful lightnings of the
spheres; now I was Apollo in his sun-gleaming
chariot, riding in the path of heaven; now I was
Phæthon, whirled onwards in a track of flame;
or Hector, following the flying Greeks, and deal-
ing death at every stroke; or the swiftly striding
son of Peleus, when he came forth like a tempest
to wreak revenge for the slain Patroclus; again

I compared myself to the Erynnes, that chased the murderous Orestes, and on his guilty eyes waved their flickering torches; or to Medea, when having slain her fated offspring by the son of Æson, she rose in dragon-harnessed car and soared homewards through the startled heaven.

Away; away; away; and as my gallant steed heard the word, he seemed to fly over the ground. I had no need to guide him with the rein, or urge him with the heel. With the quick intelligence of his kind, he thoroughly understood my motive and my heart. Yes! thou glorious child of the desert, I see in thy shining eyes, and haughty neck, that thou also dost hate this accursed wretch; thy blood is up against him; thou knowest that he has wronged me, and that he merits death. Even now thy brain pants with the anticipated rapture of my revenge. Thou shalt be known to all time; thou shalt be honoured as the most glorious steed. Away; away; away; and like a comet we were borne, scarcely touching the ignoble earth, but armed, and winged, and swelling with exultant joy and hope, we outstripped the very winds in speed.

What object stops me in my path? It is a woman and a child; they are lying straight before me. Are they asleep or dead? Stay, stay, thou noble steed. Let us not trample down the slumberers. Mayhap the fiery heat has stricken them, and they are resting fatigued after a hard day's wandering. Stay, stay, and I reined him in, but gently, gently, for his Arab blood was up, and it was with difficulty that he could even stay himself. But when the beast of noble heart saw my object, and that in the narrow path we must crush the prostrate woman and her babe if we stopped not, he needed no further word from me, but gradually subsided into a gentle trot, and from that into a slow but haughty pace. No, not even for my sacred vengeance will I forget the rights that even the lowliest claim. She was lying in the middle of the bridle path—it was no better. A deep wound was in her head, from which the blood was flowing freely. She was a beggar — God help her! — and had wandered hither from Gibraltar with her babe. She told me she had seen Dom Balthazar, and had endeavoured to get out of his way, but failing, she had lifted her hands to warn him, but he had ridden her down with the relentless fury of a beast of prey. Good heavens! how my rage rose. The baby was killed; its brain was spattered on the rough stones; she herself, in striving to protect the innocent infant, was hurled against a heap of rock and rendered

senseless; but the rider laughed, she said, and
heedless of her screams, urged his reeking steed
yet faster. I could not linger long—but I endeavoured all I could to soothe the poor mother's
heart. I had a few silver coins which I bestowed
on her; but she regarded only her dead baby,
with a kind of stupor of grief, that filled my
heart with black, undying rage. On, Selim,
onward yet—onward! onward! brave and gallant
steed; let us stay the mad career of this un-
pitying demon.

The sun was setting as I rode into Huelma, and
baited for a short space at the solitary inn. I
inquired after my flying foe; he had passed
through the town an hour before, both horse and
man evidently fatigued, but had only stayed two
or three moments to procure some wine and
brandy, and a draught for his panting steed. He
had told the people he was an Englishman pursued by robbers, but nobody believed his story;
and when I briefly mentioned his crime and my
pursuit, concluding with his wanton murder of
the innocent child, I was hailed with shouts and
vivas, and God bless you's, quite sufficient for
my vanity, if vanity I had. From this place to
Alhama, which is the next town, is fifteen miles,
and these I got over so rapidly, though the town
itself is on the summit of a mountain peak, that

I learned that Dom Balthazar had but left at
one gate of the town as I entered at the other.
It was at this time nearly night; but still I
determined to go on until I came up with him.
And now there was a steep descending road of
some miles, through horrible passes, and even
deserts, bounded on the one side by the sea, and
on the other by a secluded valley, where witches
might have dwelt and held their horrid orgies.
The moon was up, the stars were overhead, and I
could see before me to a great extent. Judge of
my joy when, about four miles in front, and in
an open path, on which the light descended
brightly, I saw Dom Balthazar riding leisurely
down the incline, as if there were no such creatures as Arab steeds and avenging Englishmen
in existence. The sight drove me mad with
excitement, and though I was now sorely fatigued,
the hope that this desperate pursuit was drawing
to a close revived me with new vigour, and
patting the neck of my glorious horse, he rose
under me with redoubled energy and power, and
visibly gained on the retreating enemy. Oh,
blessed moon, still shine on me as now, and soon
shall I overtake this flying assassin! and ye, O
stars, lend me still your virgin light! Francesca's
name crossed my lips, and at that blessed word

I felt new courage, new hope, new certainty. And I was within a mile of Balthazar before he knew that I was nigh.

Oh! how he fled! God in Heaven, there is indeed a conscience and a fear, even in the most hellish-hearted. Aye, aye, disguise it from thee as thou wilt, O wicked one, thou knowest in thine inmost soul the mighty power of Heaven and truth, and innocence. Thou mayest laugh their holy names to scorn in thy drunken moments with thy mad companions, but when thou art alone at midnight, with the stars of light above, the solemn silence of the hour around, the visible presence of the Infinite and Unknown above thee, over thee, and all-embracing, then indeed thou confessest their power, and art constrained to bow before their awful sanctity. So felt this horrid wretch. Casting one quick and fearful glance backwards, he saw the Just Avenger on his track. I could feel magnetically that he shuddered, even to his heart's core. I could feel as it were in my own vital being, that a mighty arrow had gone forth from me, and smitten him with icy coldness. He fled; but his steed evidently flagged; and when my glorious Selim knew that the hated enemy was at hand, he snorted like a mighty spirit of thunder, and redoubled his fierce pursuit. He tore up the earth; he flung the stones beneath his feet, like so many straws; the ground flashed in the dark night, as if the Cyclopes were beating it with their steel hammers. The rapidity, the dreadful energy of his wild course was something supernatural. He seemed animated by a spirit which belonged not to the earth. The whole landscape ran past me; it whirled in mine eye, and was gone. I was no longer master of myself. The demoniac wildness of my horse entered into, and became part of my own being. I was the Wild Huntsman of the Black Forest. I was bent on Death, and I fled with the speed of Death. I lifted up my eyes to heaven, and the stars themselves whirled by and were outstript. I was close upon him, and my heart began at length to beat.

And now the final struggle evidently was at hand. I knew that we must meet for life or death in less than half-an-hour, and I rejoiced that the encounter was so near. But Balthazar had evidently no relish for fighting. On the contrary, the moment that he heard my horse's hoofs and looking back, guessed by the uncertain light that I was on his track, he urged on his jaded steed as hardly as he could, hoping to reach Velez, where he might probably claim the aid of

the authorities, and involve me in fresh troubles.
But he reckoned without his host in this.   I
gained upon him so rapidly that he struck out of
the high road, and fled across the country, making towards the terrible deserts of the Sierra de
Tepida, where doubtless he hoped from his knowledge of the place to bewilder and mislead me.
The sky now became overcast, and I lost sight of
him for some time; I could not even hear his
horse's hoofs upon the soft herbage; but my
steed knew, as if by divine instinct that I was
pursuing him to death, and I left t· him to follow
in the other courser's footsteps, anu admirably he
did so.   His sagacity was perfect.   The first
moment that the moon emerged from behind the
cloud I saw we were close upon Balthazar, and a
more rugged, wild, or lonely scene could scarcely
be presented than that which met my eye.   For
it was nothing but a medley of rocks, and tors,
and hissing mountain streams, with scarcely any
vegetation—the very place that a bravo would
select for a murder, or a novelist for a ghost
story.   Nature herself seemed to have heaped
every given accessory about it that could lend to
solitude and desolation their most imposing
features.

"In this place," I said, "shall this man die;

and fit it is for such a fiend. The vulture and the wolf shall have his body; as for his soul, the devil will take care of that."

His horse was now wholly knocked up, and could not move a foot farther. All further flight was useless. He whirled round and faced me. He was deadly pale; but his eyes were an image of hell fire. In his hand he held a sword; he had no firearms: this was perhaps lucky for me; but Satan generally deserts these fellows in the end, and they want the very implement of devil-dom which would serve them most. But his courage was as usual unflinching, and as he could not murder, he resolved to fight me. He re-mained on his steed awaiting my attack. He had not long to do so. My horse was already going at a furious pace, and I resolved not to check him. On the contrary, I had no doubt I should bear him down like a whirlwind before me. So far, therefore, from reining in my steed, I urged him still more resolutely with voice, and hand, and heel, and rode him right against Balthazar. The shock was dreadful. He flew out of the saddle like a rocket, and fell heavily on the ground. As he did so, the sword which he held still in his hand entered his heart, and he was dead in an instant. Thus perished Dom Balthazar. I left him to the wolves, and rode back to Granada, much more satisfied than when I left it. I was cool enough to lead back to Captain Bermudez the footsore Arab, which the dead devil had run away with ; and we both rejoiced merrily over many a flask of sunny Val de Penas.

NOTES.

NOTE U.—CHAPTER XXVIII.—PAGE 28.—HENRY FIELD-
ING.—The following anecdote is not generally known   H. F.,
hearing from a friend that a third person was very much
dejected, asked the cause. "Because," said the friend, "he is
deeply in debt."   " Is that all ?" replied Fielding.   "You
surprise me that he should mind it. How happy should I
be, could I find means to get £500 deeper in debt than I am."
—*Memoirs by Letitia Matilda Hawkins.*

NOTE V.—CHAPTER   XXIX.—P.   101.—LADY TOWNS-
HEND AND LADY ORFORD.—There is a slight sketch of
Lady Townshend, and the times in the " History of
Pompey the Little," where a conversation between herself and a nobleman called Hillario, is described. "From
this time," it says, "the conversation began to grow much
too loose to be reported in this work. They congratulated
each other on the felicity of living in an age that allows such
indulgence to women, and gives them leave to break loose from
their husbands, whenever they grow morose or disagreeable, or
attempt to interrupt their pleasures. They laughed at con-
stancy in marriage as the most ridiculous thing in nature,
exploded the very notion of matrimonial happiness ; and were
most fashionably pleasant in decrying everything that is serious,
virtuous, and religious."—Page, 36. In the same work Lady
Orford is described. The lady who now arrived, came directly
up to Lady Tempest, and made her compliments ; then sitting
down, and addressing herself, after some little pause to one of
the physicians, asked him, *If he believed in the immortality of
the soul?* But before we answer this extraordinary question, or
relate the conversation that ensued upon it, it will be for the
reader's ease to receive a short sketch of her character. In
many respects this Lady was in similar circumstances with
Lady Tempest, only with this difference, that the one had been

separated from her husband by his death ; the other was
divorced from hers by Act of Parliament ; the one was famous
for wit, and the other affected the character of wisdom ; Lady
Sophister (for that was her name), as soon as she was released
from the matrimonial fetters, set out to visit foreign parts, and
displayed her charms in most of the courts of Europe. There,
in many parts of her tour, she had kept company with Literati,
and particularly in France, where the ladies affect a reputation
of science, and are able to discourse on the profoundest questions
of theology and philosophy The labyrinths of a female brain
are so various and intricate, that it is difficult to say what first
suggested the opinion to her, whether caprice or vanity, of
being singular ; but all on a sudden, her ladyship took a fancy
into her head, to disbelieve the immortality of the soul, and
never came into the company of learned men, without display-
ing her talents on this wonderful subject. She would, indeed,
ascribe the rise of this opinion in her ladyship's brain to self-
interest, for said they, *It is much better to perish than to burn ;*
but for my part, I chose rather to impute it to absolute whim
and caprice, or rather an absurd and ridiculous love of paradox.
But whatever started the thought first in her imagination, she
had been at the pains of great reading to confirm her in it, and
could appeal to the greatest authorities in defence of it. She
had read Hobbes, Malbranche, Locke, Shaftesbury, Woolaston,
and many more, all of whom she obliged to give testimony to
her paradox, and perverted passages out of their works with a
facility very easy to be imagined.—Page, 60. " When first she
broke loose from all restraint," says Lord Wharncliffe, " while
still very young, separating from her husband to seek adventures abroad, some patriot bade her God speed in these lines —

> ' Go sprightly, Rolle, and traverse earth and sea ;
> Go, fly the land where beauty mayn't be free ;
> Admired and pitied, seek some friendly shore,
> Where not a Walpole shall approach thee more.' "

The following memoranda of some of the *Dramatis Personæ*
of this autobiography may not be uninteresting :—

HENRIETTA LOUISA, only daughter and heiress of John Lord
Jefferies, Baron of Wem, married July, 1720, to Lord Pomfret.
She and Lady Mary M. W. corresponded for some years.

LORD WILLIAM HAMILTON, son of James, Duke of Hamilton, married Anne, daughter and heiress of Francis Hawes, of
Purley Hall, near Reading, one of the South Sea directors.
Lord W. died in 1734, his widow, the celebrated Lady Vane,
married (when she was only 21), William, Viscount Vane in
the peerage of Ireland. She died in London, March 31st, 1788.
Smollett has published her memoirs in Peregrine Pickle.

SEWALLIS SHIRLEY, born 1709, M.P. for Callington, one of Lady Vane's lovers, married 25th May, 1751, Margaret, Countess Dowager of Orford, and died October 31st, 1765, Comptroller of her Majesty's household. An admirable and characteristic portrait of him by Knapton was exhibited at Kensington in 1868, among the members of the Dilettanti Society. There is an entry in Bubb Dodington's Diary under date, June 19th, 1754. " Lady Orford staid with me above three hours. Her business was to lament her misfortunes, for that Mr. Shirley and she were parted, of which she gave me a long account ; the whole of which was that he insisted upon something independent, and that she would part with nothing out of her own power." He refused to lend poor Vane fifty pounds when she was in great distress.

JOHN, LORD HERVEY, born 15th October, 1696, died 5th August, 1743. Sat in the House of Lords as a peer after the death of his elder brother, Carr, the father of Horace Walpole, according to the statement of Lady Louisa Stuart, in her anecdotes of her grandmother, Lady M. W. M. In 1720 he married Mary Lepel, with a major's commission and pay on the Irish establishment, and maid of honour to the Princess of Wales, afterwards Queen Caroline. He is base enough to divulge his intrigue with Miss Vane in his memoirs (Vol ii.. p. 20), but he aided, it is supposed, in getting her brother made Earl of Darlington ; a title of one of King George the First's mistresses—Madam Platen. Lord Vane, poor Lady V.'s second husband, was one of this family.

LADY DELORAINE was generally believed to have poisoned Miss McKenzie.

WORTLEY MONTAGU, the father of E. W. M., died 22nd January, 1761, aged 80. Lady Mary died 21st August, 1762. Her farewell to Bath, which appears in her son's memoir, is printed in the Gentleman's Magazine, Vol. i., p. 305.

LADY MARY WORTLEY MONTAGU TO MR. WORTLEY MONTAGU.

" Avignon, June 10th, N.S., 1742.

" I am just returned from passing two days with our son, of whom I will give you the most exact account I am capable of. He is so altered in person, I should scarcely have known him. He has entirely lost his beauty, and looks at least seven years older than he did ; and the wildness that he always had in his eye is so much increased ; it is downright shocking, and I am afraid it will end fatally. He is grown fat ; but he is still genteel, and has an air of politeness that is agreeable. He speaks French like a Frenchman, and has got all the fashionable expressions of that language, and a volubility of words, which he always had, and which I do not wonder should pass for wit with inconsiderate people. His behaviour is perfectly civil, and I found him very submissive; but in the main no way really improved in his understanding, which is exceedingly weak ; and I am convinced he will always be led by the person he converses with, either right or wrong not being capable of forming any fixed judgment of his own. As to his enthusiasm, if he had it, I suppose he has already lost it, since I could perceive no turn of it in all his conversation. But with his head I believe it is possible to make him a monk one day, and a Turk three days after. He has a flattering, insinuating manner, which naturally prejudices strangers in his favour. He began to talk to me in the usual silly cant I have so often heard from him, which I shortened by telling him I desired not to be troubled with it ; that professions were of no use when actions were expected, and that the only thing could give me hopes of a good conduct was regularity and truth. He very readily agreed to all I said (as indeed he has always done when he has not been hot-headed) I endeavoured to convince him how favourably he has been dealt with—his allowance being much more than, had I been his father, I would have given in the same case. The Prince of Hesse, who is now married to the Princess of England, lived some years at Geneva on £500 per annum. Lord Hervey sent his son at sixteen thither, and to travel afterwards, on no larger pension than £200 ; and though without a governor he had reason enough not only to live within the compass of it, but carried home little presents to his father and mother, which he showed me at Turin. In short, I know there is no place so expensive, but a prudent single man may live on £300 per annum, and an extravagant one may run out ten thousand in the cheapest. Had you (I said to him) thought rightly, or would have regarded the advice I gave you in all my letters while in the little town of Holstein, you would have laid up £150 per annum ; you would now have £750 in your pocket, which would have almost paid your debts, and such a management would have gained you the esteem of the reasonable part of the world. I perceived this reflection, which he had never made himself, had very great weight with him. He would have excused part of his follies by saying, Mr. G. had told him it became Mr. Wortley's son to live handsomely. I answered that, whether Mr. G. had said so or not, the good sense of the thing was in no way altered by it ; that the true figure of a man was the opinion the world had of his sense and probity, and not the idle expenses, which were only respected by foolish and ignorant people ; that his case was particular ; he had but too publicly shown his inclination to vanities, and the most becoming part he could now act would be, owning the

ill use he had made of his father's indulgence, and professing
to endeavour to be no further expense to him, instead of scandalous complaints, and being always at his last shirt and last
guinea, which any man of spirit would be ashamed to own.   I
prevailed so far with him that he seemed very willing to follow
this advice ; and I gave him a paragraph to write to G., which
I suppose you will easily distinguish from the rest of his letter.
He asked me whether you had settled your estate   I made
answer that I did not doubt (like all other wise men) you always
had a will by you ; but that you had certainly not put anything
out of your power to change   On that he began to insinuate
that if I could prevail on you to settle the estate on him, I
might expect anything from his gratitude.   I made him a very
clear and positive answer in these words : 'I hope your father
will outlive me, and if I should be so unfortunate to have it otherwise, I do not believe he will leave me in your power. But was
I sure of the contrary, no interest, nor no necessity, shall
ever make me act against my honour and conscience ; and I
plainly tell you that I will never persuade your father to do
anything for you till I think you deserve it.'   He answered by
great promises of good behaviour and economy. He is delighted
with the prospect of going into the army, and mightily pleased
with the good reception he got from Lord Stair, though I find
it amounts to no more than telling him he was sorry he had
already appointed his aide-de-camp, and otherwise should have
been very glad of him in that post. He says Lord Carteret has
confirmed to him his promise of a commission.

" The rest of his conversation was extremely gay. The various
things he has seen have given him a superficial universal knowledge. He really knows most of the modern languages, and if
I could believe him, can read Arabic, and has read the Bible in
Hebrew. He said it was impossible for him to avoid going
back to Paris ; but he promised me to lie but one night there,
and to go to a town six posts from thence on the Flanders road,
where he would wait your orders, and go by the name of Mons.
du Durand, a Dutch officer ; under which name I saw him.
These are the most material passages, and my eyes are so much
tired I can write no more at this time.   I gave him 240 livres
for his journey."

Mr. Montagu, writing of himself to Father Lami   at
Florence, says, " I have been making some trials that have not
a little contributed to the improvement of my organic system.
I have conversed with the nobles of Germany, and served my
apprenticeship in the science of horsemanship at their country
seats. I have been a labourer in the fields of Switzerland and
Holland, and have not disdained the humble profession of a
postillion and ploughman.   I assumed at Paris the ridiculous
character of a *petit maître.* I was an Abbé at Rome. I put on

at Hamburg the Lutheran ruff, and with a triple chin and a
formal countenance, I dealt about me the word of God, so as to
excite the envy of the clergy. I acted successively all the parts
that Fielding has described in his Julian. My fate was similar
to that of a guinea, which is at one time in the hands of a
Queen, and at another in the fob of a greasy Israelite."

Writing from Rosetta in Egypt in 1773, he again describes
himself. "I am much obliged for the compliment that you
pay my beard, and to my good friend Dr. Mackenzie for having
given you an account of its advantages enough to merit the
panegyrick. I have followed Ulysses and Eneas. I have seen
all they are said to have visited ; the territories of the allies of
the Greeks, as well as those of old Priam, with less ease
though with more pleasure than most of our travellers traverse
France and Italy. I have had many a weary step, but never a
tiresome hour, and however disagreeable and dangerous the
adventures I may have had, none could ever deter me from my
point ; but on the contrary, they were only stimulants. I have
certainly many materials and classical ones too ; but I am always
a bad workman ; and a sexagenary one is of all workmen the
worst, as perhaps with truth the fair sex say. This is very true,
but the patriarchs only began life at that time of the day, and
I find that I have a patriarchal constitution. I live as hardly
and simply as they did. Inured to hardships, I despise
luxury ; my only luxury is coffee, and the concomitant of
claret—*exceptis excipiendis*. I stayed a considerable time at
Epirus and Thessalia—theatres on which the fate of the world
was the drama. I took exact plans of Actium and Pharsalia.
I am totally taken up with the study of the Arabic language."

Dr Moore, the author of Zeluco, paid him a visit at Venice,
in company with the Duke of Hamilton. He thus describes it.

" Hearing that Mr. Montagu resided at Venice, the Duke of
Hamilton has had the curiosity to wait on that extraordinary
man. He met his grace at the stair head, and led us through
some apartments, furnished in the Venetian style, into an inner
room in quite a different style. There were no chairs, but he
desired us to seat ourselves on a sofa, whilst he placed himself
on a cushion on the floor, with his legs crossed in the Turkish
fashion. A young black slave sat by him, and a venerable old
man with a long beard served us with coffee. After this colla-
tion some aromatic gums were brought, and burnt in a little
silver vessel. Mr. Montagu held his nose over the steam for
some minutes, and snuffed up the perfume with peculiar
satisfaction ; he afterwards endeavoured to collect the smoke
with his hands, spreading and rubbing it carefully along his
beard which hung in hoary ringlets to his girdle. This
manner of perfuming the beard seems more cleanly and
rather an improvement upon that used by the Jews in ancient

times, as described in the Psalms translated by Sternhold and
Hopkins—

> " 'Tis like the precious ointment that
> Was poured on Aaron's head,
> Which from the beard down to the skirts
> Of his rich garment spread."

Or as the Scotch translation has it—

> " Like precious ointment on the head,
> That down the beard did flow,
> Even Aaron's beard unto the skirts,
> Did of his garments go."

Which of these versions is preferable I leave to the critics in
Hebrew and English poesy to determine. I hope for the sake
of David's reputation as a poet, that neither has retained all
the spirit of the original. We had a great deal of conversation with this venerable looking person, who is to the last degree acute, communicative, and entertaining, and in whose
discourse and manners are blended the vivacity of a Frenchman with the gravity of a Turk. We found him, however,
wonderfully prejudiced in favour of the Turkish character and
manners, which he thinks infinitely preferable to the European,
or those of any other nation. He describes the Turks in
general as a people of great sense and integrity, the most hos-
pitable, generous, and the happiest of mankind. He talks of
returning as soon as possible to Egypt, which he paints as a
perfect paradise, and thinks that had it not been otherwise ordered for wise purposes, of which it does not become us to judge,
the children of Israel would certainly have chosen to remain
where they were, and have endeavoured to drive the Egyptians
to the land of Canaan. Though Mr. Montagu hardly ever stirs
abroad he returned the Duke's visit, and as we were not provided with cushions, he sat while he stayed upon a sofa with
his legs under him, as he had done at his own house. This
posture by long habit is now become the most agreeable to him,
and he insists on its being by far the most natural and con-
venient ; but indeed he seems to cherish the same opinion with
regard to all the customs which prevail among the Turks. I
could not help mentioning one which I suspected would be
thought both unnatural and inconvenient by at least one half
of the human race, that of the men being allowed to engross
as many women as they can maintain, and confining them to
the most insipid of all lives within their hareems. " No
doubt," replied he, " the women are all enemies to polygamy
and concubinage, and there is reason to imagine that this
aversion of theirs, joined to the great influence they have in
all Christian countries, has prevented Mohammedanism from
making any progress in Europe. The Turkish men, on the

other hand," continued he, "have an aversion to Christianity equal to that which the Christian women have to the religion of Mohammed; auricular confession is perfectly horrible to their imagination. No Turk of any delicacy would ever allow his wife, particularly if he had but one, to hold private conference with a man, on any pretext whatever."

"I took notice that this aversion to auricular confession could not be a reason for the Turks' dislike to the Protestant religion. 'That is true,' said he; 'but you have other tenets in common with the Catholics, which renders your religion as odious as theirs. You forbid polygamy and concubinage, which in the eyes of the Turks, who obey the dictates of the religion they embrace, is considered an intolerable hardshp. Besides the idea which your religion gives of Heaven, is by no means to their taste. If they believed your account they would think it the most tiresome and comfortless place in the universe, and not one Turk among a thousand would go to the Christian heaven if he had it in his choice. Lastly, the Christian religion considers women as creatures upon a level with men, and equally entitled to any enjoyment both here and hereafter. When the Turks are told this, added he, they are not surprised at being informed also, that women in general are better Christians than men: but they are perfectly astonished that an opinion which they think so contrary to common sense should subsist among the rational, that is to say, the male part of Christians. It is impossible,' added Mr. Montagu, 'to drive it out of the head of a Mussulman that women are creatures of a subordinate species, created merely to comfort and amuse men during their journey through this vain world; but by no means worthy of accompanying believers to Paradise, where females of a nature far superior to women, wait with impatience to receive all pious Moslems into their arms.'

"It is needless to relate to you any more of our conversation. A lady to whom I was giving account of it on the day on which it happened could with difficulty allow me to proceed thus far in my narrative; but interrupting me with impatience, she said she was surprised I could repeat all the nonsensical, detestable, impious maxims of those odious Mohammedans; and she thought Mr. Montagu should be sent back to Egypt with his long beard, and not be allowed to propagate opinions, the bare mention of which, however, reasonable they might appear to Turks, ought not to be tolerated in any Christian land."

So far Mr. Moore. It may be doubted, however, whether Mr. Montagu was accurately understood by his hearer, as the doctrine of the inferiority of women is no part of the Mohammedan creed, as truly understood or expounded; though like many of the traditions and fictions which prevail among

Europeans, and are thought to be truly Christian, they are held by great numbers of the vulgar.

Mr. Montagu did not long survive this visit. In 1776 while dining at Padua with Romney, the artist, a partridge bone stuck in his throat. His attendants thinking he was about to die, called in a priest, at which he was highly indignant ; and being asked in what faith he would leave the world, he replied, "I hope a good Mussulman." Inflammation came on, and he died in a few days. He is buried under a plain slab in the cloisters of the Hermitants at Padua.

A few dates may be added :—

In 1747 he was M.P. for Huntingdonshire.

In 1754, M.P. for Bossiney.

In 1759 he published " Reflections on the Rise and Fall of Ancient Republics."

THE END.

T. C. NEWBY, 30, Welbeck Street, Cavendish Square, London.